Three Wishes

River of Time: California

LISA T. BERGREN

THREE WISHES

Published by Bergren Creative Group, Inc.
Colorado Springs, CO, USA

Cover design: Bergren Creative Group, Inc.
Cover images: Jennifer Ilene Photography

Printed in the United States of America

CHAPTER 1

"It's all yours. The apartment. The restaurant. She left it all to you."

I stared at him. I knew I was doing little more than blinking, but so many words came to my head at once...and yet none seemed to add up to complete sentences.

"I'm only seventeen," I finally spit out. Which pretty much summed up all my scattered thoughts. There was no way I could do this alone. How was I supposed to figure out my next steps without my *abuela*?

Señor Rodriguez blinked back at me, his bushy gray eyebrows like caterpillars above his eyes. "You'll be eighteen in a couple of months, Zara. Graduated. By the time the state catches up, you'll be officially independent." He said it as though this was the best news possible.

He reached out and patted my hand, this lawyer who had been to mass with us every Sunday of my life. His knuckles were thick with age, as my abuela's had been. "Your cousin, Mirabel. You can live with her a few months?"

"They have no room," I said, my eyes shifting to the window, with my guitar perched beside the frame. I thought of Mirabel's tiny two-bedroom apartment and three children under the age of five. Her husband, who drank tequila from the time he came through the door after work until he passed out on the couch. "She said she'd look in on me here," I said, forcing a confident nod. "I'll be fine."

"Well, better here," he said, putting some of his papers in an old briefcase, "than in a foster home or orphanage. I see no sense in that for two months. Your abuela…" He made the sign of the cross from his forehead to his ample belly and then from shoulder to shoulder and shook his head once. "She wouldn't have wanted that for you."

I frowned. She wouldn't. Neither would I.

"But what about the restaurant?" I asked.

He shrugged, raising ham-like shoulders to his ears. "Run it. Your abuela taught you everything she knew, *sí*? You're young. Strong." He lifted a hand and made a sweeping motion. "Or sell it. I know of some people—"

"Sell it," I said firmly. "I'll sell it," I said, more softly this time. I looked to the window again. "It's too much, you know? Too much hers. To be in that kitchen, without her there…" I shook my head. "I think I'd cry every day." Even the thought of it brought tears to my eyes. I'd be rolling out masa for tortillas but missing her beside me—poking me when I left it too thick, swatting me on the butt when I got it too thin. Making me smile through it all.

"The sale could help a little with college, though after we pay all your abuela's bills, I wouldn't count on much." He patted my hand again. "There's no need to rush. Shut the doors for a while. Wait to make a decision until you're certain. There's no hurry. But now, dear girl, I must go." He rose wearily. "It's very late."

"Sí, sí," I said, rising with him, guiltily glancing at the clock. It was past three in the morning. My grandmother's friends and family had stayed until after two, drinking up her tequila, eating everything I put out. Few made an effort to help clean up. The restaurant downstairs was a disaster.

I followed him to the door. "*Gracias*, Señor Rodriguez. I appreciate your guidance."

He turned and gave me a weary smile. "When you decide on the restaurant, I'll help you through. And if you need me, you call. For anything."

"I will."

He paused, looking out to the empty, dimly lit street. We heard nothing but the sound of crickets and distant waves on the beach. He looked back to me. "You'll be okay, Zara?"

"I'll be okay," I said, with more confidence than I felt. "I'll just pretend she's here."

He nodded, as if that was all he needed to hear, and walked down the steps with a lurching gait. His knees must hurt. It was so much like the way Abuela had moved…I hurriedly turned away and shut the door, leaning my head against it, my hand still on the cold knob. The tears flowed then. I'd last watched my grandmother climb those stairs three days ago. After a long night in the restaurant below. It had taken us forever to climb the fifteen steps, and I wanted to scream in frustration. And now—now, all I wanted was to watch her do it again. To feel her pat my cheeks. See her look on me with love. Hear her soft *goodnight*. "*Buenas noches, Grillita*."

Grillita. "Little cricket." She'd always called me that, for as long as I could remember. And as much as we hated finding the noisy nasties in our apartment, she always made my nickname sound like something admired and cherished. Like no one else had ever made me feel.

I straightened and moved woodenly toward her rocker, her knitting half-finished in the basket beside it. Forever unfinished now, because I never was any good at that kind of thing. But I picked it up and pulled out the long needles, setting them on my lap, yarn still looped around one, and lifted the finished portion up to my cheek, closing my eyes. "Oh, Abuela, Abuela," I said, more tears running down my face. "How could you leave me?"

I cried for hours, until the tiniest glimmer of pink began to light the eastern horizon, and knew I needed to get out of the apartment. To walk. Run. Then and only then might I sleep. The memories in here, her presence, felt smothering, as if they were closing in on me, wanted and yet unwanted. I needed some space to breathe before I could find my way into and through them.

Rising, I pulled off my sweater, which smelled of yesterday's work in the kitchen—smoke and lard and onion and cumin—and reached for my abuela's thick shawl, beautifully knitted from soft black and red yarn, and wrapped it around me like a hug. I still wore the black cami and long maxiskirt from yesterday's funeral and figured I'd be warm enough on the beach. If I kept moving, anyway. Even if I got chilled, it'd be good in a way. It'd remind me I was alive, through and through—that a part of me hadn't died with my grandmother.

I hurried down the street in the near-dark, glancing into shadowed doorways, keeping an eye out for troublemakers, thinking I ought to have brought my pocket knife. But most everybody was asleep at this hour. At the bottom of the street, I turned right and walked along much finer homes that lined the beach and those across the street, forced to content themselves with peekaboo views over their neighbors' rooftops. The houses here were big and stood inches away from their million-dollar neighbors, in an effort to make the most of the space. But up ahead, a wide public beach loomed, the white of cresting waves visible even in the relative dark.

As I got closer, I thought about visiting here with my grandmother. Collecting shells and sea glass—a mound that began to dominate our entire coffee table over the years. And yet she never complained. She'd encouraged it. *Ooh*ed and *ahh*ed over each find like it might bring us money, in time. Loved me, and loved my passions. Whatever they were. Playing the guitar. Singing. Clouds. Weather.

If it hadn't been for her… My dad was in prison for life, a murderer. My mom had been young when she got pregnant with me. Dumped me with her mother and ran away, then never saw either of us again. I don't think Abuela ever got over that. That, more than anything, made me tear up. To the very end, I think Abuela waited for the phone to ring. For a knock at the door. For a sweet reunion. Somehow, she thought that if Mom came home, everything would fall back into place. The family would draw together. We would all find a measure of peace.

But it wasn't to be.

I wiped angry tears from my eyes, rubbing them as if I was mad at myself for grieving Mom's absence again—even if it was for my grandmother, who believed until the end it was all going to work out.

I knew what Abuela craved. She wanted something like we saw every night in the restaurant. Families, thick with children of all ages, doting grandparents, playfully bickering parents, aunts and uncles and cousins. It seemed the birthright of a hundred families we knew. But not ours. *Not ours.*

I kicked off my flats and picked them up with two fingers, loving the feel of cool, damp sand squishing between my toes. I could see the horizon now with the rising sun behind me, even with the dense morning marine layer that shrouded the sea in billowing, misty clouds. They rolled inward, past me, over me, bathing my skin in moisture, like Neptune's own cold breath.

My feet moved as they always did, toward the rocks at the far end of the bay. There I'd find the tide pools my grandmother had loved.

Perhaps some sea urchins or anemones. Bright orange or deep purple starfish. Those had been her favorites, which had become mine. How dedicated she'd been, I thought. Raising a baby, a toddler, a girl, a teen. Keeping the restaurant going, to bring us income, when she should have been sitting back, relaxing.

But she'd done it all. For me.

Where would I have been without her?

"Thanks, Father," I whispered skyward, taking a deep breath past the lump in my throat and crossing myself, as Señor Rodriguez had done. "For giving me Abuela. Even if I wanted her longer. Take care of her for me, okay?"

I thought about the last conversation I'd had with her, three nights past, when we'd finally made it upstairs. I helped her to her rocker, took off her shoes as she asked, and rubbed her swollen feet, something I'd always hated. But she loved it so much, was so appreciative, I'd never had the guts to admit my reluctance. She sat back and closed her eyes, her face a mixture of pain and glory as I rubbed the knots from her arches, from her heel.

"What is it you want most, Grillita?" she asked.

"What do you mean?" I returned, tired and wanting only to slip into my bed.

"From life. If I could give you anything, what would you want?"

"Besides a scholarship to UCLA or Texas A&M?" *Or even an acceptance letter…*

"After a couple of years at the community college, they will accept you. You'll see."

Abuela had more faith in the system than I did, given my 3.5 GPA. But I was sick of worrying about it. "How 'bout an introduction to a handsome prince?"

"You don't have to wish for that," she said, her brown eyes twinkling as she peeked at me. "A girl as pretty as you—"

"I want adventure," I said, giving in to her little dream-session at last. "To experience more than this little town. To see the world and learn more about the people in it."

Her gray eyebrows shot up as she considered me. She'd spent her whole life here, never left the county. Then she nodded once. "That's good, yes. It is common for the young to hunger for such things. *Pero Grillita, a veces la aventura se puede hallar exactamente en el lugar donde te encuentres." But Cricket, sometimes adventure can be found right where you are.*

"Right," I said, squinting at her. This was a different sort of conversation than our usual chatter. She didn't understand. I wanted adventure-adventure. To be the Next Big Thing on the Weather Channel. Chasing tornadoes, on a raft in a flood zone, picking up a handful of dust in a drought-ridden field, riding in a helicopter over houses leveled by a tsunami, looking for survivors to save…

"How 'bout we play cards for a while? Gin rummy?" I asked her, trying to bring my head back to the present.

"No." She snapped her fingers in front of my face, nodding her gray head. "*¿Qué más?*"

"What else do I want?"

"Sí, sí," she said, waving at me in irritation for not continuing.

"Okay, uh… Love, I guess," I said. "You know. I'm not really after a handsome *prince*. He doesn't even have to be handsome, although if he was, that'd be cool. I just want to know what it is to really fall in love. And for a guy to fall in love with me. Real love, you know? Not the teenage stuff."

"It's as good as done," she said with her gap-toothed smile. "We simply have to wait for the one worthy of my girl."

I smiled with her and shook my head. My grandmother had always thought I should be the target of every man's affections. Whether the dude was eighteen or eighty-three, she'd routinely ask, "Isn't my granddaughter beautiful? And she's *smart*, too."

So crazy-embarrassing…

"What else?" she asked, sitting back and closing her eyes.

It was then that I noticed the color of her skin, oddly gray. And she was way more tired than she usually was after closing. "Abuela, are you okay?"

"Sí, sí," she said, waving away my concern, still with her eyes closed. "What else, Grillita? What is your third wish?"

I hesitated. The thought was clear in my head, but I didn't want to bring her pain in voicing it.

She peered at me through one squinted eye. "Zara? Tell me," she said softly.

"Family." I shrugged and rubbed a bit harder. "I mean, family like you and I both wanted, forever. Like the Medinas and the Garcias. Good families. Loving families. Families all up in each other's business. And yet willing to do anything for each other. You know," I said.

"*Yo lo sé*," she agreed softly, reaching out to touch my cheek.

"I don't mean to make you feel bad, Abuela," I said, guilt flooding through me.

"You don't make me feel bad," she said, patting my cheek and leaning back. "I wanted it once too. And someday, Grillita, you shall have it for both of us."

I smiled. "There you go again, promising me the moon, Abuela."

"You will have the moon, Zara," she said, head against the back of her rocking chair, eyes closed, even as she lifted her index finger. "Trust your abuela. When you get to a certain age, you know such things."

"Does my abuela know she must get to bed?" I asked.

"Sí, sí, she knows it."

I helped her stand and walk to her room, wincing with her as her legs, stiff after sitting, objected to the exertion. She'd been so tired, she insisted in getting into bed without undressing. Without brushing her teeth or her hair, something I'd never seen her do before. "Just leave me, Zara," she said, pulling up the blanket to her wrinkled cheek. "I only need to rest."

Should I have done something then? I'd known something was wrong. I felt it. But I was so tired myself, so bone weary, I could barely cover her and make it to my own room. So I bent and kissed her forehead, whispered good night. Perhaps she whispered the same, but to my shame, I couldn't remember.

And when I awoke, she was dead.

The EMT said she passed peacefully, never waking. It looked like she had. Like she'd just been dreaming about heaven and walked right on up there. It made me a little angry, actually. That she hadn't tried to fight it. To call out to me. Given me a chance to call 911 before it was too late. Tried to stay with me. Sure, I was almost eighteen. But eighteen really wasn't that old. I was old enough to strike out on my own. Go to college. Find a job. But not really old enough to be without anyone at all who loved me, truly loved me.

I reached the dark lava rocks, pockmarked by the sea's constant rub and wash, and made out the dim silhouette of a fisherman about twenty yards away, casting his line off a long rod. Beside him was the five-gallon painter's bucket the locals favored, probably full of surf perch or croakers by now. He looked about fifty years old, short and spry. Asian.

I'd never seen him here before, and I thought I knew all the locals. Maybe he usually was done fishing before I got to the rocks during my morning walks. After all, I'd never been here this early.

He glanced in my direction, and I lifted a hand in greeting. Then I crouched to peer into the first tide pool. Three massive starfish, two purple and one orange, clung to the edge, half in the water. I smiled and moved on to the next. There I found four orangies and two purplies. I gasped and looked up at the fisherman as he moved past, hauling his heavy bucket. I'd never seen six in one pool before. Abuela would have loved it…

"You like sta'fish?" he asked in a heavy Asian accent.

"I do. They…they remind me of someone I loved very much. There are six here!"

"Hmm," he said, studying me with a stroke of his beardless chin. He moved away, suddenly, when a wave crashed toward us. The wash narrowly missed him. I watched it recede, and then felt the older man's gaze still on me. A shiver ran down my back, and I slowly rose. What was his deal? What did he want?

"You like sta'fish, go to pool over there," he said, nodding to one closer to the water. "Befo' tide comes in."

I smiled, relaxing as he moved on, wondering why I'd suspected the gentle old dude was up to anything bad at all. Another wave washed over the rocks. With a glance out toward the water, I thought I might have just enough time to check out the pool the fisherman had gestured toward before the next big wave came through. I picked my way forward, jumping from high point to high point among the rocks. When I arrived, I looked down and let out a small cry.

He'd been right. The pool was teeming with starfish, several layers thick. Orange and purple, and a couple that were red and gold.

Even a few brittle stars, with their long arms. I'd never seen anything so amazing in all my life. It was so beautiful, so cool, that I ignored the wave that came in then, striking the boulders in front of me. I barely felt the spray across my face and hair. A wash of water covered the pool and went up to my knees. When the bubbling foam receded, I laughed at the massive starfish, all moving at once at surprising speed.

But then I frowned as two edged in opposite directions. *Was that…?*

Another wave crashed against the boulders, the tide clearly intent on retaking the rocks. Again I ignored it, intent on the pool before me, waiting for the white froth to recede and clear water to show me I'd been wrong…seeing things. I squeezed my fingers impatiently, waiting, waiting.

But when the water was once again clear to the bottom, I saw that the starfish had moved away from the center, all clinging to the edges now. It made no sense. Starfish were too slow, edging quietly over a rock in the course of an hour, not minutes. I looked to the center of the pool and frowned. There, nestled among the rocks and sand was the glint of gold.

Not starfish gold. Gold-gold.

I didn't hesitate. I stepped down and into the pool, my skirt rising around me, and leaned down and grabbed the edge of the object. It lifted easily, as if it'd been placed there just for me, and I looked around for the fisherman, now gone, even as another wave crashed against the rocks and thoroughly soaked me.

I clambered out of the pool and waited for the wave to recede back to the sea, leaving my path exposed. Then I hopped from rock to rock again, until I was at last climbing on soft sand between the big boulders that rose on this side of the beach. Safe from view of any early-morning runners, I sat down heavily, pushed aside my dripping curls, and studied the golden object. It looked like a small oil lamp, encrusted by a bunch of tiny white sea creatures of some sort on one side. It was clearly old, really old. I looked out to the Pacific, wondering if it was a remnant of some ancient galleon that had run aground, crashing on the reef that bordered the coast or even in our small cove. In all my years of walking this beach, I'd never found such an object—or heard of anyone else finding one like it either.

I used my nails to try and pry off some of the ocean muck that clung to it, then ran my fingertips over the soft, golden lip and then across the worn, foreign lettering that wound around the width of it. The lid was missing, and there had clearly been a spout at one time, giving it almost a genie-lamp feel, making me think of my abuela and her questions. *What do you want most, Grillita?*

I cradled the lamp to my chest, memories of her so vivid, her voice in my head so loud, it was like I was with her again.

What had I said? What had she said?

Adventure…to know true love…to discover what it meant to have a real family.

A blinding flash of light made me blink, and the ground seemed to shift. I reached for the nearest boulder, wondering if we were having an earthquake. My stomach twisted, and I felt a wave of nausea. Then my ears popped, and popped again, like when we were driving up and down from the mountains. But as I waited, there was nothing more.

Well, that was weird. Seriously weird.

I winced, holding my stomach as it settled, wondering what exactly was going on with my body. But then the heavy object in my hands distracted me again. What would a treasure like this be worth? Could it pay for my college? Maybe the guy at the pawn shop could tell me something…

I rose and walked around the boulder, looking down to the main part of the beach, wondering when Glen, the old leather-skinned lifeguard, would show up for duty. He'd think this thing was cool.

I sucked in a quick breath, blinking rapidly.

There was no lifeguard tower.

No runners on the beach, like there usually were by this time.

The million-dollar houses that had lined the cliffs above the beach when I got here were gone—only waving grass greeted my eyes on the bluff above. I glanced out to sea, wondering if somehow, I had walked up the wrong beach, distracted by the golden object in my hands.

I turned in a slow circle, eying the cliffs and the water. It was my beach for sure. It had to be. Except it didn't look like my beach. The tide pools were gone. The beach was wider and strewn with washed-up logs. And halfway across the broad expanse was the broken, skeletal frame of a shipwreck.

A shipwreck.

I frowned, shook my head and turned around in another slow three-sixty. "Wh-what's going on?" I muttered, now thinking I was hallucinating or something. Maybe I was just so tired…maybe this was some weird response to grief over my abuela…

I studied the bluff and the rocks beside me. It *was* the same cove, the same beach. My cove. *My cove.* It had to be.

But it wasn't. It was different. Radically different. Raw and undeveloped and—

A gunshot startled me—*a gunshot?* I flinched and peeked around the big volcanic boulder, down toward the long stretch of beach the surfers favored. Now what? Some sort of gang—

My eyes widened in shock. In the distance, there was a man on horseback, charging in my direction, four men on horseback behind him—in pursuit?—galloping at the same pace, hooves tossing up clods of sand behind them. Another gunshot cracked through the air, the only other sound besides the wash of the waves.

I could feel the rumble of the horses' hooves beneath my own bare feet and saw the men approaching at a frightening pace.

Everything was wrong. Terribly wrong.

I sank back between the big rocks, desperately seeking some sort of shelter. I glanced up the dunes to the bluff above and knew there was no way I'd make it up there in time. And even if I did, there wasn't a house to run to, a door to knock on…

I peeked around the edge of the big boulder again, watching as the first guy galloped ever nearer. I took in his tailored, tightly buttoned jacket and his dark good looks before pulling back around the rock, attempting to hide. I crouched down, eyes wide, waiting for him to pass.

The mare kicked up clods of sand that pelted the rock beside and above me. I thought the rider glanced under his arm at me, our eyes meeting for a second, but he never paused. He definitely wanted to get away from those who pursued him, which made my heart pound. *What is happening?* His saddle was clearly an antique, all gorgeous tooled leather, inlaid with gold and red in an old-Mexico feel. *Everything* about him and his horse said Old Mexico, when I thought about it.

Maybe they're shooting a movie. Maybe this isn't my beach. Maybe I passed out, the waves moved my unconscious body to another beach…one I haven't ever been to.

But I'd been on every beach within twenty miles. I looked up the bluff again. This was my cove. Tainter Cove. It had to be. It had to be, but…

I sank back an inch further, wishing I could become one with the rock as the others finally passed by me, in pursuit of the first man. There were four of them, and as they passed, they were shouting in Spanish. "*¡Cerrémosle el paso! ¡Separémonos! Debemos matarlo antes que llegue al límite del rancho.*"

Cut him off, I translated in my head. *Divide up. We must kill him before he reaches the rancho border.*

Rancho? There hadn't been ranchos in this part of California for more than a century. I remembered that much from my state history class. Sure, there was Rancho Cucamonga, and Rancho Santa Margarita and Rancho Palos Verdes, but those were just nods to the past…a developer's romantic name for sprawling subdivisions of suburban houses. Right?

But their Spanish had sounded odd to my ears. Crisp. Formal. Not anything like our slurred, local Spanglish. Not even like the Spanish they spoke down across the border, in Tijuana. More like Spanish-Spanish. Old Spanish.

And they had been in odd clothing too. Tight pants, worn boots, cropped jackets, and trim hats like the vaqueros used to wear. And one had passed near enough for me to take in more finely tooled stirrups and another saddle like I'd never seen—not that I'd seen a ton of variation when I worked at camp one summer and hung out with the girls who ran the trail rides. The saddle hadn't been as elegant and elaborate as the first man's, the one they pursued. But old.

Movie. I have to be on a movie set. The director dude is going to be so pissed when he finds me here. They'll have to crop me out, or shoot this whole scene again…

But then where were the cameras? The track running alongside the horses to catch the shot? The sound guys with those long sticks and microphones?

On shaking legs, I rose and dared to edge out again, looking up the beach, where the four in pursuit were just urging the horses up the dunes and over the edge, never looking back. I had to figure this out. Maybe I was dreaming.

I gathered up Abuela's shawl, shook it out, and wrapped it around my shoulders. It was like she was with me now, giving me courage, comfort. I grabbed the golden lamp and, crouching over, scurried away from the rocks and toward the nearest dune. There I hunkered down, panting, my heart thundering in my chest, waiting. But there was no sound other than waves on the shore and wind rustling the summer-dry grasses by my head. Except for…the lowing of cows?

No honking of horns or traffic.

No thunder of a train racing down the tracks that bordered the beach.

Cows.

I swallowed hard, then forced myself to scurry up the next dune and the next, until I reached the top and peered over toward the PCH.

I gasped and blinked.

There was no Pacific Coast Highway. No buildings. No railroad track. Just miles and miles of grass and trees. A herd of cattle, not too far off.

In the distance, I could see the men, still in pursuit of the other. But now more men were riding toward him, down from another hill, as if to meet them. In battle? To defend the first? Or to finish him off?

I turned in a slow circle, letting the shawl fall, trying to make sense of what was all around me. It felt like home, but it was all so very different.

So wrong. So foreign…and yet so familiar, too.

My knees gave way, and I collapsed to the sand and rocks, cutting my hand as I fell. But I gave it little notice, grabbing hold of the golden lamp and staring furiously at it. Intuitively, I knew that all of *this*… around me…had something to do with *this*, in my hands.

I thought back to the flash of light, the popping of my ears. What I'd been thinking right before that. About Abuela. About what I'd wished for most. A passionate, adventurous life. True love. Family.

And what had I gotten?

Some sort of odd transport to a place that seemed farther from those things than ever before.

CHAPTER 2

I have to get back. Reverse whatever's happened here.

I forced myself to rise, stumbling back to the rocks below, to the place I'd been when all of this began. Dimly I realized that I was leaving Abuela's shawl behind, but I was so focused on what was ahead, so driven, that I couldn't seem to stop myself. I was totally desperate.

Panting, I knelt on the sand between the rocks. No, I'd been sitting. Quickly I shifted, trying to get exactly back in position. Like I'd been before all of this crazy stuff started happening. *My fingers had been holding it like this... No, like that...* I shifted the object in my hands, trying to get it right. But nothing felt right. I couldn't quite remember.

Focus on the familiar, Zara. I looked outward. To the tide, now receding. Then upward to the clouds I liked to study. Cirrus clouds. Usually forming above 18,000 feet and sometimes called "mare's tails." Floating west to east...

It's all right, I told myself. *It's all right. You're still you. You're not crazy. Just take a deep breath. Close your eyes. This will all be over in a sec.*

But when I opened my eyes, all was the same.

Over and over I tried. Waiting for hours for another flash of light, the popping of my ears. Waited as the cirrus clouds gave way to a brilliant, blue sky and I had to shelter in the shade of the rock. Seeing no one in all that time and getting nowhere in my concentrate-my-way-back scheme, I ventured down the beach and wandered through the bones of the old ship, running my hands over the beams to confirm they were real. I went to the other end, where I'd found the lamp in the tide pools, thinking that if I set it back in the pool among the starfish, then Scotty might beam me back. *That's it. I've landed in some weird Star Trek episode…*

But there were no pools to be found. Just a wide band of sand.

I shielded my eyes and waded partway out, wondering if the pools were here, just covered by the tide. But then I realized, by studying the cliffs, that the pools were buried by a good fifty feet of sand beneath my feet, yet to be exposed by the ravages of time.

I wandered back, feeling oddly separate from myself, distantly thinking that I was probably in some sort of shock. Mostly I felt beat, so tired I had a hard time putting one foot in front of the other, until I reached the sheltering boulders again. It was as if I'd run a marathon or had to stay late at the restaurant, closing after 2 a.m.

Nestling close to the sun-warmed rock and hugging the golden lamp close to my chest, I lay back, praying that if I just slept for a bit, I'd wake up to the familiar.

It's okay, Zara. You're just dreaming. That's why you're so tired. You'll just have to give in to this nightmare a bit more, and then you can wake up.

So I allowed it, drifting off in a moment.

I awoke to the prick of a knife at my throat.

"*¿Quién eres tú?*" a man barked at me. *Who are you?*

I blinked, trying to focus, staring up at silhouette of a man, standing against a high-noon sun. I saw first his blade—not a knife, but a long, thin, silver sword. The handle was all ornate, elegant coils and curves around his strong, brown hand. He shifted, and I could see his face better.

It was the first man, the one the others had pursued.

"What is this?" he continued in Spanish, reaching down and grabbing my lamp.

"No!" I cried, pushing away his blade and rising, wincing as I noted how it sliced through the same hand I'd injured earlier. But I was wholly focused on the golden treasure. "Give it back to me!" I shouted in English.

He frowned and brought the tip of his sword toward me again. "*¡Quédate atrás!*" *Stay back.* He glanced at the lamp, turning it in his hands a bit, but I seemed to be his main focus.

He looked me over from head to toe, and I felt the spare cami above the long, black maxiskirt that had dried, clinging to my legs. He was movie-star handsome, but that didn't give him the right to look me over like my abuela used to look at a perfect pork butt before she put it in the pot. I crossed my arms. "Give that back to me," I said, gesturing toward the lamp.

He frowned again. "*¿Por qué hablas inglés?*" he said, taking a turn around me, the sword still between us. *Why are you speaking English?* "You look like a Mexican maiden," he continued in Spanish, "but your clothing is…foreign." Was that a hint of a blush in his dark cheeks? The way he'd said *foreign*, and kept his eyes just on my face now, made me feel half-naked. I glanced around for Abuela's shawl.

"I am a Mexican maiden," I said, trying to make my Spanish match his in clarity. His accent was so weird.

"A spy," he said, bringing the tip of his sword below my chin and lifting it, forcing me to look at him again.

"No," I said, guessing from his tone that that would be the worst. "I…I fell off a ship in the night and washed ashore."

"Oh?" he said, slowly lowering his sword. "Which ship?"

"The…the *Santa Maria*." It was all I could think of on the spur of the moment. Columbus's ship.

He squinted at me, and I stared back. About twenty or twenty-one. Over six feet tall. Broad shoulders, accentuated by the tailored, tight jacket. Scruffy, short facial hair around full lips and over his chin and cheeks—like he hadn't shaved in a few days. Shoulder-length, curly black hair, partially covering one eye. Dark lashes lacing steamy eyes that seemed to see far more than I wanted. Almost into me and through my lie.

"The *Santa Maria*," he repeated dully, tossing my lamp in one hand. I moved to grab it, but he swiftly brought the sword up between us again.

He's big, but he's fast, I decided. But I'd taken on guys this big before in Krav Maga. I lifted my chin and stared back at him, forcing myself to drop my shoulders.

A tiny smile tugged at his lips. "And just who is the…*Santa Maria*'s captain?"

"Capitán DiCaprio," I said without pause. "Leonardo DiCaprio."

"And from where does she hail?"

"Puerto Vallarta," I said blithely.

Again, he squinted at me, as if trying to figure me out. "There is no such port in all of Mexico. Nor is there such a ship. About thirty ships pass these shores this time of year, and the *Santa Maria* is not one of them. And I know a hundred seafaring families and merchants who hail from Mexico, and this…*Leonardo DiCaprio* is not one of their captains." He turned, tossed my lamp to the sand next to his horse, sheathed his sword at his waist, and crossed his arms. "Now you shall tell me the truth, girl. Who are you, really? What are you doing here?"

The truth. I vacillated. Lay it on him, all of it? Or refuse to speak at all? Tell him I was a mermaid, looking for her man? Maybe that'd make him freak and run off, leaving me to find my way back to my own time.

He stepped forward, and I tensed. "Tell me, girl. Or I will tie you up and take you back to my rancho, keeping you there until you tell me. Were you with those men who gave me chase?"

"Wh-what? No!"

He stepped even closer, taking hold of my arms. "Tell me the truth!"

I was about to take him down when a low growl behind me made us both freeze.

He looked over my shoulder and then slowly pulled me to his side, as if he wished to protect me.

But the wolf seemed to be looking only at him, baring her teeth.

The young man slowly withdrew a pistol from his side, pulled back the hammer, and aimed.

"No!" I cried, pushing up his arm at the last second, finally understanding that he meant to kill the animal. The crack of gunfire made my ears ring.

"Why did you do that?" he asked, turning to face me. He gestured toward the wolf, now tearing up the dunes, running away from us as fast as she could. "Those filthy beasts cost me countless sheep every year!"

"Well, she was not attacking one of your sheep right now," I said, hands on my hips. "It looked like she was trying to protect me from *you*."

"Nonsense!" He grimaced and grabbed my arm again. "Enough. You shall come with me."

I acted without thinking. Two years of the best self-defense training—at my grandmother's insistence—had given me what I needed. *Awareness, assertiveness, technique,* my instructor whispered in my mind. I whipped my arm out of his hands and punched him in the gut, and when he bent over, I brought my knee up hard, connecting with his cheek. When he straightened, I brought my knee up again, this time to his groin.

He fell to the ground, utterly surprised, his breath whooshing from his lungs in a terrible gasp. I raced for his horse and then forced myself to slow as the mare skittered ten feet away, wary of my actions. I edged closer, glancing back to the young man writhing on the sand, his handsome face a mask of pain and fury. Then I dared to go back and grab hold of the golden lamp, just a few feet away from him.

Again I advanced toward the mare, calmer this time, knowing it wouldn't be long before the man stumbled after me with sword drawn again. I glanced over my shoulder at him again.

"*¡Detente!*" he gasped, reaching toward me, clearly furious. "*¡Vuelve acá!*" *Stop! Come back here!*

Ignoring him, I managed to grab hold of one of the mare's reins, then the other. I dropped the lamp in a saddlebag, lifted my skirt, put my bare foot in the stirrup, and wrenched myself up and across her back. It had been a couple of years since I'd ridden a horse, and I never was particularly comfortable doing it. I wavered and held on tight to the horn as the mare pranced left and right, whinnying her complaint. She brought us closer to the dude, who now was trying to rise, and my heart tripled its beat. *If he got ahold of me again…*

I tightened the reins, clenched my thighs against her sides and then rammed my heels into her flanks. She hesitated a sec and then took off, nearly unseating me. I wished the stirrups weren't too long for my feet to reach. But I leaned down and tried to catch her rhythm, odd on the sandy beach. I directed her lower, closer to the waves, where the sand was firmer, and fell more into stride with her, churning along the beach, up toward George Point.

I glanced to my right and saw the wolf, matching our pace. It felt like she was happy, cheering me on, not any sort of threat to me. Just another weird element during my weirdest day ever… I passed the ribs of the shipwreck, startling a nearby flock of seagulls into the sky. But I didn't pause until I reached the end of the beach. There, I pulled up on the reins and turned back.

The wolf was gone, sending a pang of strange sorrow through me. The man, tiny in the distance, was up on his feet and running after me, one arm outstretched.

"Sorry, handsome," I muttered in English, feeling a little bad now for stealing his horse. "But I don't know who to trust around here. And I gotta get home."

I urged the mare forward, over the black lava rocks that separated one cove from the next. At least this was the same as I remembered.

But as I rounded the point, the next cove was as foreign as the last. I mean, there were parts that seemed the same, but there were no houses, no people. *Nothing.* Again I sank my heels into the mare's flanks and rode to the next point, and then the next, until I reached Bonita Harbor. But when I could at last view that old, wide curve of beach, I paused again, trying to make sense of what I saw.

The familiar, big pier with the burger restaurant at the end wasn't there. The only thing visible along the beach was a large adobe building at the center, with an open front and tall roof. Beside it were six rowboats on the sand.

Moored at the center of the teal-green bay was a ship with three masts, sails furled. On the beach were six men, yanking a rowboat ashore. More were milling higher up, around crates that they were either loading or unloading. Others walked down a steep path, bundles of something tan across their shoulders. It looked like leather…

"She's a sight to behold, isn't she?"

I whirled, and saw a new man emerging from the cliffs behind me. *Pirates Cave*, I remembered, an old haunt we'd favored as kids. He'd been inside it, hidden from view. I steadied the horse and turned to face him again. He didn't look like a pirate. Just a tall, average-looking seaman, about twenty-five years old. "You're a sight to behold too," he said appreciatively, continuing in English, eyes scanning my bare legs. He switched to Spanish. "But this is hardly the place to be half-dressed. If my men see you… But then perhaps male company is what you seek?"

I swallowed hard. Behind me, down the beach, were the men he referenced. Now he—and the guy I stole a horse from—blocked the other way. He was armed, with a pistol on one hip and a sword on the other.

"Isn't that Javier de la Ventura's mount?" he asked in Spanish, coming closer.

"Stay where you are," I returned, in English.

His pale brows arched in surprise, and he stopped short. "You speak English."

"Yes, I do," I said.

"And you speak it well," he said, smiling in admiration. "Forgive me, miss. I mistook you for a woman seeking…masculine companionship." This, he said in Spanish.

I blinked. Had he really just said that? "Assume that again," I began, in Spanish, "and I'll have to teach you some manners, " I finished, in English.

He laughed then, so hard he bent backward and then straightened, chin in hand, looking at me in delight. He had sandy-colored hair that he wore pulled back in a leather band. His eyes were blue, the color of the Pacific, and his skin deeply tanned. "I must say"—he laughed again—"you are the biggest surprise of my voyage so far. And I've had many this year."

"I could tell you a few stories that would surprise you further," I returned.

"Oh?"

I took in his fine clothes—worn but of good quality. The longer cut of his jacket, his gloves. He, too, was like someone out of a historical film, but there was something about him—his use of English? His Midwest looks?—that made me decide to trust him. After all, if that Javier dude caught up to us, he might slice me to ribbons with his sword. Here before me was the captain of the ship in the cove—a man with the power to protect me, if necessary. Maybe even with the power to take me someplace else, someplace familiar…

He paused, brought one hand to the lapel of his jacket, and gave me a slight bow. "Perhaps we should begin again. I am Captain John Worthington, hailing from Bangor, Maine, and I am captain of that ship, the *Emma Jane*. We are here to trade goods and will set sail come morn. And you are?"

I studied him. "Señorita Zara Ruiz," I said at last.

"I am pleased to make your acquaintance, Señorita Ruiz," he said, again with a slight bow. His inquisitive eyes ran down my hair to my cami and skirt, and once again I was aware that I had far too few clothes on to be around a man of any sort in this…time? Place? "And just where do you hail from?" he asked.

"This is my difficulty, Captain, and a part of the stories I might tell, in time," I said, trying to match his formal tone and old way of speaking. "But as you noted, I am improperly dressed and in grave distress. I'm a…castaway of sorts. Perhaps in your trading you have clothes that might fit me? A bit of water? I would gladly trade you tales for some of each."

"What transpired with your clothes, Miss Ruiz? And why do you ride Javier's mount? Did that scoundrel—"

"Tales in exchange for a proper dress," I interrupted, "and water…and a bit of food if you have it," I added, suddenly feeling the rumble of my belly as well as my terribly parched throat.

He squinted at me, and an easy smile broadened across his face. "Most intriguing," he said. "Fortunately for you, I have access to all, aboard the *Emma Jane*. Perhaps you can remain here, in this cave, while I go and fetch them? As I said, if my men…"

I nodded. "Thank you. I'd be grateful for your assistance." The words rolled off my tongue as if I'd always spoken in his odd, formal manner. But they seemed right. Less foreign, perhaps, to him. Maybe it was the name of the ship, the *Emma Jane*, that had allowed me to channel my inner Latina Jane Austen. Whatever it was, it seemed to work, and the man strode off down the beach.

I dismounted and tugged the mare toward the cave, hoping to keep her out of sight in case Javier-what's-his-name made it closer. But he had to still be a couple of miles behind me now and on foot. Maybe he'd even given up the chase and was hiking home. And how did Captain John know him?

I secured the mare's reins around a rock and paced near the cave entrance, waiting for John to return. Now that I knew he was off to fetch food and water, I was all the hungrier and thirstier. *And chilly*, I thought, rubbing my arms. Abuela's shawl…I'd left it somewhere back at Tainter Cove. *Maybe I can go back and get it at some point.*

After another half hour, John returned to the cave, this time using a rowboat, arriving alone. He bent, grabbed hold of a bundle, and then splashed into the shallow water, hauling the boat higher up on the beach before turning to trudge toward me. "At your service," he said gallantly, rolling out the bundle. Inside was a deep green and black dress, a cork-topped jug that I assumed was full of water, bread, and a bit of dried meat and fruit. Desperate, I hurriedly lifted the jug, uncorked it, and drank for a long time before I straightened to see he'd been offering me a tin cup.

"Oh, sorry," I said, wiping my mouth with the back of my hand.

"Sorry?" he repeated.

"Uh, forgive me," I said. "I didn't know you'd brought a cup too."

He squinted at me. "Just who saw to your English education, Señorita Ruiz?"

"I learned it in school," I said, frowning a little.

"A Mexican girl who attended school?"

I paused. This was apparently weird. "It was important to my abuela. My grandmother."

"I speak Spanish as well as I do English," he said, proving his point in Spanish. "So use whichever tongue you choose. But I must say, I have never met a Mexican woman who can do the same. And your accent is…unlike any I've ever heard."

"As is yours," I retorted, but then instantly regretted it. I didn't need to make this guy mad. I needed him to be my new BFF.

He frowned. "I assure you, I had the finest tutors and instructors in Maine. And I keep company with many fine Castilian families, both here in Alta California and in Mexico."

I swallowed another sip of water, this time pouring it first into a cup, thinking about what he'd said. Castilian families—old Spanish families, he meant. And *Alta* California? The old name for the upper part of the state—not to be confused with Baja California below. "Forgive me. I'm certain they were. Likely far better than my own."

He stared at me, clearly trying to discern if I lied or told the truth, then inhaled slowly. "Yes, well, there is time enough to debate educational veracity. For now, you'd likely appreciate a bit more clothing and then some of this food."

I nodded and immediately bent to take hold of the huge dress—yards and yards of emerald green silk and black lace. Underneath was another skirt, in ivory silk, obviously worn beneath to poof out the green. A petticoat, I thought they were called. John turned slightly away, his cheek coloring as if embarrassed that we looked upon underclothes together. I huffed a laugh and turned, trudging up and into the cave. Once there, I pulled on the dress over my cami and maxiskirt, thinking I wasn't ready to give them up. It was a bit big, but that was better than it being a bit small. I played with the neckline, unsure of whether it was supposed to be worn on top of the shoulder or down, electing to take the safe route and leave it up.

Inside the dress, I'd found a comb that appeared to be made of bone or ivory, each tooth of the comb hand-carved from the bigger object. *Apparently, this is Captain John's hint to fix my hair*, I thought. I set about working the comb through my wild curls, feeling bits of sand fall to my shoulders. Then, feeling like a girl in costume, I edged back out into the sunlight.

John turned, and his face broke out into that easy smile. "Miss Ruiz, you are a vision. And a proper-looking lady now."

"Thank you, Captain Worthington," I said, deciding he might not appreciate my casual use of his first name. I was talking to Captain John. A real-life sea captain. While clothed in what felt like a Halloween costume.

"Before we sit down, I brought this too," he said, fishing out a clean strip of white cloth from his jacket pocket. He reached down and lifted the water jug. "I saw that you had injured your hand?"

"Oh. Yes," I said, lifting my palm up to see the rough gash from the rocks and a longer, thinner cut from Javier's sharp blade. In the midst of everything else, I'd forgotten about it—other than to try and keep blood from getting on the new gown. "They look worse than they are."

"Yes, well, we don't want them to fester, do we? Hold still." He splashed water over my palm and gently washed away the blood. His eyes narrowed as he noted the clean cut of a blade, but he said nothing, just wrapped the strip of cloth around my hand until he reached the end, tucking it into the last loop around my palm. "That should hold you."

"Thank you," I said, touched by his thoughtfulness.

He gestured toward a cloth, spread across the sand like it was a picnic blanket, and I sank down, aware of how the skirt circled me in an arc. It really was beautiful, with a pretty shimmer that reminded me of the tide pools at twilight. "So…how is it that a sea captain has such a dress aboard his ship? I assume there are only men with you?" I bit into a chunk of stale bread, waiting on his answer.

He quirked a rueful smile. "It was meant for my younger sister, who wanted 'something unique' from Mexico. But I decided I could stop for another upon our return voyage."

I felt instantly guilty. "I only need to borrow it, Captain. I can return it just as soon as…just as soon as…" As what? When? Where?

"Never mind that. It is my good pleasure to come to your aid. It will make this tale better for the telling. And speaking of tales, a strange girl I met on the beach made a certain promise to me…" He lifted one of his light brows, lips in a teasing grin, then raised his hands. "So tell me, Señorita Ruiz, what you must."

"I…I…" I swallowed, not sure where to begin. What to say, how much, or whether I should say anything at all. "Captain, please tell me three things, first." I took a drink of water, forcing down the dry bread and then a bite of the dried meat.

"That was not our bargain," he said lightly. "But as I am a gentleman, I shall submit to your request. Ask away." He waved one hand and reached for his own strip of meat.

The questions I needed answered would make him think I was crazy, so I tried a story I'd concocted while he was gone. "I believe I fell from a ship," I said, "and struck my head. My memory is sketchy."

"Sketchy?" he repeated with a frown.

"Spare," I amended, remembering my Latina Austen. "I actually remember very little, I fear."

His frown deepened. He stopped chewing. "That is grave indeed."

"Tell me, Captain…what year is it?"

"1840," he said soberly. "Do you not remember that?"

1840.

He wasn't joking.

1840, I thought again, trying to make it sink into my brain, ignoring his question.

"And…where are we, exactly?"

His blue eyes did not leave mine, alarm growing behind them.

"We are in Alta California, of course. About sixty miles north of Santa Barbara."

"Alta California," I repeated. The name the Spaniards and Mexicans gave this territory before it became a state. *1840…*

"And where is the nearest American government office?" I forced out.

He blinked slowly and shifted, leaning back, as if trying to be outwardly casual when he felt uneasy within. "There is an embassy in Mexico, as well as in Panama. But the nearest United States government officials, on their own soil, are likely in Louisiana."

"Louisiana," I muttered. I'd not even driven as far east as Arizona. How far was Louisiana?

"Louisiana," he repeated gently, tucking his chin. "You've heard of it, yes?"

"Yes," I whispered, looking out to sea, and we both stayed silent for a while. What had I been thinking? Did I think government officials could tell me where I was and how to get home to my own time? I cradled my head in my hands.

"Miss Ruiz, do you remember where your home is?"

"I do," I said quickly, but then paused. "Or did."

"Did?"

"I…I used to live just up the hill from that cove, several down," I said, gesturing southward.

"That is Rancho Ventura land." When my expression didn't change, he tried, "Or perhaps you lived just south of the ranch border, on Vargas land? Were you employed by the Venturas or Vargases?" He was obviously trying to jog my memory. His frown returned. "But you said you were a castaway, I thought. You fell from a ship?"

"Yes. And I think I hit my head. I cannot remember much

of my past."

"You must have taken a fearsome blow to your skull, indeed," he said, instantly nodding, as if now my odd talk about living on Ventura or Vargas land made sense to him. "I've seen it once or twice before with sailors. Both had their memories return within a day or two. Perhaps you shall experience the same."

"Yes, perhaps," I said.

"Which ship were you on? Perhaps I can assist you in getting back to her. The captain could likely tell us more about you."

I shook my head as if I couldn't remember. That Leonardo-DiCaprio-track hadn't gone well with Javier.

"Or do you remember the name of your school? Where you received instruction in English? Or who your governess or tutor was? Clearly, you must have been the daughter of a fine Mexican gentleman to command such skills."

That made me giggle. And then laugh. My father a fine Mexican gentleman? I pictured the faceless man—a relative I'd never met—strolling around the yard at San Quentin. Nothing could be farther from the truth. "Forgive me," I said, gathering myself as I caught his puzzled expression. "No, it wasn't due to my father. It was due to my grandmother. She gave me…everything."

Thinking about her made me so sad that I teared up. I swallowed hard, not wanting to cry in front of this man, but failing. Wordlessly, he fished a handkerchief from his pocket and handed it to me. I had to look away again, his kind gesture making me want to cry all the more. Tears slipped down my cheeks.

"I take it she has…passed?"

"Yes," I said. "Just—" *What? A hundred-and-eighty-ish years in the future?* "Yesterday."

"How dreadful for you," he said gravely, seeming not to notice my odd pause. "But you remember that much. That is a good sign. She must have been traveling with you. Perhaps in your grief, you tripped over something and fell overboard?"

"Perhaps." I cast him a grateful smile, aware that he was treating me like a kind older brother would.

"Do you remember where your *grandmother* lived?" he asked, trying a different tack. "Rancho Ventura covers that cove and many more, including this one. Perhaps the ship was bringing you and your grandmother home. Do you think you are employed there? Perhaps that is why you have Javier's mare? Did he lend her to you?"

"No," I said, shaking my head and blowing my nose loudly, hoping he'd forget about Javier. I crumpled the handkerchief in my hand, embarrassed. What was a girl supposed to do with a handkerchief that had been used? Give it back?

We sat there in companionable silence for a bit, feeling the wind blow over our faces. "Is there more you wish to tell me?" he said at last.

I paused, still not sure of what else to say. What else could I tell him that wouldn't paint me into a corner? But there was something trustworthy about John, something that told me that he really did look at me as he might his younger sister. I rose and went to the mare, petting her nose and then moved to the saddlebag. I wondered if it was wise to show him the lamp, but I desperately needed another person's opinion, and he seemed to be a thoughtful kind of guy. Maybe he'd know what it was…and how I might use it to get back to my own time.

I pulled out the lamp and turned back toward him to find he'd followed me. "Señorita Ruiz…if I may," he said, clearly feeling awkward.

"Your neckline…The seamstress showed me the dress on a mannequin when I purchased it, and I believe…Well, I believe that the top is meant to be worn…" He coughed, and I saw the tinge of red at his lower cheeks again.

Oh. Got it. My earlier question answered at last. I pulled down the edges of the lace at my neck—noticing in relief that it alleviated some cleavage—and then looked to him for approval.

His color deepened, and he looked embarrassed over his own response.

What? Yeah, there was more shoulder-skin visible now, but far less boobage. What was the deal?

"Señorita Ruiz," he said, his tone suddenly more firm. "We are scheduled to weigh anchor come daybreak. I believe…" His eyes fell on the object in my hands. "What is that?"

"It—it's something I found on the beach," I said.

He took it from my hands and shifted it, taking in the circumference, pulling it closer to his eyes to peer at the worn lettering. I waited, holding my breath. I wanted him to tell me he recognized it. Knew what it was and how I might use it to get home.

Instead he reluctantly handed it back to me. "It's valuable. Clearly gold. Hold on to it. It could purchase you transport or supplies. You found it on the beach?" he added, looking out to sea.

"I did. But about four coves to the south. Do you suppose it came from that old shipwreck?"

He paused, thinking. "Possibly. Most wrecks are thoroughly salvaged, but valuables can always be missed."

"Hmmm," I murmured, rolling the lamp around in my hands anew. If I could just make out what the writing had once said…

"Miss Ruiz," he said, after a pause, "as I was saying, we are poised to weigh anchor come morn. I cannot leave you here, a woman alone, injured. I must take you to friends, where you might find shelter and succor until your memory is fully restored."

I had no idea what *succor* meant, but I could read his expression. His intent was to find me protection, help.

"Can I…can I not travel with you? To wherever you are going? Or even to…Maine?" He was at once my lifeline, my last hope. The thought of him leaving made my heart triple its beat.

"Ahhh, no," he said firmly, turning his face toward the *Emma Jane.* "A ship is no place for a woman."

No place for a woman. His words registered on several levels. As a woman—*What, I couldn't go wherever I wanted? Anytime I wanted? Try me…*—as a girl lost in time—*should I stay right here, closest to the doorway to my own?*—and as just a normal human…wondering if I should pay attention to his cautious tone.

"You can protect me," I said, looking up into his face, wanting to bring out that older brother mode again. "Take me with you."

"No," he said abruptly, reaching out as if to lay a hand on my shoulder and then thinking better of it when his eyes took in my bare skin. "No," he said, more softly, shaking his head. "I will take you someplace you will be safe, protected, until your head clears. My friends will watch over you. I know a family. Within their walls, they shall treat you as their own."

I stared into his blue eyes, feeling his words as a promise.

"All right," I said, looking up into his face. "I am trusting you."

"Your trust, Señorita Ruiz," he said, swallowing visibly, "shall not be misplaced."

CHAPTER 3

I began to doubt Captain Worthington's decision as we passed by several doleful vaqueros that evening, watching me with suspicious eyes. It was clear that they recognized my stolen mare, and I saw at last that her brand matched their own.

"Captain," I said to him in alarm as he rode ahead of me, "you are taking me to Rancho *Ventura*?"

He cast me a soft smile. "We've been on their land since we met. Indeed, we'd be hard-pressed to pass *out* of their boundaries. I thought you would be eager to return the mare to them." He dropped back, letting me catch up. I struggled with riding bareback in the luxurious gown, with my legs to one side, as was apparently the polite way to do it. Javier's fine saddle was strapped behind John's. "Trust me, Señorita Ruiz. It is far better for you to find rest at Rancho Ventura, rather than in a town such as Santa Barbara. The priests have abandoned their missions. Mexico does precious little to support the presidios, and what soldiers remain are disreputable. And therefore, all that is left to us..." He took a deep breath. "There are far more women here," he said, nodding ahead of us, "than you'd find in town. And where there are women, there is civility."

I swallowed my sarcastic retort. *You'd be surprised.* I'd always gotten along better with boys than girls...

With each hill we crossed between the harbor and where we were going—deeper and deeper into the hills—I paused and looked back, trying to keep track of the way back to the beach. And with each hill we crested, John nodded, as if coaxing me forward.

"This is *all* Ventura land?" I asked, letting my eyes sweep across the hills that seemed to go on for miles.

"Indeed," John said. "And a good portion of that beach too, including Bonita Harbor. That's the real prize. The only decent land-approach beach between Santa Barbara and Monterey. Everywhere else we trade along the coast is far more challenging for my men. They have to carry hides and crates of tallow above their heads and through big waves to the boats."

I absorbed that, but mostly I was trying to keep my mouth from falling open. The rancho was huge. As in humongous-huge. I was pretty sure a hundred subdivisions could fit in it in modern times, and that was only the land I could see. I got the impression that it went on from there.

We passed hundreds upon hundreds of cattle, tended by half-naked, brown-skinned Indian boys atop mules, then followed a serpentine river north and east, toward the mountains in the far distance. After half an hour or so of riding, we at last saw a sprawling, three-story villa, nestled against a bank of rolling hills. In the distance, behind it, the mountains rose. Their familiar presence helped me breathe.

"Javier de la Ventura is the eldest living son of a soldier who helped establish this territory," John said. "His father secured this tremendous land grant—but then he died a few years later. Javier went to Mexico to study at university. But when his elder brother died last year, he had to return home to see to the rancho. Javier is by turns a rake and an honest man, yet I am honored to call him a friend. But then you likely know that already, on account of the fact that he lent you his horse."

I rolled his words over in my mind, unsure of what a *rake* was, but pretty sure it was the opposite of an *honest man.*

"My uh…last encounter with Señor de la Ventura didn't go well," I said nervously, remembering him writhing on the ground, "despite the fact that he lent me his horse. Are you certain he will welcome me?"

John looked me in the eye, clearly wondering just what had passed between me and Javier and how I ended up with the mare. "All I know is that *Don* de la Ventura will be relieved to have his fine mount back," he said at last. "He takes great pride in her. Whatever transpired between you, that will buy you a certain amount of grace."

Don de la Ventura. As in, The Man. The dude who claimed all of this—I paused to look around again—as his own.

We rode between two crude posts and down a road that I supposed marked the formal entry, following along two tracks cut by wagons, closer to the U-shaped house in the distance. As we drew nearer, I could see that the gates could be closed and fortified, but were now open to us in welcome. A massive, twisting bougainvillea vine—heavy with purple flowers—climbed to one side of the front door, nearly reaching the top of the second story. I noted two armed men on the roof—clearly guarding the villa. Were we in danger here? Did it have to do with the guys who'd been chasing Javier early this morning? A stately, silver-haired woman, a younger woman with a baby on her hip, and four children gathered in the center of the U, turning to look our way, but it was Javier who strode forward. Behind him, the older woman—his mother?—and the others hung back, near a bank of rose bushes.

Javier was in a clean jacket, his curly hair pulled into a ribbon at the nape of his neck. But seeing the man I'd met on the beach again, with the bruise from my knee clearly visible on his face, made my heart race.

John and I both spoke at once. But I pushed through when he hesitated. "I wished to return your horse," I repeated in Spanish, aware, now more than ever, that I needed Javier to think of me as a friend. "Thank you for lending her to me."

He paused, looking from my bare feet, then across my fine gown, his eyes seeming not to miss an inch of it, to my face. "I do not recall *lending* her to you."

I tried to swallow again, but found my mouth was dry. "I…well, I—Yes. But is it not better that I brought her to you than had I not?"

"Or would it have been better for you not to *steal* her at all?" he said, moving closer to yank the mare's reins from my hand. He rubbed his hand along her head and neck and then stooped to examine her legs as if he suspected I'd injured her somehow. "Theft of a man's horse is a hanging offense."

My eyes moved to the captain.

"Come now, Javier," John said, dismounting. "Cease your press. No matter what has transpired, a horse rustler never returns what he captures, does he? You and Señorita Ruiz clearly got off on the wrong foot. And this young woman is in need of your hospitality… she's been injured in a fall and cannot quite remember all she ought." He handed his reins to an Indian child dressed in a jacket far too small for him, with no shirt beneath, and only a leather-like diaper below. "Perhaps that led her to act rashly. I thought your mother and sisters might see to her until she regains her full faculties."

He strode toward me and reached up, taking hold of my hips. *He wants to help me down,* I belatedly realized, when he glanced up, a puzzled look in his eyes over my hesitation. I took hold of his shoulders, and he lowered me gently to the ground, giving me a small, encouraging smile. Urging me to continue to trust his decision in this, no matter how it might feel at the moment.

"Now. Shall we begin again? Don Javier de la Ventura, master of Rancho Ventura, may I present to you Señorita Zara Ruiz?" John asked, his voice high and tight. I wanted to look his way, but my eyes were drawn solely to this Javier de la Ventura. The guy I'd kneed in a *couple* of different ways. Luckily, he appeared to have made more than a full recovery, other than the bruised cheek. He sniffed, straightened, and peered down at me intently, as if deciding whether or not we could begin again.

I fought to not squirm under his heated gaze.

Suddenly deciding, he took my hand, bent and slowly kissed it, looking at my face all the while. He knew he was making me feel uncomfortable, but still he lingered, clearly loving that it threw me. There was something tangible between us, a pull that both drew and repelled me in panic.

I hurriedly pulled my hand from his and took a step away.

But he followed after, his fingers sprawling across my lower back, gently guiding me forward. "*Please*, Señorita Ruiz. Captain Worthington is correct. Accept my hospitality, and we shall begin again. You are welcome here at my home," he said, in a falsely sweet tone, gesturing toward the villa, "for as long as you have need of shelter and support."

"Thank you," I said, taking hesitant steps forward as he pressed. We paused to meet his mother, Doña Elena, dressed in a severe, black gown; his black-clad sister-in-law, Adalia—a pretty, round-faced girl with baby Álvaro in her arms; and his sisters, Francesca and Estrella, as well as his brothers, Mateo and Jacinto. The girls—about twelve and fourteen—each curtsied to me. The boys—maybe ten and fifteen—both gave me a bow. But his mother…she only stared at me. She reminded me of a couple old ladies in our *barrio*, exuding power with only the use of her eyes. Javier pressed my back again. "This way, Señorita Ruiz."

"Zara," I said. "You may call me Zara."

He lifted one perfect black brow, and his dark, chocolate-colored eyes twinkled with curious mischief. "So informal, Señorita! Are you certain? We've but just met."

"Yes, I'm certain," I insisted, irritated that he seemed to be reveling in any chance he could grab to unnerve me—his own special brand of payback? I didn't miss the fact that he did not invite me to call him *Javier* as we continued to walk down the hall and into a grand sitting room.

"Please, sit," he said, gesturing to a chair before us, with leather stretched across the seat, a cowhide pillow at the back. All of the furniture appeared as such—handmade of rustic pine and leather. But of good quality. At last his hot hand left my back, and I sat down across from John.

The captain pulled off his gloves and set them on the table between us. "Thank you for looking beyond your unfortunate introduction," John said to Javier, glancing toward me. "I knew I could count on you to look after Señorita Ruiz."

I am right here, I thought, irritated that they talked about me as if I wasn't. And I didn't need a babysitter! Why did they talk about me like that? Everyone seemed to be staring at me—the maids, the manservants, as well as Javier's mom and sisters and brothers as they took their seats. I imagined Doña Elena had x-ray vision, she was staring at me so hard.

"I am more than capable of discussing my predicament myself, Captain."

"But will you freely discuss it?" Javier jumped in. "When we first met, it seemed that you had your share of secrets."

"Not secrets," I said, gratefully taking a cup of tea from a maidservant. "It was only that I was confused, my memories largely absent. You alarmed me with your advances."

Doña Elena's laser vision shifted to her son.

"No, Mamá," he said, lifting a hand to her. "It is not as it sounds."

"No?" Her dark eyes shifted to his cheek.

"No," he said firmly.

It warmed me, her sudden shift, the protective stance, her willingness to believe that I might have had cause to strike him. That wasn't like any Mexican mama I knew, but there was something in that automatic belief in me and my intentions that reminded me of my own abuela. Still, thinking back, I did regret hurting Javier. In all fairness, he likely had reason to doubt me. My abrupt appearance, right after he'd been chased? A strange girl miles away from any known town?

But why would Doña Elena take my side? Be willing to doubt her own son? Unless her son was a troublemaker...

"Who was it that was chasing you this morning?" I said to him sweetly, reaching for my teacup to take a sip and praying no one noticed my trembling.

"Chasing?" he said, leaning back and taking a sip from his own cup. "There was no one chasing me this morning. We were but a few friends out for a morning's race." His dancing eyes settled on mine. *Leave it alone. Say nothing more.* Doña Elena's narrowed, keen gaze surveyed us both.

"Oh, I, uh…of course. A race. I was mistaken." I let out a hollow laugh. "It appears my head is more muddled than I thought."

I felt a tiny glimmer of appreciation from Javier. I'd covered for him. He was keeping some sort of secret from his mother in regard to those guys…

John leaned forward, nodding encouragingly. "Don't fret overmuch," he encouraged. "As I said, it will likely all come back to you in time. And then Javier and his family can help you get back home to your own."

"Sí, sí, my own," I repeated. They moved on to the subject of tallow and whether the ranch could sell him ten more crates of candles, but my mind kept repeating his last words to me: *your own.*

Who exactly would that be? I had no grandmother, no parents to speak of. My friends were graduating in a month, heading off to seek jobs or to go to college, not one of them planning to stay in our neighborhood. I'd planned to go to the community college… then eventually transfer to another school to study atmospheric science and meteorology. A teacher had encouraged me, said I had a face for television and the smarts to get me through school, and I'd always had a thing for clouds and weather. But now, with my abuela gone and no one to run the restaurant, I had no idea how I could swing even community college, financially. She'd been my sole support, my only hope on that front. And the restaurant brought in only enough to pay the mortgage, food, and an occasional bill. College would have been a stretch, with Abuela around.

Now, without her, it seemed impossible.

"Miss Ruiz has a fine command of the English language," John said, continuing in Spanish, as we rose to move to the dining room when it became clear that dinner was about to be served.

Doña Elena coughed as if startled. I dared not look in her direction.

"I've heard her use the foreigners' tongue," Javier said, arcing an eyebrow and glancing at me as if wondering about that anew. Apparently English or even Spanglish wasn't a thing yet.

"Indeed," John returned in perfect Spanish. "She may prove useful to you in your negotiations this summer with other captains. I know for certain that some will carry translators of their own; not all are scrupulous. Some are known to skim a portion of the profits for themselves. Having someone on your side who speaks both languages might prove a boon to you. Who knows?" he said, waiting as Javier pulled out my chair and then helped me scoot toward the rough-hewn table. "Her beauty could do more than sway a few more captains into your harbor. And her intellect could help you land better deals than ever before."

Y*o! Right here with ya*, I wanted to interject.

But I managed to hold my tongue. John meant well. He was trying to secure my position here, give me some power. I was grateful. I needed any edge I could find.

Javier flicked a dismissive glance over me. "The last thing I need is a woman's meddling in my business."

I literally bit my tongue that time, rather than let out some sassy retort.

"This is *Mexican* territory," Doña Elena added, as Javier pushed her chair in toward the table across from me. "Our guests," she paused to arrow a look at me, "are expected to speak the language of our people. We do not require translators."

"Indeed, Doña Elena," John said amiably. "It behooves the finest captains to speak the language. But there are more coming your way this summer than ever before. I know from my own native Maine that more than three score were scheduled to set sail for the West Coast. And that only accounts for those from Maine. Would it not be beneficial to your rancho? To have options to circumvent any obstacles to trade? It appears you have more hides and tallow in your storehouse than I've ever seen before."

Javier nodded. "It's been a good year for us."

"If my son doesn't gamble away all our profits," Doña Elena grumbled, "it shall be the best yet."

Javier and John kept silent.

"Perhaps you can speak some sense into him before you set sail," Doña Elena went on, riveting the captain with a scowl. "It is time for my son to take a wife. To begin having children. It is time for the next generation to begin, to help populate this rich land we've been given. Dante and Adalia had their start, but—" She paused, bit her lip, wiped an eye. But she didn't even look Adalia's way. The baby had been spirited away by a maid when we reached the table. I thought it kind of awful, the way Doña Elena seemed to write off Adalia as dead too. As if all her hopes had died with her son, Dante.

"Mamá, please," Javier said sternly. "This is a conversation for family only, not anything John wishes to take part in. Nor Señorita Ruiz."

She lifted her goblet as soon as a servant poured her wine, taking a big gulp as if to distract herself, and then looked my way again. I hurriedly glanced away.

"Oh, I wouldn't rush to such a conclusion," John said, lifting a teasing brow at Javier. "Your mother makes an interesting point. What keeps you from taking a bride, my friend? You have this fine rancho, more than enough food, one of the finest villas in either Baja or Alta California…"

Javier turned his goblet in a circle and cast him a flinty look. "I could ask the same of you. A man of a certain age, with six fine ships now to his family's name…"

"Ah, yes, but months at sea. I fear I'd miss a wife too much, and it would end my seafaring days. In time, I shall take a wife. Just not yet," he said, lifting his goblet.

Javier lifted his own, and they clinked them together, as if in silent toast to bachelorhood.

I understood then. Confirmed bachelorhood was bound to make Doña Elena crazy. Every Mexican mama I knew wanted nothing more than babies and grandbabies and great-grandbabies. It had been my own abuela's great sadness that I was her only family not in prison or on the run. To her, it meant she was poor in the only way that mattered.

We bowed our heads for grace, and then servants arrived with steaming platters holding roast chicken covered in a rich-smelling sauce full of cumin, *arroz con mariscos*, with mussel shells artfully popping up through the mound of garlic-infused rice and between the shrimp, and lastly, tons of tamales. I swallowed hard, realizing I was hungry again.

By the time all the platters had been passed, my plate was crazy-full. Javier gave me a wry look. "It has been some time since you ate, I assume?"

"Captain Worthington fed me upon the beach, but yes, I seem to have quite the appetite. It all looks and smells so wonderful," I said, mostly to Doña Elena, trying to win her over some with praise, even if it was her staff who'd done all the work.

She didn't respond.

"This is my favorite," little Estrella said, beside her grandmother, holding a whole shrimp by the tail to show me.

"*Estrella*," Doña Elena scolded in a whisper, shooting her a look that seemed to say *children are to be seen but not heard.* I pretended not to notice. "I believe that might be my favorite too," I said, stabbing a shrimp with my odd, two-tined fork and cutting off a bite. Estrella shot me a shy smile but then quickly returned her gaze to her plate, as her elder sister was carefully doing.

"This is my favorite," said the youngest, Jacinto, lifting a spoon full of tamale. He flashed me a gap-toothed grin. "With cheese it's—"

Doña Elena leaned forward in her chair and looked down the table, and little Jacinto abruptly shoved the spoon in his mouth. I waited until I could catch his eye and gave him a quick smile, taking a bite of my tamale right afterward and nodding appreciatively. The elder sister and brother, Francesca and Mateo, both took in my friendly gestures. I could feel them soften a bit toward me.

Making progress with the kids...but what about the matron of the family? I'd find my way with her in time. Abuela always told me I was good with customers at the restaurant, and I thought she was right. I could read a man's mood, a woman's tone, and find my way in response.

Javier de la Ventura, on the other hand, was hard for me to read. One moment he seemed to be testing me, the next irritated by my presence, and the next, flirting. I refused to look his way but instead said to John, "How long does the voyage from Maine take, to get here?"

"It is a two-to-three-month journey around the Cape," he said, looking like I ought to clearly know such a thing. "Depending on the winds, of course."

I blinked, considering that long aboard a ship. Three months?

"But this summer, we've established a cargo train across Panama, so that three of my family's ships shall continue to import and export from the East Coast, while three more shall import and export here along the West. In so doing, I believe I'll be here five, maybe six times this summer, depending on how long the weather holds."

He'll be back. That news made me take a deep breath of relief. It was ridiculous, really, me pinning so much on a man I'd just met. But while I couldn't read Javier very well, John was an open book to me. Caring, polite, protective. And if he thought I was best situated here, with the Venturas, I really had no choice but to trust him. No matter how much Javier unnerved me.

But the thought that John was going to return, that I could convince him to take me to another place if it wasn't working out, regardless of how he felt about women aboard his ship, comforted me.

All that said, I knew I'd likely be outta here by the time he got back. I'd ride back to that beach every day if I had to, hold my little golden lamp, and wait for the poppy-noise-blasty-light-nausea weirdness to happen again, taking me home.

Because as fascinating as all of this was—some wild dreamscape—this was *not* where I belonged.

CHAPTER 4

We finished our supper, and the servants, who all appeared to be Native Americans—which made me feel a little strange—cleared away our dishes. They seemed content with their tasks, even happy. But what had life been like for them before Spain encouraged Mexico to send people northward? I remembered from my state history class that the missions hadn't all been unicorns and rainbows. At some, the natives had been little more than indentured servants. And now, as John had said, with the missions being abandoned, many were likely displaced. No longer either master *or* servant in their own land.

But that had been the way of America from before colonial times: move in, dominate, take over. And it appeared that the Mexicans were no different. Maybe it was the same everywhere. Fortune favored the strongest.

Mexico ruled this territory for now. But a few years down the line, gold would be discovered, and California would become much, much more interesting to the old dudes back in DC. If I remembered right, there was still the Mexican-American War to come and that battle at the Alamo. Or had that already happened?

All I knew was that, as much as the Ventura family thought they were All That, there would be some rough times ahead for them. I could see it unfolding before me as clearly as paging through my California-history textbook.

But it wasn't my place to interfere. My only role here, now, was to ride out this particular experience and wait for my return back to my own world of problems. I didn't need to adopt theirs too.

All at once it became clear that John was preparing to take his leave. My heart pitter-pattered in alarm, but I knew he couldn't do anything about it, and neither could I. His world called him to take to the sea; mine called me to remain as close to my own land as possible. There just really was no other option. I followed him and Javier out of the dining room, ignoring the fact that Doña Elena and the children remained behind. Perhaps it was the way of gentlemen in this era to say farewell without distraction, but I pretty much didn't care. There was no way Captain Worthington was going to leave without remembering me…and remembering me well.

I needed him in my corner. If I didn't succeed in getting home before he returned, there was a whole list of reasons I needed him. And I owed him. He'd taken me under his wing with little hesitation. Just took care of me from start to finish, giving all he had. Who did that kind of thing?

He'd found me this dress and a place to stay—perhaps the only place to stay in over a hundred miles.

John turned toward me and took my hand in both of his. "My prayer is that you will heal and flourish here, Señorita Ruiz."

"Zara," I said. "Please call me Zara. I owe you a great deal."

"You owe me nothing at all," he said, leaning toward me in that Older Brother sort of conspiratorial way, still holding my hand in his. "It has been my good pleasure. And stories of you shall fuel our voyage northward. The men shall allow me to speak of little else, I assume, wanting to know all about the girl I found on the beach. The girl who managed to finagle my own sister's dress as a gift of her own—and to relieve Don Javier of his horse. Oh, how the tongues shall wag…" He turned toward Javier. "Treat this one as you would my sister, Javier." He lifted a warning finger toward him. "Truly. My *sister*. I shall hold you accountable."

"Of course," Javier said with a crisp nod, hands behind his waist. But his lush lips quirked to one side, as if holding back a grin.

"Javier…," John said, instantly sober and serious. "I shall hold you accountable. If anything untoward happens to Señorita Ruiz—"

Javier lifted his hands. "You doubt me? You are as dear to me as a brother. Trust me when I say I will treat this one as our sister."

They both looked at me then, and I wondered at the odd twisting of displeasure I felt in my heart when I heard Javier utter those words. Surely I didn't want anything else from him…the thought of it made my cheeks burn.

The same stable boy in the too-small jacket brought back John's mount. I saw then that two men from the ship had arrived after us. Had they trailed us all along, an escort of sorts? Or guards? They mounted and glanced my way as their captain neatly pulled astride his own horse.

Impulsively, I moved toward John and looked up, aware that I was wringing my hands. "I shall look forward to your return, Captain Worthington."

He stiffened, looked a little confused, but then smiled. "Be well, Señorita Ruiz. This is a land of bounty and a fine home. Relish it as you take your recovery. I shall see you soon."

Then I took a step back, and the three men turned and rode off at a gallop. I saw now that the sun was hanging low on the horizon—maybe six o'clock. I instinctively reached for a pocket, where my cell phone always was, to check. But of course there was nothing.

"What do you search for among your skirts?" Javier asked, stepping beside me.

"Nothing," I muttered. "Nothing at all." It was only then that I thought of it. I'd been so distracted, so focused on meeting up with Javier again, and then his fam, and then distracted by this new place, I'd forgotten. "Where is your mare?" I said, turning toward him. But my mind was screaming, *Where is that saddlebag? My golden lamp?*

"In the stables, of course," he said casually.

I turned, lifted my skirts, and practically ran to where he had gestured, a long, single-level barn sort of structure. I knew he followed behind me, but I didn't care. *How could I have let it out of my sight?* I berated myself. *My only link to my own time?*

I was an idiot. *¡Que idiota!* For a moment, I wondered if I had really hit my head on something, keeping me from thinking clearly.

I pushed up the crossbeam and let the doors swing open before me, rushing through. He entered behind me, almost lackadaisical, but I ignored him. Madly I looked left and right, searching for Javier's mare. But it wasn't until I reached the very end that I saw her, in a larger stall, saddle off, munching on hay at her feet. I swallowed an angry accusation—he could've told me she was at the end, rather than watching me search each stall in a panic—in favor of finding the saddlebag.

But as I craned my neck to search each corner of the mare's stall, I could see it was gone. I whirled, feeling my skirts follow behind, an odd, foreign sensation. "Where is the saddlebag?"

He leaned his shoulder against the wooden beams of his mare's stable and crossed his arms. "Why do you ask?"

"You *know* why I ask," I returned furiously, stepping toward him.

I noted he kept his legs together this time, but he didn't flinch at my advance, just watched me through curious, suspicious eyes.

"You clearly know what's inside the bag, Don de la Ventura. Where is it?" I asked, stepping closer to him. "Tell me."

"It is in my safekeeping," he said, looking down at me. The shadows were long, hiding half his face from me now. "Such a valuable object…it belongs in the ranchero's hands. You wouldn't want such a thing stolen, would you? It's worth more than a year's pay for most. I've locked it securely away in my safe."

"But, but it's *mine*," I sputtered lamely.

He studied me a moment. "And I shall keep it safe for you," he declared.

I stared up at him, willing myself not to react, not to attack him like some sort of crazy person. No matter how badly I wanted to.

"Who are you, Zara?" he whispered, leaning a little closer to me. "Tell me. Tell me the truth, and I might consider giving your little lamp back to you." He shook his head. "Beautiful, educated women with such unique objects do not just fall off a passing ship—unless they are planted for some other purpose." He straightened and circled me slowly, looking me over. A nervous shiver ran down my back. "By someone who knows my taste in women? You come here, having charmed my friend, John, and win over my mother, my siblings in the space of an hour."

His words were complimentary, but his tone was nothing but accusatory. Who did he *think* I was? Who did he so fear? Suspect?

"I am Zara Ruiz," I returned. "And you know all that I know about how I got here and who I am."

"Hmm," he said doubtfully. "So until you can tell me more," he said thoughtfully, looking at my lips in a way that made my stomach flip. "I'll hold on to your treasure."

"Then you hold it as *ransom*," I said, "more than any true desire to keep it *safe*."

"For both," he returned.

"You cannot. It is mine!"

"I can. And I will." He quirked a brow. "Besides, what need of it have you? Here? Now? Do you not trust me with it? I promise I will not sell it. I have all the gold a man could need from our trade in tallow and hide."

I frowned up at him, wishing he'd make some advance that would allow me to bring him down again, right here in the middle of his own stables. But he stayed stubbornly in place, not even reaching out to touch my face again. "I will trust you with it for now, Don Ventura," I said, speaking as if I was uttering a blood oath. "But when I am ready to leave, you shall give it to me."

"Of course," he said easily. "When you are ready to go, I shall give it to you."

I stared back at him. He knew I had nowhere else to go. But to be without the only key to that invisible doorway to my own time made me feel crazed with worry, with frustration. Never had I felt so trapped in all my life and I hated that hot, angry tears threatened behind my eyes. "If you allow anything to happen to it, I shall make you *pay*."

His full lips pulled to one side, and he reached up and cradled his bruised cheek. "Believe me, beautiful Zara," he whispered slowly, ever so slowly, not letting his stare leave my eyes. "I'll remember."

I knew he meant to make me falter, unnerve me. Instead I leaned closer and took hold of his arm. "Please do," I hissed. "Because if you forget, I promise it shall come back to bite you."

And then I made myself stride out. It pleased me that I'd felt his arm tighten beneath my hold, seen his jaw muscle clench. *He's a little scared of me*, I thought with pleasure.

But the man still held my Golden Ticket out of this place.

It was he who held power over me. Really, it was he who seemed to hold all kinds of weird power over me.

And I had to find some way, somehow, to get it back.

CHAPTER 5

Francesca and Estrella Ventura waited for me back at the villa, practically wringing their hands in worry.

"Ah, Señorita Ruiz," Estrella began, "I'm so glad to see you. Mamá was about to send the boys to fetch you."

I turned halfway toward her, still partially lost in my fury over her eldest brother's decisions. "I'm capable of making my own way."

Francesca stiffened, coming up to my shoulder in height. "Clearly," she said, and suddenly seeming far more mature in tone. "But it is our duty to see to you, a woman alone in a land not her own."

I blinked at her, thinking over her words. She wasn't a part of whatever was making me feel trapped. Not like Javier. These girls were just trying to make me feel at home. "Thank you for that," I said abruptly. "Your brother…I'm not certain he feels the same way."

Francesca's dark chocolate eyes, so much like her brother's, stared into mine. "He's like that, you know. He likes to keep us guessing. All of us, including Mamá."

I let out a swift snort through my nostrils, all the pieces finally settling into place. Figured. A player. On all levels. *Well, Javier, let me introduce you to Miss Zara Ruiz, a girl like no other you've yet met…and I know your game.*

I was used to guys like him coming into the restaurant. Handsome, with money in their pockets. Thinking they could do whatever they wanted with me, because of course I'd be drooling over them. Telling their mamas what they wanted to hear, pretending to be someone they weren't, and then following whatever whim that came their way when their mama's head was turned.

B*ut that has come to an end, Javier,* I vowed. He could have his way with whomever he wished. But with me?

With me, it would be different.

So different.

Little Estrella showed me to my room, a spare ten-by-ten with ivory adobe walls, a narrow bed, a small table and an oil lamp. The floor was of wide pine planks. On another side table was a pitcher and basin, for washing up. At the base of the bed was a chest. Estrella went to it and opened it. "Mamá found a couple more dresses for you," she said, her dark eyes slipping down my fine, green gown. "You'll want to save that one for special occasions. There's a shift in here too, as well as more underthings."

I smiled at her in gratitude. But I had more pressing matters at the moment. "Where is the bathroom?" I asked, shifting.

She frowned in confusion. "You shall take your bath in here, once a week. Usually Saturdays, so you're fresh for Sunday mass."

"No, I, uh…" I shifted again until understanding dawned and she lifted her brows.

"The privy is outside," she said slowly, as if I was a child in need of some basic explanations. "Or if you prefer, there's the chamber pot," she added, gesturing to a wide-brimmed copper pot in the corner of the room, a sponge in a bowl beside it. "The servants will see to it twice a day, midmorning and evening, before you go to sleep."

I looked back at her in alarm. She wasn't serious… But then I managed to get a grip and pretend this was no surprise at all.

"Do you need anything else before morning?" she asked, politely preparing to take her leave so I could see to my business.

"No—no, I'll be fine," I said, walking her to the door. "Gracias, Estrella."

"Sleep well, Señorita Ruiz," she said with a short curtsy.

I didn't have time to think of it much. *When a girl has to go, she has to go.* And with some relief, I used a chamber pot for the first time ever, trying not to miss as I squatted. I'd hate it if I messed up my dress *peeing*, of all things.

I hoped it'd be the last time I'd have to use it. I'd sleep, find something to tell Javier that would convince him to give me my golden lamp back, then ride for the beach and exit this nightmare, stage left.

Okay, so I'll probably have to use it one more time in the morning, I admitted to myself. *But then…*

I pulled off the dress and laid it across the foot of my bed, then untied the petticoat beneath. My black cami was bundled at my waist, and I pulled that and my maxiskirt off too, then donned the shift that Estrella had mentioned. It was not the butter-soft nightgown I had at home, but it was something, and it felt good to be in something shapeless and roomy, out of all those…skirts. *That's a lot of skirt for any girl*, I thought, gazing from the green silk to my maxi. People of this time, this place, all wore so many clothes. Layer upon layer. And without the aid of washing machines…It all seemed like a lot of work to me.

I moved over to my window, which faced west. The sun was setting, and a pang of panic rang through me as I thought of John and his crew preparing to leave come morning. How was I going to find my way out too? I was so dreadfully tired, I thought, my eyelids feeling like a hundred pounds each. Maybe all I had to do was sleep, and I'd wake come morning in my own bed, in my own abuela's apartment, and this whole, weird, wild adventure would be over.

I pulled back the heavy woolen blanket and climbed into the bed. It smelled of hay—*is this what they called a straw tick?*—and I had a flashback to reading *Little House on the Prairie.* I thought, *That's it. I've morphed into Laura Ingalls Wilder. A Latina Lara.* In Old California rather than the Old Midwest.

The sheet beneath me was scratchy, but it was clean, and I let my eyelids fall at last. I'd dream of Pa and Mary and that evil Nellie. That was a story I could handle this night, something familiar, rather than this new story spinning out of control before me. And when I woke, everything would be right…

But when I woke the next morning, all was the same. The chamber pot, the pitcher and basin on the nightstand, the view out my window—miles and miles of grassy hills and cattle, stretching toward the sea, not a suburban home with the familiar tile roofs and stucco walls to be seen.

I groaned in dismay.

It seemed that I wasn't going to wake my way outta here. I'd have to find the secret doorway and open it again myself.

And when I went to change into one of the other dresses that Doña Elena had found for me, I really did start to feel like Laura Ingalls Wilder. One was a plain, drab brown, with poufy sleeves and a white apron-like overlay, and the other was a deep, dark blue with a high neck and long sleeves. At the bottom of the chest were a couple pair of worn boots, and woolen socks. It all looked hot—as in heat-hot, not style-hot—and I groaned. I'd always been a flip-flop and shorts kind of girl, six months out of the year. But here on the ranch, there was no way I'd get away with that. Not that there were any flip-flops or shorts within reach.

I tried one pair of the lace-up boots, but they were too small. Then the other, which were a bit big…I stuffed some handkerchiefs into the toes, then pulled on the woolen socks and the boots. I chose the brown dress, thinking it was a bit softer and lighter than the other, and managed to slip it over my head, leaving only two buttons at the upper-center of my back in need of fastening. Then I ran my hands over my wild hair and wondered if I should braid it, like Laura would have.

A small knock sounded at my door, and I moved over to answer it. "*Buenos días*, Señorita Ruiz," twelve-year-old Estrella said, grinning up at me. "Frani wondered if you might need help with your hair before breakfast, and Captain Worthington left this for you." She lifted the big-toothed bone comb I'd used on the beach yesterday.

"Oh, yes," I said. "Thank you." I gestured for her to come in, and I sat down on the corner of the bed. "Would you do it for me? I'd be so grateful."

"Of course," she said, flashing a gap-toothed grin at me. It was just like her little brother Jacinto's smile, only more seldom seen. Maybe she hid it because of the gap? Her own hair, black and straight, was tied into a neat, thick knot at the nape of her neck. I didn't know what she was going to do with mine, without aid of a hair product, a straightener, and elastic bands, but she seemed game to try.

As Estrella worked, I unwound the bandage from my hand and asked her question after question, realizing this was a rare opportunity to do some research and get some sort of grip on this place, this family.

"How long have you lived here, Estrella?" I said, wincing a bit as she tugged through a knot in my hair.

"Here? On Rancho Ventura? All my life," she said.

Well, duh, I chided myself. *Way to go, Captain Obvious.* "Do you go to school?"

"No. We had a tutor one year, and a governess for three, when I was little. I know how to do arithmetic," she said proudly, "and I read quite well. It's only that I tire of our books. I'm always begging Javier to trade for new books when he goes to the harbor. He gets me one every Christmas. Novels are my favorite."

"Mine too," I said.

"My *papá* used to buy me a novel every time he could."

"What happened to your papá?"

"He died five years ago. It was his heart. Then Dante, our oldest brother, last year…" Her voice cracked and I turned to take her hand for a moment.

"My abuela died…recently," I said, tearing up. "She was dear to me. Losing her has been the hardest thing. Were you close to Dante?"

"Close to him?" she asked in confusion over my phrasing.

I took a breath. "Was he…dear to you?"

She nodded, blinking back tears in her beautiful dark eyes. Then she resumed her combing of my hair. "Javier had to come back from Mexico when Dante died."

A college boy, I thought. *No, probably more like a frat boy. Forced to return home. Maybe that's why he's a little rebellious.* I thought back to the men chasing him on the beach yesterday and the secret he'd convinced me to keep.

"Where are your neighbors, Estrella? Do you ever see them?"

"Oh yes," she said enthusiastically. "Every few months at the *charreada*, near town. The Vargases and Fuenteses and Herreras are always there. They are our nearest neighbors. But many others come too."

The charreada, I repeated silently. An old Mexican rodeo sort of event, if I remembered right. "And how far away is your nearest neighbor?"

"Oh, it's no more than twenty miles south or so to the Vargases, but we don't get along with them very well. Javier thinks they have stolen some of our cattle."

I took a moment to absorb that. The nearest neighbors were twenty miles away. "And…to your north?"

She paused. "There is no one up there other than Indians, I think. For a while, the Losas ran a rancho up there, but they grew old and had no children. So they returned to Mexico." She shoved a last pin in my hair and stepped back. I glanced at her pleased face. "There. *Muy bonita.* Javier will not be able to keep his eyes from you. But Adalia says you need no help when it comes to him. He's already smitten."

Smitten? My eyes widened in surprise. "I'm sure I'm the last thing on your brother's mind today."

"Don't be silly," she said, her brows lowering in confusion. "A pretty girl like you? Arriving in such a mysterious way? And stealing his horse out from under him? Frani says she doubts he's thought of anything but you ever since. No girl we've ever known would ever dare to strike him."

"He deserved it," I put in, eager for the family not to blame me. "He scared me."

"I don't doubt it. Adalia thought that must be the case. But he didn't do it on purpose. Javier would never scare a girl on purpose."

I wasn't so sure she was right about that. Clearly, she had a sort of hero-worship thing going on with her Big Bro.

"But Frani thinks that that just helped pique his interest," she yammered on, making it clear that the girls had had quite the gab-fest about me, which came as a surprise. While Estrella was a chatterbox, the older two girls were fairly quiet, especially Adalia. I'd decided she was still grieving, as well as shy. "Just like Frani said, he likes to keep us guessing," Estrella was saying. "The girls who fall all over him never keep his interest. And every girl in the last year has done everything she could to try and catch his eye. You," she said, leaning forward excitedly, "are the first to make him stare."

"You've read too many novels, my young friend," I said, quickly rising and straightening my skirts. I didn't like how her words made my heart pound. Worse, how I liked hearing them.

"Never," she grinned happily, her round cheeks betraying two deep dimples. The thought finally got her off the subject of Javier. "I don't suppose you brought any books with you…"

"I'm afraid not. I only arrived with that dress, and a special treasure, in hand." I bent to fold my nightshirt on the bed and then placed it in my chest. "Javier said he's keeping my treasure for me in his safe. Do you know where that is?"

"Yes, of course," she said, pouring water from the pitcher into the basin. "In the library."

"Is it quite secure?" I asked, picturing big old black safes in the spaghetti Westerns my abuela had loved. "Can anyone open it for me, other than him?"

"No," she said, turning to take a towel from her waistband and offer it to me. "Don't fret, Señorita Ruiz. It is the best safe in all of Alta California. Papá had it brought to us, special, from the East. Your treasure will be safe."

"Good, good," I said, pretending relief. I obediently bent over the makeshift sink and washed my face, then took the small towel from her hands to dry it. Then I used the damp towel to rub over the back of my neck and hands. *I guess sponge-baths are the way to go around here…*

"Can you show me around the rancho after breakfast, Estrella?"

"Of course. But it's pretty much like every rancho you've ever been on. Just bigger and nicer." She sounded kind of bored, like most kids in their own homes.

"I've never been on a rancho before. At least, that I can remember."

She glanced back at me in confusion, but I didn't try and explain.

I followed her along the hall and down a tiled staircase that turned at a forty-five-degree angle halfway down, widening and spilling into the front receiving foyer. The walls of the hallway and main rooms of the house were a brick-red rough adobe, with white plaster on the high ceiling between exposed beams that looked hand-cut. *Well, duh, Zara,* I told myself. *Of course they're hand-cut.* Everything about this part of the world, in this time, was the product of hard manual labor. Only the fabric of our gowns was made somewhere back East or in Mexico, I assumed, and imported by ship.

It was as if I could really *see* it all this morning, whereas last night my head was spinning so much, I could barely take in the basics. In the main sitting room at the bottom of the stairs—the library—

there were men talking and laughing, and as we passed, I saw Javier and two young men leaning over what looked like a yellowed map spread across a table, its edges curling.

One looked up at me. He was tall and thin and angular, everything about him elegant, I registered, in a clean, black coat, crisp white shirt, and tie. How did anyone stay that clean here, in this land of dust, without showers and washers?

"Who is that with Javier?" I whispered to Estrella, as we paused a moment.

"Oh, that is his friend, Rafael Vasquez, the youngest son on Rancho Vasquez, near Santa Barbara. He's always up here, trading on behalf of his family." She gave me an impish grin. "He's taken notice of you, too."

"I don't need any more notice," I grumbled as Javier straightened and followed Rafael's gaze to give me a piercing, searching, curious look that made my pulse immediately pick up speed. I hurriedly pushed Estrella onward. We moved down the hall, and I checked out the tall, substantial doors of each room, carved in simple but pleasing patterns, but my head was frustratingly back on Javier.

He's just another obstacle in your path, Zara, I told myself sternly.

I was used to Obstacles in my own neighborhood looking my way, trying to flirt with me at school. Or in the restaurant, after I played my guitar or served them a particularly delicious meal. More handsome Obstacles at the beach, when I went swimming. But I'd never had time for any of them. They were just boys. And I was a girl with a dream. Of college. Of studying science and the weather. Of finding my way toward a full, adventurous life. To love. A family of my own. I'd seen more than enough teen girls, saddled with a baby, the result of being with boys they thought they loved…boys who disappeared as soon as it Got Serious. No, I was waiting for love, the man who would help me accomplish my dreams, not become an Obstacle, keeping me from them.

It would take *true* love, *forever* love, before any guy was getting anywhere close to my heart.

And this place? It was temporary. No *forever* for me here.

I just had to find my way home.

CHAPTER 6

I noted a music room, a small chapel and a closed door on our way to the dining hall. A fire crackled merrily in the fireplace at the far end, chasing away the morning's chill. As much as I wanted to go to it, it was clear we were to wait by our chairs for the men to join us for breakfast. Doña Elena stood across from me in another immaculate black dress—how long would she and Adalia wear mourning gowns?—and Estrella and Mateo on either side of her. I hadn't really talked to fifteen-year-old Mateo yet; he seemed very quiet and subdued, but he gave me a brief, shy smile along with a gentle "*Buenos días*." Adalia and her baby sat at the head of the table, where she had more room to feed him. Francesca and Jacinto flanked me, leaving the end of the table for Javier and his visitors, I assumed.

"Did you sleep well, Señorita Ruiz?" Doña Elena asked, as servants brought in heaps of scrambled eggs and piles of fresh tortillas and stood waiting for everyone to be seated. The men entered the dining room then, as if they'd smelled the food. Álvaro, the little, chubby baby, squawked angrily, as if smelling it too. Adalia bent to shush him, but I saw the flash of her smile.

"I slept well," I returned. "Thank you for asking."

"Of course," she said.

"Gentlemen, you know my family," Javier said, "but allow me to introduce our guest, Señorita Ruiz. She will be staying with us for a while as she recuperates from an injury."

Rafael Vasquez edged over to me and took my uninjured hand in his, bowing to give it a quick kiss. "Please tell me it shall be a *long* while, Javier," he said, never releasing my hand or gaze.

"Oh, I quite doubt it," I returned, forcing a demure smile. "I must be on my way at the earliest opportunity." The other man, named Patricio Casales, gave me a happy nod and waited his turn to take my hand. While Rafael was all smooth movement, like a star dancer, Patricio was like an exuberant puppy.

"What is your rush, dear woman?" Patricio asked, helping me scoot my chair farther in as Javier and Rafael took their seats. "This is one of the finest ranchos in all of Alta California. You would be hard-pressed to find better accommodations."

"Unless, of course, you chose to sojourn on Rancho Vasquez," interjected Rafael, nodding my way as a maid poured steaming coffee into his cup. "An invitation that I hope you shall accept, my lady, if your host proves…difficult."

Javier's eyes shifted toward him for a second. Did I read irritation in his expression? But he only sat back as the maid moved on to fill his cup and then Patricio's. Javier glanced my way then, casually lifting his cup. "By all means, you should visit Rancho Vasquez and witness for yourself the second-best rancho in Alta California."

Rafael smiled good-naturedly over the jibe. After all, he'd baited his host, but it didn't take a weather expert to feel the cooling mist move in among the men.

"Forgive them, Señorita," Patricio said. "It is rare for us to have a female guest at any of the ranchos, and such a beautiful guest tends to make my friends…contentious."

I gave him a grateful smile. He was round-faced and yet strong, with the shadow of a beard clinging to his curved cheeks. But I liked his tone, his demeanor, utterly lacking in the competition that the other two seemed all tied up in. He was pure, friendly gentility.

The men began to speak of the ships that had just left and who was due in the following week. The rest of us dived into our breakfast, which included fresh oranges. I'd glimpsed a vineyard on the way in, but there were also orchards? I lifted a segment on my fork and leaned toward Francesca. "There is an orchard on Rancho Ventura?"

"Indeed," she said primly. "We raise apples and oranges. Even some tangerines. The ship captains pay a pretty penny for them, when Mamá allows them to leave our storerooms."

Doña Elena let a small, proud smile tickle her lips and stabbed a juicy bite, leaning down the table to hand it to her gleeful grandson, who immediately stuffed it into his mouth. "They are good for the bones, as well as the blood."

"The sailors want them to avoid scurvy, of course," Jacinto said earnestly. "Scurvy makes them so ill they can barely walk!"

"I'll show you the orchards when we go out later this morning," Estrella said to me excitedly, her cheeks dimpling.

Javier shifted in his seat down the table. "You intend to go out today?"

"Is that not allowed?" I said. I thought his tone odd. "Estrella offered to give me a tour of the rancho."

"Why wander about?" he asked, sipping from his cup. "I thought you didn't intend to tarry long."

"Yes, well," I said, "as long as I'm here…I'd love to see what your family has built."

He visibly took this in and seemed oddly miffed. Because he thought me nosy? Or still considered me some sort of potential spy—

for who, exactly? Or because he regretted he wouldn't be my escort? I had no idea. I really couldn't figure him out. I just seemed to agitate him at every turn.

"I can go with you," Francesca offered.

"You must see to your chores first," Doña Elena said to her daughters. "Then you may go."

"I'll help," I said. "We'll be twice as fast together."

But Estrella frowned. She shook her head. "Oh no, Señorita Ruiz. It's improper for a woman of your age, and a guest of this house, to do such a thing."

I opened my mouth to argue, but with one look at Francesca and Doña Elena—so similar in their prim, grand countenance—I took a bite of egg instead. As I chewed, my mind whirled. So I was supposed to just sit around and look pretty? It'd be impossible. All my life, I had worked from sunup to sundown. In the restaurant. At school. Back at the restaurant after school. At the county shelter, feeding the homeless, cleaning, cooking. In Abuela's apartment. My only break had been my early morning runs or late night swims. The prospect of having nothing to occupy my time but thoughts of home…

No. I'd have to find something to do. Maybe our tour today would give me some ideas.

The men talked among themselves, occasionally drawing in each of the children or Adalia or Doña Elena into the discussion but clearly avoiding me. It was as if none of them knew what to ask me for openers, which was fine by me. It left me clear to just observe the connections between them all, here an intimacy, there a friction. It was like watching the hundred-plus families that had come to eat at my abuela's restaurant, ignoring me as I served beyond a few curious glances. When we were done eating, we all waited. It was only when

Doña Elena set down her fork that Javier said, "Mamá?"

She waved at him in dismissal, and all three young men rose at once. I liked his deference toward his mother. Asking to be excused, in his own way. It made me feel like he couldn't be all bad, despite the way he unnerved me.

Servants came and cleared our plates, and eventually the rest of us rose and followed the men out. Only Patricio looked my way as he exited, casting me a playful two-fingered salute. Estrella and Francesca walked out with me, and I glimpsed the young men leaving through the front door. Apparently, they were free to do as they wished, and they had plans. Adalia, who seemed to be kind of depressed, carried the fussy Álvaro up the stairs, apparently to change his diaper or put him down for a nap.

"Here," Estrella said, taking my arm. Francesca followed behind us. "You can wait in here for us to be done with our chores." She led me into a sprawling library, with the embers of a morning fire dying in the hearth and a strong shaft of sunlight streaming through the open window. On one side of the room a towering bookcase held hundreds of leather-bound volumes. Beside it stood a wide desk and two chairs. Several melting candles were at its center, under glass hurricanes. And the safe had to be behind the massive oil painting behind it… I stepped toward it as if called, knowing my golden lamp was inside.

"You might find a new novel to entertain you," Estrella said.

"What?" I asked, distracted, then, "Oh, yes."

"Come along, Estie," Francesca said from the doorway, urging her little sister to hurry, rather than linger here with me.

I turned toward the older girl, just a few years younger than I. *About the age of a freshman,* I judged. "What are the chores you must do?"

"I must see to some correspondence for Mamá while she

oversees the kitchen and discusses the supper menu with Cook. Estrella is to make her bed and refold her clothes in her trunk that got rumpled when she undressed last night, then she will play with Álvaro for a while to give Adalia some rest." She turned to her sister, and they exchanged a few words I couldn't hear. Apparently in agreement, she turned back to me. "We should be back with you in no longer than an hour or two. Do you need anything else to be comfortable in our absence?"

"No," I said, swallowing a desire to beg them to let me do something to help. Anything. But my first offer had been turned down—I sensed that Francesca would frown upon a second. And there was the safe… when else might I have the chance to check it out? "I'll see you soon. Thank you."

They left, and alone again, I moved over to the window, observing how thick the walls of this place were. Deep enough to hold in the heat through the damp of winter…or keep it out during the hottest summer day.

I saw a group of men and women trudging down the road toward the vineyard, half of them carrying hoes over their shoulders. Off to do some weeding, apparently. And then Javier and his friends came into view, reaching for their horses' reins, tied to the posts out front.

It was the baby's squawk that alerted me to Adalia's presence, and I turned in surprise. She stood beside me, looking out at the men too. "Do you fancy him?" she asked me soberly.

I blinked rapidly, trying to come up with a suitable answer. "You mean Javier?"

"Of course," she said, giving me a quizzical look. "Or was it Rafael who caught your eye?"

"None of them!" I sputtered. "I was simply looking out the

window and they came into view."

"Mm-hmm," she said, moving to the settee and setting Álvaro down beside the table. He stood there, slapping the wood with his pudgy, open palm, then shifted down the edge, big, brown eyes focused on a delicate pitcher at the end. "Uh-uh," she clucked, smoothly lifting it out of harm's way, placing it on the mantel above the fireplace. She fished a leather disc out of her pocket, which she handed to him. The toddler immediately thrust it into his drooling mouth, gnawing at it. Some sort of primitive teether, I assumed.

I sat down across from her. "It must be difficult for you, caring for Álvaro by yourself."

Her sad eyes met mine, and she tilted her head to the side. "It makes me miss Dante all the more," she said quietly, eyes darting toward the open door to the hallway as if afraid she might be overheard. "While he wouldn't have been much good at caring for the child, he would have been grand at loving him alongside me." She cast a wistful gaze at Álvaro, as he took out the damp leather disc and rammed it against the table.

I nodded. How many times had I caught myself over the last two days, thinking I needed to share this or that with Abuela? Wondering if she could help me think through this crazy situation, and help me get back home, only to remember that she was gone. Farther from me than ever, never to return, even if I did get back to my own time.

"At least you have the Venturas. They seem to love you both." I'd watched the children make faces and kiss the baby every chance they had.

"That's true," she said, "but without Dante…" I felt the grief in her then, like a yawning chasm. Perhaps Dante had been her bridge to this family, and without him, she felt somewhat alone, even surrounded by them all. But wasn't that a choice? Couldn't an adopted member of the family feel as much a part of them as blood kin?

Adalia seemed to remember herself, as if she felt she'd said too much, and abruptly shut her mouth. "Never mind me. I just wanted to tell you, Zara, warn you…" Again, her words trailed off, as if she wondered if she should say anything at all.

I frowned. "Warn me of what?"

"The Venturas can be very charming. Javier even more than my husband was," she said softly. "Guard your heart, if you wish to leave this place. Because it may surprise you how quickly you find yourself marooned here in the villa, with little hope of escape."

I stared at her. Did she know? Know the truth of how I got here? "Believe me, I don't have any intention of staying."

"Nor did I, when I first visited. And then one thing led to another…"

"Where did you live, before this?" I asked, as a servant came in, swooped up the baby after a nod from Adalia, and wordlessly left the room.

"South of here, in a town called Los Angeles. My family lives there still," she said wistfully.

I glanced to the doorway myself then. "Could you not return to them?" I asked in a whisper. "If you are so unhappy here?"

"Oh, I am not unhappy, really." She sighed. "I'm not sure I can be happy anywhere again. Love is like that, you know. True love. When you love a man and you allow him to hold your heart in his hands, and then he dies…he takes a piece of your heart with him. So it's not that I'm unhappy. It's only as if I'm not quite *whole* anymore."

I nodded. "It must hurt a great deal."

"More than you can imagine." Her eyes met mine again. "So that is what I wished to tell you. Hold on to your heart, if you wish to leave this place. Because no one is better at wooing a girl than one of the Venturas."

"You don't have to tell me that twice," I said, smiling a little. "Jacinto, with that gap-toothed grin? He had my heart from the start."

She laughed, surprised, and then covered her mouth as if embarrassed. "Forgive me. I've said far too much." She rose as if to leave. "It's just that…when I saw Javier look at you yesterday…and then this morning—"

"No, thank you. Thank you for sharing. And Adalia, I think… I think you will find wholeness, in time. I think you might even find love again, after your grieving eases. And maybe in that love, you will find that missing piece of your heart restored. Maybe, maybe you just need a fresh start."

Her sad eyes blinked in surprise, as if absorbing that thought. She nodded and then bustled away, as if suddenly wanting to flee from me, leaving me to think that it had been my turn to say too much.

I sat there for a time, thinking about what she'd said. I had to leave this place, escape myself. And to do that, I needed to get my gold lamp back. I stood and moved toward the oil painting behind the desk. I'd seen the hinges, and knew it must hide the safe behind it.

But then two servants walked past the door, eying me curiously, and I lost my nerve. Instead, I moved toward the bookcase on the other side of the room, cocking my head sideways to read the gilt-inlaid titles, all in Spanish. *The Count of Monte Cristo. The Inferno. Songs of Robert Burns. Highland Warrior.* I mused over that one. Sounded like a modern Scottish romance, not something from the 1800s. I would've laid a bet that Estrella had read that one for sure. She'd likely read everything here…I stepped back and looked over the shelves, wondering about a world in which this was the max of what they could read. What they could buy. What they could lend. We had…what? Thousands of books at our fingertips, between libraries and e-books and used books and Barnes & Noble…

But staring at these precious, honored tomes on the shelves, I felt the weight of their value. It made me appreciate all the more everything I'd read in the past. My breath caught as I wondered if my TBR stack would consist of one preciously obtained book at a time from here on out, rather than the five or six library books I routinely had waiting for me at home. *Library books.* What would the fines be like if I didn't get back to return them for weeks? Or months? Or…ever?

The thought made me a little sick to my stomach, and I reached out to grab hold of a shelf, forcing myself to breathe. *Of course you'll get back. Somehow, Zara, you'll get back. And you'll go to college. And buy that Kindle you've been wanting, and have gobs upon gobs of books to read. Stacks…*

But my ears were ringing, as if I were reaching across time for that segment of space, that lost era of my own, and yet couldn't quite make out the voices that would help me find it again. It felt farther away than ever. As if it was disappearing…a sand castle disintegrating behind me in the waves. I sat down heavily as my vision tunneled, and I knew I was dangerously close to fainting. I leaned over, forcing myself to take deep breaths. I wasn't the sort of girl to panic. I was Zara Ruiz, a good student, a level-headed girl. *Breathe, girl, breathe…*

"Señorita?" said a tentative voice from the doorway. I straightened, too fast, and had to lean over and force myself to breathe some more. The servant girl—one I recognized from the dining room—rushed over to me, setting down a tray with teapot and cups beside me on the table. She touched my back. "Are you all right? Should I fetch Doña Elena?"

"No! No," I repeated, softening my tone. The last thing I wanted was the grand old lady coming in here, seeing me as pale as a ghost, when nothing had happened to me at all that I could even explain. *Add it to the list...*

"Here," she said, pouring a cup of tea. "Sip from this," she said, placing the cup in my trembling hands.

Obediently I drank some of it and then set it on the table, irritated that my hand shook so much that I could barely center the cup on the saucer.

"Did something happen, Señorita?" she asked, kneeling before me. "Are you ill?"

No, unless you believe getting catapulted across almost two hundred years is a form of illness... I stared at her helplessly, then forced myself to shake my head. I moved my fingers around the cup, concentrated, and brought it to my lips again, letting the hot liquid remind me that I was alive, that none of this was a dream.

But why? Why had I been sent here? Now?

I focused in on her. "Thank you for your help. I am Zara. What is your name?"

"Maria," she said. She was clearly native to this land, and it was likely a name imposed by Spanish missionaries, not her own Chumash family.

"Maria," I repeated. "I am pleased to meet you."

"Thank you, Señorita."

"Zara," I said, leaning back in the chair. "Please call me Zara."

"Oh, I couldn't," she said, quickly rising, rubbing one hand with the other.

I took a deep breath, suddenly too weary to say more. There might be time in the days to come for me to woo Maria...to show her that although I might appear a "lady," an esteemed visitor to this fine house, I was really no more than a girl who could dice ten onions in ten minutes.

Awkwardly, she curtsied and left me. I leaned to my right, grabbed the first volume that I could lay my fingers on, and opened it. *A Brief History of Alta California.* I blinked. Here was the perfect book for me. The Cliff Notes of early California history, giving me everything that everyone around me would assume I knew or remembered. Except printed on, you know, thick, soft rough-edged paper and bound in a soft leather cover that felt like it had been an animal hide not too long ago…

Hurriedly, I opened the pages, took another quick sip of tea, and began reading. The language was formal, archaic even, but I could follow along well enough. The author began back more than a hundred years ago and clearly thought the Spanish had some divine right to this land. The missionaries came then, led by Father Junípero Serra, establishing their outposts and presidios all the way up the coast. There'd apparently been one up north, in Santa Leon, that I didn't remember from my history class, but it had been abandoned in the 1820s…

"What has caught your attention so?" Doña Elena said, striding into the library.

I started and stared at her a moment before finding the words to respond. "A volume on California history," I said, lifting it up. "I've always liked history."

"Hmm," she said, bustling over to the table. "An odd choice for a young woman."

Is it? I wondered silently. *Then you don't know the half of it, lady…*

She bent to pour herself a cup of tea and then sat in the other chair beside the table. I stifled a sigh, realizing that it'd be a while before I could check out the safe but also glad that I hadn't been doing so when my hostess walked in.

She took a sip, staring at me over the rim the whole time. "So you are an educated girl," she said.

I nodded. Not a college girl, not yet. But educated? In comparison to a few years of tutoring and governess for her girls? "Yes," I said.

"How many years of schooling have you?" she said, setting down her cup in her saucer. Her thick silver hair was in an immaculate bun, and she held her chin at an angle that told me she was The Boss. I could see that some of Javier's good looks had come from her, despite the losses she'd suffered that had left her forehead a mass of wrinkles and deep frown lines around her mouth.

"Years of schooling? Uh…almost twelve."

Her lips clamped together, and her eyes flashed with disbelief. "Twelve?"

I paused. Apparently this was the wrong answer. "My…my abuela was a firm believer in a proper education," I tried, hoping to reach out to her, bonding one old lady to another. "She sent me to the local school."

"A school, you say? Where?"

It was my turn to clamp my lips in a thin line. I gestured toward my head. "I don't remember, Doña Elena."

"And yet you remember receiving twelve years of tutelage," she said, squinting at me.

"I do," I said.

"Even my own Javier only had eight years of tutelage, before heading to university," she said doubtfully. "Perhaps you've dreamed it. Or it's a part of your head injury?"

"No," I returned, feeling as if this was a line I had to hold. "I am quite certain. I know quite a bit of literature, math, science. History and language too."

"Science!" she scoffed. "They do not teach such things to girls."

"They do where…I came from."

She stared me down a moment, then sniffed. "A most odd occurrence. Your family must be very well-to-do."

This made me want to laugh aloud. But I managed to hold it back. "You might be surprised."

She took this as affirmation that I was some rich chick, apparently, rather than absorbing my note of sarcasm. I let it go, aware that it was likely safer for her to think that way.

"So you are beautiful," she said, looking over my face as if seeking any imperfection, "and clever. You lack certain social graces, but it isn't anything that we cannot overcome. A few weeks under my wing, and I can train you well, my dear."

"Train me for what?" I blurted out, thoroughly confused.

"Well, is it not obvious?" She set down her cup. "To be my future daughter-in-law."

And for the very first time, I saw a full smile on her lips.

CHAPTER 7

"Wh-what?" I sputtered, gaping at her. "Doña Elena," I hurried on, "I am more than honored that you should think of me in such a way, but—"

The grand old lady stood, hands held before her, and turned and looked down her nose at me, as proper and imposing as a portrait. "It is as good as done," she said. "One look at my son, and I knew he was smitten."

I blinked several times, knew my mouth had fallen open. Did she just say what I thought she'd said? *Javier, smitten? This is the second time I've heard that…*

She lifted a single finger, shushing me when I tried to speak. "I have prayed to Our Lady, night after night, for years now, for the right woman to capture his heart. And here you are," she said, gesturing toward me, eyes wide. "A gift from God, as assuredly as each of my children were to me, as well as my own husband." With this last word, she crossed herself. "Delivered to the sands of our very beach!"

I, too, rose, distantly aware that my legs were shaking a little. "Doña Elena, thank you," I said, using my old skills at reading people. This woman needed to know she was respected, more than anything else. I brought a hand to my chest. "The thought that you would consider someone like me, as the…bride of your dear son is an honor beyond any I could imagine." I paused, trying to gather my thoughts.

"Forgive me, but I cannot remain here. My home is somewhere else. Somewhere my mind has forgotten. But surely you understand this," I said, reaching out to her. "If your own family were lost to you—the town of your birth," I added, trying new phrases on for size that sounded vaguely historical, "as they have been to me, would you not wish to find them? After all, how can I press forward when I do not quite fully know what I've left behind?"

"I understand it more than you can imagine," she said with an odd quaver to her voice, her eyes moving to the window, as if lost in memory. Her eyes shifted back to mine, as if she was trying to ferret out the truth within me, and I saw a glimpse of where Javier got it. But then she relented, thank God. At least I thought she had.

"We shall summon a doctor," she said, ignoring me as I narrowed my eyes. "From Santa Barbara. He shall tell us whether your memory will return," she said confidently, "or whether you simply need to press on from this point forward, knowing what you know. But realize this, dear girl," she said, stepping forward and taking one of my cold hands in both of her warm, soft ones. "The honor of my son's hand in marriage is something that daughters of many nobles have sought for years, and even more in this last year when he became the leader of this household. Yet I wanted something else for him. Something as unique and special as I shared with his father."

I gaped at her. She didn't even know me. She was crazy. And yet she seemed so, so sure that this was right. Why?

"And Javier?" I managed, the only civil thing I could utter. "What does he wish?"

She let out a hollow laugh. "He wishes for the extraordinary to capture his heart. Settle him." She lifted one brow and then my hand. "And here you are. Trust me, you are the answer to both our prayers." I gaped at her, and she dropped my hand. "Go and explore with Estrella and Francesca. My daughters will show you the bounty that God has bestowed at your feet. All here," she said, lifting her hands, "for the taking. You need only accept the path that the Lord has opened to you."

With that she strode out, and I continued to stare at the empty doorway. I let out a hollow laugh and turned halfway around, palms on my cheeks. What had just happened? What in the heck had just happened? And how was I supposed to get myself out of it? When Javier found out, he'd be furious. At his mother. Even with me. The last thing he wanted—the *last*—would be me, some poor chick who, when the truth came out, everyone would think was *loca*. If Doña Elena was right…if every girl was after Mr. Ranchero with his hot good looks and steamy eyes and brash ways…then why on earth would he choose me? The girl who had hit him in the face and nether regions…

I turned back around and found the girls waiting for me with expectant faces. They'd been quick about their chores. Or maybe Doña Elena had let them go early—part of her whack-a-doodle plan to make me an insta-member of the clan.

"Ready?" Francesca asked crisply, her hands folded before her waist. "What part of the rancho do you wish to see? Do you wish to ride? Or simply see the closest buildings on foot?"

"I'd like to see all of it," I said, trying to concentrate on the girls, who led me out, rather than the strange things their mother had just told me. "But we can begin here, close in."

She nodded. "That is good. If we go far or wish to ride, we'll have to bring the boys or a guard with us. Javier and Mamá don't like us riding alone."

"Kidnappers might get us," Estrella added, eyes round and earnest.

"Kidnappers?" I smiled, thinking she was joking. But in a sec, I realized she wasn't.

"It's why we cannot go to boarding school in Mexico," Francesca said, obviously reading my expression. "Coming from Rancho Ventura, we could be kidnapped and held for ransom."

"I think it would be an adventure to be kidnapped," Estrella said, looping her arm through mine.

"Estie! Such silly words!" her sister chastised her.

"It's not silly, Frani. To want to see other places, meet new people. Why, Zara is the first new person I've met in years." She drew out that last word in dramatic fashion.

"That is only because you are not yet of age. When that day comes, you'll be able to meet many people. Many *boys* too." She bumped her sister with a teasing hip. I liked seeing this new, softer side of the girl. Obviously, her little sister brought out the best in her.

"It is not boys I wish to meet!"

"Of course it isn't," her sister continued to tease. "That's why you read every novel, yes? For the setting, correct? *Never* the *love* story."

Estrella frowned, and I hid a smile. It was clear that her big sis had nailed it. But the young girl was so adorable…I hated for her to think that I was anything but her staunch friend. We moved to the stables, and when Francesca turned to enter, I said, "Oh, it's all right. I've been in there already." I wasn't ready to relive the memory of my heated discussion with Javier in there—for many reasons.

So we went on to one of the four other outbuildings, all as big as the stables. The first proved to be a butchering shed, where we didn't linger long. I quickly saw the blood and recoiled at the horrendous odor of piles of red meat for drying and cubes of fat—to be rendered into tallow, Francesca explained, confused by my utter lack of knowledge—as well as hides being scraped and taken out to dry flat in the sun. I hurriedly urged the girls onward. In the next shed was the second stage of curing hides, which appeared to involve covering them with disgusting, mashed cow-brains and working them smooth, and again, I rushed them on, practically gagging over the smell.

"Do you have a sensitive stomach, Zara?" Estrella asked, staring up at me in concern as we walked.

"I suppose you could put it that way."

"Was your father not a rancher?"

"No," I said. "I never knew my father or mother. I lived with my abuela, and she ran a restaurant."

"A restaurant!" Francesca said. "Then you must come from a very big city."

"It wasn't all that big," I said.

She turned to me excitedly. "So you remember it? What was the name?"

I lifted a hand to my temples and rubbed. To answer her truthfully might only lead to more questions, and then still more when Javier and his mother learned of it. No one would recognize it. The town probably wasn't even founded for another fifty or a hundred years. "I remember what it looked like. That's all I can share," I said, lifting my hands helplessly. It was true. It *was* all I could share.

The girls looked upon me with sincere empathy.

"What kind of food did your abuela cook?" asked Estrella, walking through the next doors. She took my hand. "And how sad for you, that your parents died! I'm only glad that you had your dear abuela."

"She cooked many of my favorites," I said, choosing to let them think my parents were dead. "*Tamales y arroz con pollo y lentejas con fruta*... And she made the most delicious tortillas." It was with some relief that I saw this next building was a storehouse, with stacks of congealed tallow, candles, and hides, as well as barrels of salt, flour, and sugar and a few crates of fruit and nuts. We walked down the length of it, and I admired the amazing stores of goods, stacked to the ceiling in places. "Is this all for trade?" I asked.

"It's mostly for the rancho," Francesca said. "We have over a hundred workers who depend on us for at least one meal a day. And then with the needs for tanning the hides and rendering the tallow..."

"It takes a great deal," I put in, understanding. This was a serious business, from start to finish. But then, if you didn't have a Walmart down the road, it all would be pretty much up to you. We exited the end of that building, and I saw there was an arc of smaller shelters, open to one side. In three, men were working on various leather goods, creating rope and bridles and, in one, what appeared to be a saddle. In the next two, fires blazed, and two blacksmiths hammered across their anvils. In neither shelter could I tell what the end product might be.

The girls led me up a hill. Across from it, in a shallow valley beside a stream and a grove of oaks, was an entire village, with hundreds of small huts. Francesca said, "This is where the servants in our house and workers on our rancho live."

"And you said you have over a hundred people who work for you?" I asked.

"Yes," she said. "They work in the fields and orchards, or across the hills as goatherds and vaqueros. Others, as you have seen, work at tanning or tallow-making—"

"And tooling leather!" Estrella put in.

"And others work in the villa," Francesca went on.

We walked down the dusty path and into the village. Chickens scattered before our feet, and doleful looking little children stared at us as we walked by. A mother pulled one into a hut, glancing back at us, partially in fear. "Do they like it here?" I asked.

"Well enough," Estrella said, looking momentarily sad for them. "They are dreadfully poor, but they are better off than when we weren't here. Now they have some steady food, work, shelter. When my grandfather came, they had none of that."

"But were they…happier?"

Her delicate brows rose and met in the middle. "Happier? How would I know that?"

"Of course," I hurried on. "I suppose I was only musing aloud." *Unless you're a time traveler too and can tell me for certain…*

"The priests brought them the sacraments, introduced them to the Holy Writ. If they were solely graced by that, then they are better off than before."

"Of course," I repeated, but as I stared into the dark, dusty doorway at a woman with a tiny baby at her bare, sagging breast, I wasn't certain at all.

On the far side, by the stream, were big cauldrons full of boiling water, in which women dipped clothing and then set them steaming on big rocks to rub clean. Some held bars of soap, scrubbing into the cloth—dresses and shirts and sheets and long underwear. Others carried the clothing to a long line strung between the trees, clipping them against the breeze to dry. Never had I been more thankful for my abuela's old washing machine and dryer that took forever. This, *this* was work like I'd never considered before.

You put a hundred-plus people together on a ranch, and there's some serious laundry. But the women here were singing, in a low, dissonant tone, which made me feel oddly welcome. It was as if I knew the tune, but couldn't quite place it. Children ran through the laundry hanging over lines, shrieking in glee, and mothers swatted them away but smiled as they did so. Here was a more familiar form of family, of work, of joy, which comforted me and made me smile with them. Maybe it was just that jobs on the ranch varied, as they did everywhere, and some were happier than others. Those in the big villa, after all, seemed pretty content.

The girls walked me through the oak grove and then up the next hill. Before us were acres upon acres of corn and wheat, planted as far as the eye could see, with irrigation trenches running in neat lines at perfect intervals. Men and women alike moved in and out of the crop parcels, carrying baskets for gathering and hoes and picks and shovels. Now that I thought about it, this was what the blacksmiths had been working on—more farming tools.

"This is about as far as we can go and still get back before noon," Estrella said. "We should head back now, or Mamá will become worried."

Thoughts of Doña Elena—and her last words to me—made me shift uneasily. I wasn't so anxious to get back. "What of the orchards? Could we not just take a quick peek at those? Aren't we close?" I could smell orange blossoms on the breeze.

Francesca hesitated, and I remembered talk of kidnappers and bringing a guard with us. But seriously, there didn't seem to be anybody but rancho workers for miles.

"We've come this far," I said. "What's the harm?"

"Well, maybe," she said reluctantly. "Just a quick peek."

Together we set off again, climbing a steep path that gave way to a rocky valley. The orange blossom scent surged before the trees came into view, and I covered my mouth. The green—the beautiful green of the leaves—was in such sharp contrast to the brown, rocky soil and rocks around the trunks that it surprised me. The trees were not the perfectly trimmed, round, fat trees I remembered from my own time, but they were very pretty in their own rustic way. Again, neat irrigation lines ran between the trees. Clearly, this ranch was blessed with an abundance of fresh water. Maybe there'd always been enough water in California, until millions of people moved in.

We heard the men talking and laughing before they came into view, walking their horses along the edge of the orchard. When they saw us, they pulled up to a stop. Javier blinked in surprise when he saw us. "You women came this far?" he said. I thought it odd that he referred to his little sisters as *women*. "Where is your guard?"

"Forgive us, hermano," Francesca said quickly. "We didn't think Señorita Ruiz would want to come this far today, so we didn't think we required one."

"But then one thing led to another," I put in, "and I wanted to see more. Forgive me, Don Ventura. It was my urging that led us here."

His eyes hovered over me as his horse stepped nervously left and right. "I thought when you said you wished to see more of the rancho, you meant the outbuildings."

"That's hardly a tour, is it?" I asked, smiling to try and hide my irritation—thinking we didn't need any babysitter, not out here in this gorgeous, open country—and reached up to pick an orange. It was small but heavy with juice. "It's even more beautiful out here." I lifted the orange to my nose, closed my eyes, and inhaled deeply. I smiled and lifted it up at him, wanting to dispel the odd tension in the air. A good piece of fruit—

But when I noted them all staring at me, I felt the heat of a blush at my cheeks again. "I-I'm sorry. Was I not supposed to pick one?" I asked, feeling terribly guilty.

"No, no," Javier said, his fine, dark-fringed eyes searching mine, as if still trying to figure me out. "Come. We shall give you a ride back to the villa. There is no way you will make it back on foot before the meal."

I swallowed my protest as Rafael and Patricio took the arms of Estrella and Francesca, neatly swinging them up and to the rear of each horse, behind the rider's saddle. Javier edged his mare toward me. "Come now, Señorita," he said, reaching down, offering his arm.

I stared up at him. He really meant to just swoop me up behind him? I was bigger, heavier than his sisters.

"Put your boot in this stirrup," he said with some agitation, "and take my hand. I will see to you." Javier didn't seem to doubt his strength or ability to handle my weight. I took hold of his hand, placed my boot in the stirrup, Javier pulled and swung, and I landed abruptly on the rump of his mare. The horse danced a little, threatening to unseat me, but he shifted his hold, grabbing my left arm and pulling it around him until we settled. "Good?" he grunted.

"Good," I said, willing as much confidence into my tone as possible, even though I was terrified. I didn't like being on top of the horse, my legs on one side. It felt unstable.

"Shift farther over," he said in irritation, as if I should know this. "And lean against me." I did as he instructed, hoping he couldn't feel my pounding heart. His hand covered mine, which rested below his sternum. My body was partially pressed against his broad back. "Better?"

"Better," I croaked. But I was uncomfortably aware of the raw physicality of him again as we set off. His wide, strong muscles, tensing and easing. The smell of orange and leather and lye soap from his clothes.

"Have you never ridden with a man, Señorita Ruiz?" he said over his shoulder in puzzlement.

"No," I answered without thinking. "I prefer my own horse."

"And with a proper side-saddle, I imagine. When you arrived bareback yesterday with John, you appeared…uncomfortable."

It was only then that I realized I was entering dangerous conversation territory. But if he tested me on it… "Actually," I gambled, "I prefer to ride astride. Not that I was ever much of a horsewoman. I was more of a…wagon girl." *As in station wagons. Or SUVs.*

"Yet you managed to steal my own mount," he said.

"Borrowed. I borrowed her," I corrected softly.

I felt the rumble of a laugh in his belly, but he uttered no sound. I smiled in spite of myself. Had I nearly made Javier de la Ventura laugh out loud? The man always seemed to be unnecessarily stern around his family. It was only with his friends that I had heard laughter from him.

"So what do you make of Rancho Ventura?" he asked over his shoulder. "Does she compare to others you've seen?"

"She is finer than any that I have seen," I said, hoping to continue to win favor from him.

"Truly? To what other ranchos would you compare her?"

"I…I would have a hard time naming any. With my head injury

and all."

He paused. "But you remember seeing other ranchos?"

"Perhaps." I tried to pull away from him a bit, sensing the trap he was laying for me.

But he held on to my hand with his own. "Hold tight, Señorita Ruiz. I don't wish for you to fall while you are in my care."

"He's never dropped a girl yet," said Patricio, pulling up alongside us, Estrella behind him. "But you may be the first girl to drop him." He grinned mischievously, and I was thankful to him for the interruption.

"Patricio, by the saints," Javier said, his belly stiffening beneath my hand, "if you weren't the best agent out of Monterey, I'd chase you from my land myself or else show you what it means to be dropped with a punch."

The man grinned, but I noted he moved his horse a few steps out of reach.

"How is it that a woman as fine as you, Señorita Ruiz, has learned to strike a man the way you did my friend?" asked Rafael as he came up on our other side. I was alternately upset by this line of questioning and pleased that Javier de la Ventura was not too prideful to admit where his bruised cheek had been earned.

"My abuela wished me to learn the ways of defense," I said. "She taught me that a small woman could still be mighty and wished me to learn every aspect of what that meant, whether in physical or mental power."

He lifted one brow in surprise and appreciation. "A wise woman, your abuela," he said. "But do you not have brothers or uncles to defend you?"

"No," I said, feeling a horrifying ball form in my throat.

There was no way I could start *crying.* "It was just me and my abuela," I managed, swallowing hard. "And she died recently."

He bowed his head, and I felt Javier's hand tighten over mine, which made the ball in my throat swell even more. "Forgive me, miss," Rafael said, "for bringing up painful memories of the dear and departed."

I forced a bright smile and took a deep breath, trying to chase away the tears. "Memories of her hurt, because I miss her so. But it is good to remember her."

"So your amnesia clearly does not preclude you from memories of her?" Javier asked, his tone a mix of curiosity and suspicion.

"No, it does not," I said, taking a chance. About this, *her*, I could not bring myself to lie. I looked past him to the sea, visible from here in the distance. "She would have enjoyed hearing me tell of the rancho and my time here. She appreciated hard workers and a family's business."

"Just the sort of woman this country needs," Rafael said. "Women civilize a land. Bring balance and order."

"At times, too much balance and order," Javier murmured before me.

"For those who chafe against the bit," Francesca said, speaking up for the first time. "Give in to what is yours, brother," she added, "rather than fighting against it."

"Truly, Javier," Patricio said, in front of her. "Men would die to win such a land, with such promise, from you."

"And someone might do so," added Rafael, "if you keep gambling. Somewhere, someone, at some point, will take from you something precious, and you will recognize what you should never have—"

"Enough!" Javier said, abruptly pulling up on his reins and turning his mare to face the others. "Who are you—any of you—to lecture me? Have I not returned here and assumed the mantle my father laid across my shoulders?"

I felt the gathering tension in his chest. Javier didn't like that I was hearing any of this.

This has to do with those dudes chasing him yesterday.

Patricio edged his mount forward. "We shall leave it, but you must promise that you will not gamble with the men of the *Guadiana*, when they pass by these shores again. They are far more dangerous, Javier, and—"

"Enough!" Javier cried again. "I am the grown lord of this rancho, not a child for you all to chastise! You weary me." He wheeled his mount around and took off at a gallop, with me bouncing around on her rump as if he'd completely forgotten that I was there.

But he hadn't forgotten. Because he held on to my forearm with an iron grip. And between that and how hard I held on to him with both arms now, willing myself to become one with him, trying to bounce back onto the center of the horse's back rather than off of it, I somehow managed miraculously to keep my seat. But it wasn't long until I felt my strength waning, the adrenaline wearing away. "Javier," I gasped, hating the soft, frightened whine in my voice. But one more big bounce would send me to the ground. I knew it. People broke their necks falling from horses… "Javier!" I cried louder.

He seemed to remember me more fully then and pulled up on the crest of a hill. We'd ridden closer to the sea and were at the edge of a bluff that overlooked an eroded arroyo which, come winter, obviously flooded with aggressive torrents that washed away at the clay like a mad sculptor. He pulled his leg over the saddle, jumped down, and strode away, leaving me stranded there, gaping after him.

His mare circled around and then turned the other way, obviously as confused as I. *Oh brother,* I thought, getting irritated with him. *So much for chivalry.* I looked down, took a breath, and slipped off the mare's rump to land heavily on the soft soil. Then I walked after him.

He stood about twenty paces away, hands on hips, staring out to sea like some freakishly good-looking historical romance cover model, now present in 3-D. I came up beside him and stood there, silent. Waiting. The guy obviously had something he needed to get off his chest.

"I wished to captain my own ship," he said, angrily rubbing his forehead between thumb and finger as if to massage away a pain. "Not to be stuck on this land. To sail as John does, up and down these shores. And beyond. *Far* beyond. I was in Mexico, training to read maps, studying the weather and nautical engineering, when my brother died. I had no choice but to return."

I took a deep breath. His tone—filled with embarrassment and sorrow—told me he regretted his rash reaction to his friends and sisters. But his words resonated with me. Had I not suffered a similar change of fate? My prospects of becoming a meteorologist in 1840 Alta California were distinctly narrow…

We stood there a moment, in silence. "Sometimes," I dared, "life takes us into waters we did not chart. Could this…could this not just be a chapter of your life, rather than the whole book?"

His chin lifted a little, and his dark eyes slid toward me, hungry with hope. Encouraging me. "Might you not still captain your own ship at some point?" I went on. "When Mateo and Francesca are a little older?"

I saw my mistake when confusion overtook hope in the lines of his face. Francesca would never be heir to this ranch. This place and time was patriarchal all the way. But I didn't correct myself. Maybe he'd chalk it up to me thinking she might marry someone who could run it. *Yeah, that's it…*

But then his brows lifted a little in surprise, wonder. As if he'd never thought about it that way. As if he'd thought that, in returning to the rancho, his fate was sealed. That it was all on his shoulders, forever. And who was I to say? Maybe it was. Maybe if a guy was called back to the ranch, he'd never escape the daily grind again. But good grief, he'd landed on a piece of property that—as his friend had noted—others would kill for. The guy had to give up the "woe is me, my treasured life plan got wrecked" act and *man up.*

You need not speak every thought that comes into your head, Grillita, Abuela whispered to me in memory. I swear it was only that, jumping into my head just then, that kept me from saying more. Maybe it was because I wasn't a sister to anyone, because I'd never been one to coddle others. Still, I just thought my thoughts for once, rather than saying them aloud, choosing to honor my abuela in this manner.

Then I noticed Javier had turned slightly toward me and gazed at me in a different way than before. With appreciation, not tolerance or disdain or suspicion. With some odd sense of wonder. *It was just that idea I'd planted,* I told myself. I've given him hope.

But I had to admit, when Javier de la Ventura looked at me like *that…holy hot tamale…*I had a hard time looking away.

CHAPTER 8

Doña Elena looked on with some satisfaction as we rode up to the villa, just as the others entered through the doors. Her dark eyes shifted back and forth between Javier and me, as if her diabolical plan for us to fall madly in love was already coming together. *Listen, lady, I just showed up for lunch, and then I'll be back to planning my way outta here…*

But when Javier dismounted and turned to help me down, I was struck by how he took his time, from the moment he placed his long, strong fingers at my waist, lifted me up and away from the horse, and then gently, slowly lifted me to the ground. It was not at all the polite, straight-to-it manner that Captain John had used to help me yesterday. No, this was a long, slow, sultry sort of move that made my heart do a weird flip. He was staring down at me, still holding my hips. I dared not look up into his face. "Gracias, Don Ventura," I said, thinking, *Okay, you can let go now…*

"Javier," he said to me, his voice low and gravelly, still holding me. "Please, Zara. Call me Javier. You did already today and I found I… liked it."

Got it. Javier. Javvy. Whatever. Just ¡Libérame! Your mom *is standing* right there, *watching all of this go down!*

"Gracias, Javier," I said quickly and turned, tearing away from his hands…those hot, wide, sprawling, possessive hands. He paused and then followed after me, as if embarrassed to be caught in that odd sort of reverie.

"Doña Elena," I greeted the grand lady as I passed. I could *feel* the glee radiating from her, as if she had orchestrated our chance meeting and the whole ride back.

I entered the villa and blinked in the sudden relative darkness. But I welcomed the cool shadows and gratefully turned toward a servant holding a copper bowl, standing beside another with a clean towel, and swiftly washed and dried my face and hands. At the end of the hall the Ventura sisters awaited me, and each took an arm as we walked to the dining room, both speaking at once.

"Was he awful?"

"He gets in such a state…"

"I'm sorry you got caught up in it. He hasn't been the same since—"

"Since Papá and Dante died, he's been like that. At one moment jovial, at another in a tempest."

"He was fine," I interjected. "He is well. We spoke, and he seemed to calm down. I think, I think he just needed a moment to pull himself together."

Both girls turned to face me. "Pull himself together," Francesca repeated quizzically.

I got it then. That was a totally modern phrase. "*¿Comprenden?*" I rushed on, as if they should understand the phrase. "Pull himself together," I repeated, more forcefully this time. "As a seamstress might do with portions of fabric. Or a maid making a bed."

Estrella paused and then nodded, as if it made sense to her. "Pull himself together," she murmured to herself. And as they turned to lead me back into the dining hall, I wondered if I'd introduced a phrase into the language of the people a good hundred or so years before it was meant to be there.

We sat down around the table, women first, and then the men.

But Javier never joined us.

In fact, I didn't see him the rest of the day. His friends did their best to fill in the awkward gap; Patricio regaled me with stories of his life as an agent dealing with more than two hundred ships that sailed past these shores, especially the neat, square-rigged *Ayacucho* with an Englishman for a captain and crew from the Sandwich Islands. According to Patricio, they could read the winds in seconds and never dropped more than a single anchor in port, and with all sails aloft, the *Ayacucho* was as agile as a Polynesian catamaran. He seemed more than a little impressed with them and went on to speak of how they narrowly avoided coming aground near Point Conception during a fierce southeaster. I soon learned that such storms apparently chased all ships at sea from November to April.

Through it all, Doña Elena ate and drank and smiled more than I'd ever seen her smile, looking down the table at me like a doting aunt, even with her son conspicuously absent. It unnerved me, but Javier's empty seat unnerved me more. *What's up with that?* I thought. After the meal, we retired for a siesta, and I pretty much ran to my room, closing the door behind me with relief.

But then the hair prickled on the back of my neck. I wasn't alone.

I turned.

But it was only him—Javier, leaning against the far wall. He was staring at me, his arms crossed, his wide-brimmed hat tossed on the foot of my bed.

"Ja-Javier," I said, my heart pounding. "What are you doing in here?"

"What are you doing here at all?" was all he said in return. He didn't make any moves on me. Just stood there, staring, as if trying to make sense of me. "Who are you, Zara? You are…different. Unlike any woman I've ever met before."

I stared at him, my mouth growing dry. *I'm Zara Ruiz. Granddaughter of a poor restaurant owner. Daughter to a prison inmate and runaway mother. Almost–high school graduate. Almost–college attender. Sudden time-traveler.*

None of that, of course, came out of my mouth.

"Tell me," he said. "Tell me the truth."

"If-if I told you," I stuttered, "you wouldn't believe me."

He squinted at me, straightened, and took a step away from the wall. I lifted my hands. "Stay where you are."

His squint deepened as he took another step. "I will not harm you, Zara. But those words…they are truth. You think that I wouldn't believe you. Why is that?"

"Because I…it's…impossible."

He took another step forward. "So you remember something."

"I remember," I said, still with my hands up. "But I am afraid."

His gaze hardened. "Because you fear how I might respond if I knew of it?"

"I'm afraid how everyone would respond," I muttered. "Stop," I said, raising my hands as he continued to advance.

"Tell me, Zara. Trust me. As I trusted you this day with something most intimate." He took another step forward, until my fingers brushed up against his chest, halting him. "As I trust you now, when I am more than aware of how you are able to…defend yourself." He stared down at me, all earnest need in his eyes. Practically begging me to be vulnerable with him here, now.

"I-I can't," I said. "Not yet," I added impulsively, when I saw the pain run across his face. But he didn't move away from me.

"Is it because of the beach? What you saw? Those men, chasing me? Is this why you don't trust me?"

N*o, you idiot,* I thought in frustration. *It's because you might take me to the local priest and have him dunk me in the river until I confess I'm a witch. Because even in my time, big guy, no one time-travels. No one.*

It was fantasy. The basis of movies. Books.

Not real life.

And surely I was going to snap out of it and return to my awful, normal, sad, transitory life any sec. And all of this would disappear. The rancho. Doña Elena. The girls. The boys. The workers and their mountains of hides. The massive herds of cattle morphing back into massive herds of suburban houses, like Cinderella's guards back into mice.

"There is a reason I gamble with men like those of the *Guadiana*," Javier said, a muscle twitching along his jaw. "But you," he said, reaching up to brush a curl away from my eye, a bit hesitant, "need to give me a chance to explain."

I stared up at him. "Javier," I whispered, half in complaint, half in warning, "truly you needn't explain yourself at all. I am but a guest in your household. Gone as soon as I'm…well."

He dropped his hand abruptly. "Of course," he said, nodding curtly. "What could possibly hold you here?"

I stared back into his eyes amid their fringes of black lashes and recognized the magnetic pull between us anew, wondering for a sec just what could possibly make me leave, with this, *this* in the mix. I sniffed and forced myself to take a step back. "I am most grateful for your hospitality. But now? Now I think I need to rest." I rubbed my forehead, feeling an ache in full-throb mode there.

He studied me and then reached for his hat and rolled it in his hands, an uncharacteristically nervous move. "Of course. Rest well, Zara."

"You as well, Javier," I said gently. I reached for the door and watched him exit. He turned in the hallway, looking back at me, and *Ay de mí,* I had to admit that I might never see another model-quality dude check me out like that again. The afternoon shadows seemed to catch every perfect curve and angle of his face, and I wished I could snap a pic of him with my phone to remember him and this crazy moment. It was like a dream.

But it wasn't a dream. This was some sort of alternate-reality life. And I had to stop this before it got completely out of hand, keeping me from returning to my real life. *My real life,* I repeated silently in my head, willing myself to remember.

So I shut the door firmly between us and, on shaking legs, made my way to the bed. I pulled down the covers and climbed in, fully dressed. I didn't care. I was wiped. The day had taken everything in me and it wasn't even over yet. But I hadn't gotten any closer to my golden lamp. "Tonight," I muttered to myself, letting my eyelids fall. *Tonight I'll find my way into that safe…*

CHAPTER 9

That night at supper Javier seemed to pointedly ignore me and focus on Patricio, Rafael, and two sea captains who had just arrived in Bonita Harbor. From what I could gather, this was much of the focus at the ranch—entertaining guests, who were either trading with the Venturas or trying to do so, brokering deals when they went back to the harbor. The household had prepared all day for the big meal, and platters upon platters of food were set before us. Javier poured the first glasses of wine—presumably imported, since I'd seen that the vines were yet young and there'd been no casks of wine on our tour—and the house servants made certain the glasses remained full.

He grew agitated every time his guests turned his attention back to me, over and over, in their hunger for any sort of female company they could get. And since young Francesca and I were the closest to eligible that they might find—with Adalia clearly in her mourning black—the two kept finding pauses in the conversation to return their focus on me, the It Girl of the moment. It had come out that I'd lost my memory and was "convalescing" here until it returned. And as more wine was swallowed, the men apparently decided that it was all a ruse, a way for me to finagle my way into the estate and close to Javier.

"I wish I'd have such luck," Captain Donnovan said in his light Irish accent, looking down the table at me and lifting his glass. "Were I to fish such a maiden as you from the sea, I'd make certain you had the best care for as long as I could manage to make you stay."

Javier cleared his throat. "That would not go over well with your men. Captain Worthington said women aboard a ship are considered bad luck. As much as he doesn't believe it, his men do."

Captain Donnovan took another sip and squinted his green eyes in my direction. "I'd wager this one would be worth risking mutiny. Especially if she *maneuvered* her way alongside *me*."

I was just thinking of my retort, enraged by what he was hinting at, when Doña Elena frowned and rose, also clearly disapproving of this line of conversation. "Yes, well, our guest is not leaving the safety of this rancho until she regains her full faculties. The good Lord has seen fit to set her upon *our* beach, and we see it as our Christian duty to care for her until she is fully recovered."

Captain Donnovan gave me an exaggerated, admiring wink, as if I had them all just where I wanted them. I was about to give him a piece of my mind when Javier rose. "Mamá, it was a fine meal as usual. Thank you, and please pass on our gratitude to the cooks." He nodded in the direction of the four servants who stood at the edge of the dining room, hands behind their backs. They gave him shy smiles. "Gentlemen, let us return to the harbor for a…nightcap."

And gambling, I figured. They would gather at the harbor house for some cards and more liquor, undoubtedly. But I'd seen Javier be very judicious about how much wine he was drinking—only a glass while his guests had four from the tiny, delicate crystal goblets. No doubt to set them in a place to negotiate the best deal possible for his goods, as well as to win at cards. Patricio and Rafael had been freer with the wine, but not nearly as free as the other two visitors.

We all stood, and I lined up alongside Estrella and Francesca. The captains said their farewells, shook the boys' hands, kissed Doña

Elena's and Adalia's, and briefly held each of ours. Captain Donnovan, as short as I was but clearly very strong, held mine longer. "Miss Ruiz," he said, covering my hand with his other. I sensed Javier stiffen behind him but didn't look his way. "Should you have any need of travel southward, I shall be returning in a month's time. Please do not hesitate if I may be of any service to you at all."

"Thank you, Captain Donnovan," I said, giving him a brief curtsy, as I'd seen Estrella do before me.

Reluctantly, he let my hand go and moved on to Francesca as I said my farewell to the other captain. I felt some relief when they all disappeared through the tall, wide front door and a servant shut it behind them. The girls asked me to play a game with them in the library, but I begged off, blaming a headache but really just wanting some time alone. I wanted to get out of this dress with its too-tight waist, open my window to the sea breeze, and try to find my breath again.

But Doña Elena was following me up the wide, curving stairs. I paused and looked back at her in question.

She took my elbow and urged me into my room, clearly not wanting the servants—or her children looking up at us from below—to hear us. She closed the door behind her and crossed her arms, reminding me of her son when he'd stood in my room that afternoon. A servant had lit a lantern beside my bed. Outside, I could hear the men's horses as they rode down the road.

"What is it, Doña Elena?" I asked.

"My son tells me he is keeping a certain item for you in the safe," she said. "I wondered if you would describe it to me."

"What? Why?"

"Because it is important that I know."

"Why not ask him to see it?" I asked, confused and frustrated. There was none of the warmth in her there'd been earlier. She was agitated, as if doubting me. Was it something Captain Donnovan had said? Did she think—as Javier did at the start—that I'd somehow planted myself here? That I was some sort of spy? Or worse, some sort of girl trying to worm her way into Javier's heart and home?

The tightening of her face made me realize that she had already asked him, and he'd refused her. Why? *Probably thought she was meddling...* I took a deep breath, let it out slowly, and lifted my hands. "It is gold, about this big. Once a teapot of sorts, I think, but it was missing its spout. With odd, foreign writing on it." I shook my head. "Barely visible writing. It is very old. Half of it is covered with white sea creatures that need to be scraped off."

"Sea creatures?" she said, her eyes distant.

"On half," I repeated. "Those hard, crusty things? It'd been in the water a very long time."

"It sounds very valuable," she said.

I nodded. "I think so."

"And how did it come into your possession?"

I swallowed hard. She was looking at me so keenly, so earnestly, that I thought about telling her. Telling anyone would be a relief to me. But no, she'd think I was crazy and probably toss me out the door. Chase me down the road with a broom. *So much for the future daughter-in-law concept...* No, I needed her, this house, this place, until I could figure out what was next. "I...I don't remember," I said.

Her eyes narrowed, and she stepped toward me. "Did someone give it to you? Tell you to come here with it?"

"What? No!"

"How did you get to Pirata Cove?"

"Pirata? Oh, I call it Tainter Cove. I…I don't remember how I got there, exactly."

"Why did you strike my son?"

"It was…instinct. I was afraid. I didn't know him. He grabbed my arm and was accusing me…like you seem to be doing now."

She looked at me as if trying to see through me—she was just an inch or so taller than I, but she felt much taller. "You do not wish to harm me or my family?"

"What? Of course not!"

"And you did not hear of Javier somehow…of his wealth? His position?"

"*No*," I said, willing every ounce of the truth into my eyes as I stared back at her. "I'd never heard of your son. *He* was the one who found *me*."

"What did you know of that lamp before it was in your hands?"

I shook my head at her, exasperated. I had to give her something to get her off my back. "I keep telling you, I knew nothing. The last thing I remember is that I found it in a tide pool. At Tainter Cove," I said. "I was walking up the beach, and I sat down with it, looking it over." I shook my head again and lifted my hands. "That's the last thing I remember. Honestly." *At least, it's the last thing I remember before I was here, in your time.*

"Tainter Cove," she repeated softly. Her dark eyes shifted over mine, searching, then grew still. It was as if something had been confirmed for her, deep within. But she gave me no indication of what that might be. "I believe you, Zara. But you must show me the spot soon. When we return from the charreada. For now, you must rest."

I held my breath, managing to nod, and she slipped out the door and shut it carefully behind her. I didn't bother to ask for specifics about the "charreada" Estrella had told me about, hoping I might be out of here before that was something I had to deal with. My mind went over our conversation, her odd reaction—so much hidden behind her eyes and that down-turned mouth—and yet her trust too. I'd just have to go through it with her. Show her the tide pools…

I sank to the edge of my bed, head dropping into my hands.

How could I show her the tide pools when they were fifty feet under the sand? Sand that wouldn't erode away for more than a hundred years?

Maria came and helped me out of my dress and into my night shift, but as soon as she was out the door, I put on my maxiskirt and cami, which I'd found washed and neatly folded in my chest, along with my other clothes. It was then that I found my abuela's shawl too. I cried out and lifted it in my hands, cradling it to my face, weeping. Javier had obviously found it and placed it in my chest, when he came to my room. Sitting there, my tears spent after a while, I started to feel a bit more like myself in my own clothes, with the shawl about my shoulders.

It was quite late, and the house had grown silent. Outside, a three-quarter moon was sinking toward the west. Leaning on the sill, I thought I heard a howl on the wind—the distant cry of the wolf dog?

Inspired, I took my lantern, opened my door with a soft creak that made me wince, and moved along the hall and then down the sweeping stairs. I thought about going outside but then recalled the guards on the roof. If they weren't dozing, they'd surely stop me and question me before I could whistle for the wolf. There seemed to be some subtle, ongoing threat for the inhabitants of this villa, and it was clearly frowned upon for girls to leave alone.

So I prowled the lower level. Wandered into the big kitchen, with a long, wide stone island, where they clearly were set up to roll out tortillas. The place smelled like home—of burned oil and onions and cumin and cinnamon. I set my lantern down and leaned to rest my cheek on the cool surface of the central island, again thinking of my grandmother and her hours and hours of cooking. I stretched my arms out, my fingers splayed, wanting to remember her, reach her across the abyss of time.

"What are you doing?" asked a small voice.

I rose, startled, wiped the tears from my face, then pulled my shawl tightly around my shoulders.

It was little Jacinto, in a nightshirt that draped to his ankles, holding his own lantern.

"I was…thinking," I said.

"In the kitchen?" he asked.

"Yes. I do some of my best thinking in the kitchen."

"But you are a lady. Kitchens are for servants."

"As well as some ladies," I said, wiping my eyes again, hoping the boy wouldn't notice. "What are you doing up at this hour?"

"I couldn't sleep. Mamá says that milk helps you go to sleep, so I came down for some." He padded over to a door in the floor and lifted the heavy wooden lid until it stood upright. A cellar, I decided. A place to keep things cool. He went down the steps and came up again with a tin can in his hand. "Want some? Are you having trouble sleeping too?"

"Yes," I said with a nod. Maybe some lukewarm, 1840 milk was exactly what I needed. If I didn't sleep, how would I deal with Doña Elena tomorrow? Or Javier? I shook my head, determined not to think of either of them any more tonight. If I did, there would be no sleeping at all.

The boy fetched us two ceramic cups without handles and, biting his lip, carefully poured from the tin can, managing to spill only a few drops. He wiped those away with his hand, licked it, and set the lid on the can again. He took it back to the cellar, closed the door, and came back over to me and the cups. He handed one to me with some ceremony.

"Gracias, Jacinto," I said, raising my cup toward his. "*Salud.*"

He gave me his gap-toothed grin. "Salud," he said, clinking his cup against mine.

I took a sip and almost spit it out.

It was thick, almost like cream, and I dimly realized that it was like whole milk. It *was* whole milk. I'd always been a one-percent girl myself. Apparently that wasn't an option among the cellar shelves. "Mmmm," I said, forcing an appreciative smile. He grinned back at me, his brown upper lip now sporting a white mustache. The kid was adorable.

"Would you like to play backgammon, Señorita?" he said. "I like backgammon."

I smiled at him. "Maybe one round. If I can recall how to play."

He led the way down the hall, across the wide red tiles, smooth beneath my bare feet, and opened a giant, carved door to the music room I'd glimpsed yesterday. Three guitars and a mandolin were on one wall, a harpsichord in the corner. I followed him in, staring at the guitars, as he rummaged through a closet for the game.

The instruments were elegant, gorgeous antiques, honey and red-hued in the lantern light. Well, not *antiques*, obviously, in this age. But I'd never seen anything like them. I lifted one that was about my size. "Who plays them?" I asked, sinking to a hide-covered stool.

Jacinto turned to me, clearly confused as I tentatively strummed the strings. "No one, since Papá died. But girls don't play guitar. Only the harpsichord."

I laughed under my breath at him. "This girl does," I said. And then I found the first chord and played my favorite old Spanish song, an intricate, gentle tune that spoke of night and stars and love on the wind…I'd always loved playing. Periodically, Abuela or others in the restaurant would convince me to play. But it'd always been more of an intimate exercise for me. An extension of my thoughts and feelings. A prayer of sorts rather than a performance. And in the welcome embrace of the song, I closed my eyes, giving myself fully to each note, building in intensity, then slowing, softening…

As the sweet sound of the last note faded in the air, I opened my eyes and saw not just Jacinto, mouth agape as he stared at me, but his big brother, Javier, standing in the doorway behind him. "That was…beautiful," Javier said, his brown eyes warm with wonder.

We stared at each other for a moment.

"Jacinto, to bed," he commanded, and the boy set aside the game and scampered off without complaint, obviously glad that I was distracting his brother, keeping him out of more serious trouble for being up at this hour.

Javier sat down on a stool a few feet away from me and swept off his hat. "When I came in and heard the music…I couldn't believe it. It…sounded like…"

"Like something your papá played?" I asked gently.

He nodded once, laid the hat on the corner of the settee behind him, and rubbed his hair. The curls bobbed around his face, partially covering one eye, but he shook it aside. "Where did a woman such as you learn to play?" His eyes slipped down to my bare shoulder, and I lifted the shawl higher up. His eyes moved down to my skirt and bare feet, and I quickly tucked my toes beneath the hem.

I didn't feel like explaining my old clothes. I hoped he wouldn't ask.

"I've always played," I said, hoping to distract him.

"Your papá taught you? A girl?"

Again, with the girl-thing. "Uh, no. My neighbor."

"So you recall your neighbor?"

I saw where he was headed. "I recall it was he who taught me."

"Do you remember his name? His house? What village it was called?"

I swallowed hard and shook my head, rising to set the guitar back on the rack.

"No," he said, lifting his hands in alarm. "Forgive me. It's late and clearly you are not in the mood for more questions. But please… would you play me another song? I—it would be a blessing to me, this night. I have not heard that guitar played in a very long time."

I paused, looking down into his face, suddenly childlike with need, and slowly sank back to my stool. He leaned forward, chin on hands, waiting.

He was so handsome, so dang *electric*, he was like interference. My mind went blank for a minute. I knew a good twenty songs by heart, but could I think of another in that instant? Not so much.

He gave me a puzzled look, his lips relaxing into a slight smile.

"Do you know 'By the Water in Seville'?"

I shook my head, but the city name jogged a song loose in my head. "Not that one, but this…" And I set my fingers confidently upon the strings and began picking it out, more gradually dissolving into the music now—with him present—than I had last time.

I closed my eyes, imagining flamenco dancers moving in their magical way as I played, as my neighbor had taught me to do. "If you imagine dancers before you, your fingers will dance too," he'd coached.

I knew Javier was watching me, absorbing every inch of my face and body and movement, almost viscerally pulling me to him. And I shared the song, fully, not holding back, finding that here, in this way, I could be open to him, bridging the gap between us.

But when the song ended, I blinked once, twice, trying to get my bearings again and yet captivated by his sober stare.

"It is a gift you have, Zara," he said softly. "My father never played like that, and he was fairly accomplished. I have heard such fine music only in Mexico, when I was at university."

"Thank you," I said, reaching for my cup of disgusting creamy milk, suddenly desperate for distraction. Anything but to look into those chocolate eyes…

"Would you play me another?"

"I…uh, it's quite late," I said. "Perhaps tomorrow?"

"Oh, yes, of course. Forgive me, making you tarry at this hour."

We both rose at once, coming closer together. "No, it's all right," I said. "I obviously couldn't sleep. But now…" *Now I need to get away from you. Before this is something I can't control…*

"Here. Allow me." He reached for the guitar and I gave it to him. Our fingers touched, sending shivers up through my elbow, my shoulder, my neck. I swiftly turned and moved toward the door, only slowing when I was a safe distance from him. "Good night, Javier."

"Good night, Zara," he returned, eyes thoughtful as they rested on me.

And then I pulled away, realizing only partway down the hall that I had no lantern. But there was no way I was going back in there. I'd fumble my way up the stairs and to my room in the near-dark, using only the scant moonlight streaming through a few windows.

Because deep down, I knew I had to stay away from Javier, as far away as possible, until I could find my way back home.

CHAPTER 10

Doña Elena didn't ask me again about the lamp, either in the morning or in the afternoon. Thankfully, she was distracted by the upcoming gathering near Santa Barbara and whipped the entire household into a frenzy of preparation—baking, cooking, washing, mending, sewing. According to the girls, we would all leave early the following morning to arrive late the day after, and there would be a rodeo and festivities for two full days.

"Jacinto," I called to the boy scampering down the hall.

He paused at the top of the stairs and grinned at me. "Yes, Señorita?"

I walked closer to him, not wanting anyone else to hear. "How are we to get to Santa Barbara?"

He squinted at me, confused. "By horse and wagon, of course!" he said, the thought of it making his eyes go wide with excitement.

"But…but isn't Santa Barbara very far?"

"Yes," he said, nodding.

"So…we will ride all day?"

"All day for two whole days!" he said, as if this was the best news he could possibly deliver.

I, on the other hand, felt a little sick. Two whole days on the saddle? *Santo cielo*, how was my backside going to handle that? I got saddle-sore after an hour or two. Maybe there'd be space in a wagon as well, what with all the food…

I glanced up and saw Francesca at the top of the stairs, hand around a ceiling-high post. She was watching me intently, and it was clear she'd heard my interchange with Jacinto and that she'd witnessed my displeasure over the news. "You don't wish to go to Santa Barbara?" she asked. "There will be so much to enjoy there! The events of the charreada and dancing, food like you've never seen before."

"Oh, yes. I look forward to seeing it. It's just that…it's an awfully long way to travel in the saddle."

A confused smile drew one side of her lips upward. "How else would we get there?"

"I…I don't know. No, of course. Never mind. It's just that I don't remember ever traveling that far on a horse. An hour's ride, maybe two. But farther?" I gave her a rueful smile. "How does one walk after more than a couple of hours in the saddle?"

"Javier has had one of our saddlers working over an old one of Mama's for you. It should be ready by tomorrow. It's a good saddle—I think you'll find it quite comfortable. But we ladies will travel part of each day in the wagons, of course."

"Oh," I breathed in relief. "Right." I thought it touching that Javier had thought about my needs. In my whole life, it felt like the only one who watched out for me, took care of me in such a manner, was Abuela. I blinked back sudden tears and moved away from Francesca, down the stairs, not wanting her to see. "I think I'll go and help in the kitchen, if I might," I muttered.

I heard her sputtering a response. I realized it wasn't The Thing around here, but with the hustle and bustle all about and the thought of Abuela, all I wanted to do right now was to work in the kitchen. I didn't care what anyone thought. I *needed* it.

I heard the singing and chatter and laughter ahead of me and moved through the dining room, down the hall, past a vast pantry full of dishes, and through two swinging doors into a sprawling kitchen. At the back were two stoves and maids stocking them with more wood. I could smell seared meat, and my mouth watered. Four Indian women were rolling out tortillas on the long stone island, tossing them in succession to a catcher, beside two women manning the stovetop. Two others were kneading dough at the end of the island beside me. In the corner, on the ground, two others appeared to be grinding corn in a mortar. At the farther end, two women were chopping onions, and in another corner, a man appeared to be butchering half a cow hanging from a hook beside a metal table. Gradually, everyone came to a standstill, staring at me, until the only sound was the crackling of wood in the fire, the sizzle of oil in pans, and the burble of boiling water.

I smiled at them all and took a fresh handkerchief from the pile nearby, pulling back my hair from my face, and then slipped on an apron. "I have cooked all my life," I said to them. "I need to cook today. How can I help you?"

They all continued to look at me, horrified. Finally, one round-faced, slit-eyed woman, who I thought might be the head cook, stepped forward. "Señorita, if Doña Elena finds you here, she will not be pleased," she said in labored Spanish, her tone pinched with fear.

"I will tell Doña Elena that I insisted on being here. I beg you," I said, reaching out to touch her wrist. "Please. Put me to work, just for a little while. I can make tortillas, or I can chop. Whatever would be most helpful. What is your name?"

She stared at me a moment longer, and I wondered if she would turn me away. Insist I go in order to avoid the Wrath of Elena.

But she didn't. "They call me Juana," she said. Then she gave me a conspiratorial smile, making her eyes almost disappear. "But my real name is Jalama." She took a rolling pin from the nearest maid and nodded her away to another task. Then she handed it to me and clapped her hands, nudging the whole group back into production.

Gradually, they all fell back to their tasks, sliding me curious glances as I formed dough into a ball and then rolled it out. The stone was perfect in temperature, the dough never sticking, and in minutes, I was moving nearly as fast as the others, tossing the disks like small Frisbees to the catcher, who placed them on the grill. There were already hundreds in stacks, but I knew it had to take hundreds to feed the entire household and rancho staff each day. And it was clear that their task was to make extra food for our travels to come.

I fell into the rhythm, and it soothed me—oh, how it soothed me—to be at work again. The pin wasn't all that different from my abuela's, the dough the same even across the centuries. Masa, water, a touch of lard. To me, it felt like being home, and as the women began to chat and laugh again, gradually accepting me, it was like being in Abuela's kitchen. There, I'd made tortillas as a kid and eventually graduated to more sophisticated cooking. *Ceviche* and *mole* were my specialties.

People came in and out of the kitchen, including servants from outside via the back door, and all cast inquiring glances my way. The others just shrugged or pushed them back out, silently encouraging them to ignore the crazy-weird houseguest who apparently just *had* to cook. I felt their grudging admiration and growing camaraderie too, as they decided I wasn't all hat, no cattle. This—*this* was in my bones.

I'd been at it for a good hour when Javier came into the kitchen.

He stood alongside me, watching for a moment, before I realized he was there. "Zara?"

"Yes?" I said, continuing at my task, fearing he'd yank me out of there because I'd crossed clear social boundaries. The other workers slowed, all listening in.

"Why are you here? My sisters are in the library, embroidering. Perhaps you'd be more comfortable with them?"

I almost laughed out loud. I grinned up at him. "Trust me when I say that I am a far better at cooking than needlepoint."

He smiled back at me, obviously confused. "My mother would prefer you were there with them. And it is cooler."

"I understand," I said as I tossed a tortilla down the island and wiped my forehead. I knew I was sweating. I didn't care. This was where I belonged. I paused and looked at him. "I need this, Javier. Just for the morning. I want to be of some use. I'm not the kind of woman who can just…sit about." I lifted my hands. "I need to use these." I shook my head. "And not to embroider a pillow. That would be disastrous."

"Not the kind of woman to sit about," he repeated thoughtfully, pinching his chin between thumb and forefinger. "Do as you must," he said with a shrug. "I will speak to my mother, so she will not vex you."

"Thank you," I said. I smiled at that. The last thing I needed was The Vexer in this kitchen.

He smiled quizzically and shook his head as if I were as odd as an ostrich. But then he put on his hat and slipped out the back door, apparently setting out on some chore. I kept smiling for some time after he left and only realized it when a couple of the women rolling tortillas with me nudged each other and cast me knowing glances and whispered things in their own language that weren't hard to figure out. *Just what I need,* I thought. *A kitchen full of matchmakers.*

But it settled me, being among them. Jalama began humming an Indian song, and the others hummed along. It was dissonant and foreign, and yet it was earthily beautiful, like a song rising from the Alta California soil itself. The scent of roasting peppers and chilis filled the air, on top of the constantly sautéing onions and meat over the grill. Back in Abuela's kitchen, it would have been Spanglish I'd heard, cooks and waitresses bantering back and forth as they carried plate after steaming plate through the metal swinging doors. It made me hungry for the rice and beans that accompanied every dish, the way Abuela cooked and crushed the beans until they were a smooth mash—mixed with a bit of *asadero*—that you could dip a tortilla chip in and die from happiness.

My mouth watered, and my stomach rumbled, but we were still a ways away from the noon meal. I went over to the stove, took a hot tortilla from the stack, and lifted an eyebrow to silently ask the cook if I might have one. She looked at me as if I were an idiot—clearly I had access to anything I wanted in the kitchen, as a "lady guest," as Maria called me.

I hurriedly bit into the soft tortilla and appreciated it anew. It was familiar enough—from dough to finished product—but clearly the effort of drying and grinding their own corn, adding a bit of lime, a bit of lard, a bit of water, all so freshly garnered from the land on which we stood…well, I didn't think that it was my imagination telling me that these were simply better. It made up for a bit of my longing for Abuela's rice and beans because *it rocked.* Totally.

Having heard I was in the kitchen, Maria came and fetched me an hour later, insisting I come upstairs and freshen up. Upstairs I found

Maria had drawn a bath for me, and she'd laid out a riding habit for me to try on, in a startling ruby red, with fresh underthings. It all made me want to cry, I was so happy. "Oh," I mused, the lamest thing I could manage in the moment. They were presumably trying to get me ready for the journey the next day and wanted to see if they had something suitable to fit. But the bath—the *bath.* Sweaty from the kitchen, with greasy hair after days of no shower, and definitely sporting a killer case of BO, I was suddenly desperate to get into the water.

Maria unbuttoned the back of my dress, batting away my hands as I tried to help her. In another minute, she had it totally undone, and I pulled it over my head as she set out a bar of soap and a towel on the edge. "I'll be back in an hour to help you with your hair," she said, nodding, and then she slipped out the door.

I probed the water with a toe and found it the perfect temperature. I clambered into the hammered copper tub, which angled back behind me. It wasn't long enough for me to submerge my legs too, but blessedly, most of my body was covered, with just my knees bobbing up. I held my breath and dunked below, urging water to reach my oily scalp. Then I emerged and peered at the soap through dripping eyelashes. With no shampoo or conditioner, it appeared the soap was my only option, from head to toe. I did my best to lather up, but it wasn't anything like modern-day suds with big, beautiful bubbles. Still, it smelled clean—with lavender mixed in—and felt smooth. I didn't want to think about what kind of fat they might use to make it so. No, I didn't want to think about that at all. I only wanted to relish the warm water and the sensation of being clean, really clean, for the first time in days.

I remained in the tub until the water grew cool and I'd washed every part of my body from ears to nails to toes. Then I reluctantly stood up, shivering as I wrapped my towel around me. In the distance, through the window, I could see tiny figures on the ridge, vaqueros driving a hundred head of cattle up and over the hills toward us. It was a peaceful, otherworldly scene, so distant that I couldn't hear the crack of a whip or the lowing of the cows, but the air was so clear and the sun so tangelo-bright—casting them in silhouette—it was as if I were watching them through a director's camera lens.

Remembering that it would soon be time for the noon meal, I turned toward the bed and slipped on the bloomers and split petticoat that went beneath the split skirt for riding. I was just eying the corset, blouse, and high-necked jacket when Maria knocked softly at my door. I lifted the towel to cover myself and went to the door to let her in, hiding behind it.

She looked from me to the bed. "I can assist you, Señorita, with the corset. I know you don't favor them, but you must if you are to fit into Doña Elena's old riding habit. You're a bit …curvier than the mistress."

"That's fine," I said hurriedly, feeling the burn of a blush. Getting help with such intimacies seemed awkward, but it was clear that I wouldn't be able to manage the contraption alone. It was true—I'd stashed away the corset in my trunk and Maria had fished it out again today.

In the other dresses, it was possible to go without. But one glance at the tight-fitting jacket, and I knew I'd need every inch-squeezing Spanx-like power I had at my disposal. *The last thing you need is to be popping those buttons on the trail*, I thought. And since I couldn't just bop on down to Target for something else for the trip, I really had no options. I lifted the corset, set it across my chest and turned obediently for Maria to do her work. I'd seen enough movies to know the basics of how to proceed.

I was just thinking, as she circled the last hooks, that it wasn't all that bad, when she went back to the bottom of the stays, obviously intent on *tightening* the laces, pressing the breath right out of my lungs. I swallowed hard, trying not to squeak out my protest. I was supposed to ride a horse in this thing? But in a minute she was done and reaching for the blouse, crisply ironed with lace at the neck that plunged low over my cleavage. The jacket made it less scandalous, covering more of my chest, but not much. She urged me to my small dressing table stool and set to combing my hair out, then pulled it into a thick braid down my back. At the end, she tied it with twine, knotted it securely, and then produced a beautiful ribbon that matched the habit, tying it over the twine to conceal it.

"The mistress has a hat to match," she said. "We will put that on you tomorrow. For today, we just wanted to make certain you could wear this. It is good?"

Well, *good* was a debatable term. Good would've been sweatpants or my old jeans or PJ pants. A sweatshirt and no bra. This was pretty much the exact opposite. An old *SpongeBob* episode leapt into my mind, "Opposite Day." *It's Opposite Day,* I told myself. "It is good, Maria," I said, trying to assure her.

"Very good, Señorita," she said, her face melting with relief. "You are ready. Don Ventura wishes to ride with you after your meal. He has a new gelding for you to try."

Riding? How did women ride horses in such a thing? The split skirt was wide, ample in fabric to allow for me to ride sidesaddle without exposing any skin, presumably. But that assumed that one didn't need to breathe while she rode.

I paused at the door, and Maria looked at me. "I don't know,

Maria. Perhaps the corset is too tight."

"No," she said firmly. "You are simply unused to it. You did not wear one where you came from. You have none of the markings the other women do that I have seen as I dress them."

Clearly the girls in this household bore some sort of bruises or scars from years in such contraptions. Only thoughts about foot-bindings in the Far East comforted me. At least my boots were big enough… "No," I said. "Not often."

Maria handed me a pair of black gloves and then gestured toward the hall and stairs. "They're likely already at table," she said, urging me forward. "Go on, Señorita."

I nodded and hurried along the hall and down the stairs, admitting to myself that I did have better posture in the corset. Stomach in, back straight, my shoulders naturally pulled back too, and my chin high. I felt like a doll in a new outfit and wondered just how many times Doña Elena had worn this "old habit," since it appeared none the worse for wear.

When I entered the dining room, Javier looked my way. His eyes widened, and he stood, as did his little brothers. "Zara, you look… quite…*prepared* for a ride," he finished awkwardly, moving to help me take my seat. But I could easily imagine the word he'd almost spoken before hesitating, as he lingered behind me a moment as if he wanted to say more. *Beautiful* had been the word in his wonder-filled eyes. I imagined that I at last looked the part of a fine Latina settled in this frontier villa, rather than an interloper. Scrubbed clean and in the impeccable riding habit, I *felt* more like I fit the part.

I accepted a bowl of soup from Francesca, who was serving from a big bowl at the center, and caught Doña Elena's gaze from the end of the table. She looked dotingly at me. "The habit fits you well," she said approvingly. "It never was quite right for me. Perhaps it was always meant for you."

"Oh," I said, not quite sure how to respond to that. "Yes. Thank you so much." I had the crazy thought that maybe she hadn't ever worn the habit—had had it made for me—but they would have had to begin *that* process the day I arrived. I was just lucky they had something for me, tight as it felt. Hopefully it would hold together over a couple of days of riding to Santa Barbara and a couple more when we returned.

I took hold of my goblet and swallowed some water. Water was about all I was going to ingest. Eating and drinking in the cursed corset were going to make it all the more miserable, I thought. But I was hungry, both breakfast and the stolen tortilla from the kitchen long since burned away. It had been a busy morning. So I ate, at least half my normal portions, and felt better for it. Also, the corset seemed to be easing a bit; perhaps it was why they laced them up so tightly from the start.

A manservant appeared in the doorway as we finished, hat in hand, waiting for Javier to notice him. Javier waved him forward, and the man bent to whisper something in his ear and then hurried out. Wiping his face with his napkin, Javier looked again to me. "I would ask you the favor of your company, Señorita," he said, rising and coming around my chair to help me up.

"Oh…yes, of course," I said, glancing at the others. They all looked our way expectantly. Estrella was grinning as widely as the kitchen maids had after he'd left me there, eyes practically big, pulsing heart-shapes like a cartoon character.

Javier offered me his arm. "I fear I'm not quite dressed to match your finery today, Señorita."

I glanced at him as I wrapped my fingers around his forearm, noting the fine muscles beneath his own crisp shirt. "I don't know," I said quietly. "I think you look quite fine."

He grinned at this as he opened the door for me, grandly gesturing me forward, and my heart skipped a beat. He was handsome, so handsome. But when he smiled…*Santos y ángeles*… every girl I knew would practically die to see a smile like that from him. He was…glorious. Almost too gorgeous. I thought I deserved an award or something for just being able to put two or three words together in his presence, let alone hold my own the way I had. But I had to keep a firm lid on things. *No more flirting, Zara.* He did not need me to lead him on. That wouldn't be cool, what with me thinking about getting home every time I had a chance to consider it.

Outside the villa, Javier offered me his arm again and led me around to the hitching posts that stood just beyond the library windows. It was here that I saw the horse, a gorgeous chestnut gelding with a white star-shape on his forehead. I hadn't seen him before. "Well, where did you come from, boy?" I asked, extending a hand to let him sniff me and then running my fingers up and down his nose.

Maria was there, then, beside me, quietly handing me my gloves with wide eyes. "Oh, yes," I said, catching her hint that it wasn't cool to go for a ride without them. "Thank you."

She bobbed a curtsey and left me, scurrying into the house as if holding her breath. I had the odd sensation that every window was filled with servants or family members watching us, and I glanced to them but saw nothing.

"This gelding is one of Rancho Castillo's finest," Javier said, running his hand along the horse's jaw and neck and watching me as

I awkwardly pulled on my gloves. "When I saw him among a brood that Rafael is taking to Santa Barbara tomorrow, I…negotiated a deal with him."

"You mean you won him?" I guessed.

Javier's melty-chocolate-beautiful-eyes widened. Was that a bit of a blush at his jaw and neck?

I smiled. "I don't think that Rafael would willingly let a horse like this go without exacting a pretty penny from you. Unless you beat him at cards last night?"

Javier huffed through his nose, lips curling upward, and he inclined his head. "You gather much in only a little time, Señorita."

"I'd like to think so," I said, taking the reins from him.

"But I'll have you know I paid my friend. I didn't win the horse outright. I just won him at a very good price."

I smiled. That felt better. I didn't want to be riding a horse stolen out from under Rafael's fingertips.

Doña Elena and Mateo strode out then to admire Javier's new purchase, *ooh*ing and *ahh*ing. "Oh, he's the perfect size for Señorita Ruiz," Doña Elena said. "You did very well, my son."

I gaped at her. "Wait," I said, looking to Javier. "You bought him for *me*?"

"And the saddle," she said, with knowing, doting eyes. "He had the saddle remade for you too."

My eyes widened as I took in the fine leather, the tooling, the flashes of silver. It was far more modest than his own, but it was beautiful. "You did this for me?" I asked, embarrassed at the squeak in my voice.

"Well, you needed a mount of your own for the trip tomorrow," he said, one brow arching saucily. "And I didn't want you to think again of taking *mine.* Come, let's ride, and you can decide for yourself whether you wish to keep him." With a swift, agile move, he was up and astride his mare, waiting on me. Flustered, I looked to my mount, wondering how I was supposed to get up on top of him without aid.

Thankfully a stable boy had brought a box made into stairs, which he gestured toward. I handed my reins to Mateo, who had come closer to stroke the horse's nose, and climbed the stairs, taking hold of the horn, studying the oddly shaped saddle, with a bump in front and a partial *U* above it. *For my front leg,* I figured, breathing a sigh of relief. It would make it much more stable, this whole riding-sidesaddle business, with that *U* helping to hold me in place.

I sat down on the central part, then lifted my left leg into the groove in front, grimacing a bit at how much that leather piece came over my leg. I supposed I'd appreciate it if I was going fast, but it was so tight, I wondered if my leg would be asleep before we reached the sea. Apparently girls in 1840 had skinnier thighs than the saddler thought I might. The stable boy hurriedly flicked my skirt down when it lifted to calf-height, as if embarrassed that I hadn't seen it myself. Mateo handed the reins up to me, and I took them in hand. I shifted, trying to find just the right placement for my rear, and then adjusted the reins as the gelding tugged downward to munch on some grass.

I saw Doña Elena studying me, missing nothing. She somehow knew I was a faker, that I didn't completely belong here. That I'd never sat on a saddle such as this. But what would she think if she found out I was a time-traveler? *Yeah, that'd put her in her place,* I thought. At least it'd end her matchmaking intentions…

"Have a lovely ride, children," she said.

"Thank you, Mamá," Javier said, dismissing her, and she turned and grandly returned to the house. Mateo retreated as far as the posts, but shyly waited around, as if he wished he was going too.

I pulled back on the reins, forcing my horse's head up, and the gelding flicked his tail and whinnied. Javier urged his mount to take a slow circle around me, eyes lit with admiration. "Ahh, sí, he is a fine mount," he said, grinning at me. But he wasn't looking at the horse at all. "And you are a vision, Señorita," he said, loud enough for Mateo to hear, but he didn't seem to care. "Come. Follow me."

He set off at a trot around the house, heading toward the mountains. I swallowed back my frustration, realizing that I'd hoped we would be heading to the beach. But my mind was occupied with figuring out how to stay in my saddle and yet keep up with him. He pulled up before long and circled back, matching my gelding's gait. "Do you not wish to give him more rein, Señorita? See what he has in him?"

"I do not," I said, swallowing hard. "I'm concentrating on getting used to…this new saddle," I finished.

"Does it not…fit you well?" he asked.

"Well, this front hook is a bit tight," I said, moving my leg with a wince.

"It has to be, in case you jump," he said, frowning. "But perhaps the saddler can ease its grip a bit." He was all adorable concern and worry, which would have normally melted my heart, but I was still thinking about his belief that I might want to *jump*.

On a *horse*. Riding *sidesaddle*.

"Yes," I said faintly. "Right."

But after a while, I realized I was getting the hang of it, as well as the finely trained horse and beautifully crafted saddle that seemed to cradle my hiney in an oddly comforting manner. The gelding was perfectly responsive, seeming to grasp what I wanted to do, when I wanted to do it. Sometimes he got distracted, but he seemed interested in pleasing me most of the time. He was so much better than the weary horses at camp, and Javier's skittish, high-spirited mare, that I was a bit lost in amazement. When we trotted, the gelding fairly *floated.* Was this the kind of thing that made a girl fall in love with horseback riding? Or was it everything…being alone with Javier? Climbing up into the hills, the mountains towering closer, on a pretty new horse in an outfit that made me feel like a character in a novel? Even the corset wasn't chafing me as much as it had earlier.

We crossed over a low point among the hills, and I gaped at what was ahead of us. Huge, cream-colored rocks rose above us, rounded as if waves had pounded them for centuries. Javier led me forward along the edge of them, allowing me to take in the wonder of their height and width, and pulled up when we were halfway down their block-long length. He dismounted and came over to me to stroke my horse's nose and then reached up to help me down. "Javier, I've never seen anything like this," I breathed, still looking up at the towering rocks, while I put my hands on his shoulders and leaned forward. He lowered me to the ground.

"Neither have I," he said intently, hands still on my hips as he gazed down at me.

My eyes moved from the rocks to him, and I smiled at the compliment, but then eased away as he hobbled the horses. I strode along the formation and felt him soon follow behind, the hairs on the back of my neck standing in rapt attention. Was there any part of me that didn't feel more *awake* with him around? I shook my head and forced myself to focus on where we were. The hills, the mountains…these were my hills, my mountains. Or at least they hadn't been far from my house. Why had I never come up here? It was what? Maybe ten, fifteen miles away? I'd seen the mountains, of course. But from the freeways. Never up close. I think we'd taken a field trip somewhere near here in second grade. But not here…

"I believe these hills and much of the mountains were once deep underwater," Javier said.

"Yes," I said, thinking this was common knowledge. But he'd looked at me with such surprise, that I realized that it was only common knowledge *later* in history. "I mean, that's an interesting thought. What makes you believe so?"

"Because of this," he said, taking my hand and leading me up a steep incline, until we were below one of the broad, leaning boulders. He seemed not to notice that he'd taken hold of my hand, so intent was he on his mission. But I could barely make myself put one foot in front of the other—all I could think about was the feel of his hand on mine. How my fingers fit with his. How it was sending all sorts of weird shocks up my arm, to my neck, down between my shoulder blades. How it felt so good that I never wanted him to let go.

But then he *did* let go, shocking me back to attention. "See? Here?" he asked, kneeling down.

He offered me his hand, but I didn't dare take it. Instead I pretended to be so distracted by his discovery that I hadn't noticed, crouching down. I ran my fingers along the imprinted remains of a massive fish's skeleton and then along the curve of a shell, as big as a melon. "Wow, that is so cool!" I said.

He smiled at me, but his eyes were confused.

"I mean…What I meant to say is that this is…completely… glorious!" I mumbled, rising and moving on, running my fingertips along lines in the rock, hoping he'd forget I'd used very odd words and phrasing for the time. "It's as if I can imagine being underwater right now." I turned to him and discovered he was *right* behind me. "I mean…can't you?" I asked, my voice a little strangled in the face of his sudden nearness.

"Yes," he said. But again, his eyes weren't on the rocks. They were on me. "Zara," he whispered, his voice low and full of wanting.

"Do you swim?" I asked brightly, edging away as if to explore further.

But he caught my hand and pulled me back around. He lifted his other hand and gently traced the line of my face, from temple to chin, eyes hovering over my lips. "*Zara,*" he whispered, clearly thinking more about kissing me than swimming. This time I knew it for sure.

"Do you? Swim?" I repeated.

He gave me a little smile, clearly well aware that I was stalling. "I do swim. Do you?" he asked, lifting his eyes to stare into mine.

"I do," I said, a second later, turning away from him and continuing my trek along the rocks. "I love to swim!" I said brightly. "I swam every night after work, back home."

I felt him abruptly pause and realized my mistake, in the midst of trying to avoid something both of us would regret in time. There was already enough of a pull between us. Kissing would just make our parting all the harder.

I turned back to him, thinking I'd say we should head back, but he was staring at me hard. "You…*worked*? You remember? What kind of employment was it?"

I swallowed. "My abuela had a restaurant. I remember that well enough," I said with a laugh. "That's why it felt good to me today, to help the maids in the kitchen. Rolling tortillas? Chopping onions? I could do that in my sleep."

He swallowed hard, as if trying to digest this fact. "Where was her restaurant? In what city?"

"I…I don't remember," I said, rubbing my head, hoping he'd think his questions were giving me a headache.

But his eyes narrowed. "You went swimming *every night after work*, you said. So you must have been near the ocean. A town by the beach. You remember waves? Or was it fresh water? A lake or pond, perhaps?"

"No, there were waves," I said, suddenly wishing I could tell him, tell him everything. "I remember that for sure." I licked my lips, now wondering if it'd be better to just kiss him and distract him from this line of questioning. Before I told him and he decided he wasn't taking me to Santa Barbara for a rodeo—he'd be taking me straight to the nearest mental hospital. Even if that was in Louisiana.

"So you worked in your grandmother's restaurant," he said slowly, hands on hips, beginning to pace. "In the kitchen. An odd occupation for ladies of your caliber. Where were your menfolk?"

"My grandfather was long dead. I'd lived with my grandmother as long as I can remember."

"But you can't remember more?" he asked me, unblinking as he awaited my response.

I shook my head. *Not that I can tell you*, I thought helplessly.

"Could your father and mother be looking for you right now? Posting handbills in every seaside town? I shall tell every captain we meet to keep watch."

"You could," I said tonelessly.

"You said you went swimming every *night* after work?" he asked, his frown deepening as he studied me. "Do you mean in the dark? Alone?"

"Yes," I said, smiling a little at his surprise. "Have you never been swimming at night? When the phosphorus alights all around you, like a thousand glittering stars?"

He blinked, those long, dark eyelashes like a thick fringe. "No, I haven't."

"It's glorious," I said, grinning now, remembering. "I'll have to take you sometime. I mean…we, uh…we should ride down to Tainter Cove some evening with the rest of your family so you *all* could experience it."

He stared at me, as if thunderstruck. I didn't know if it was because my suggestion had been completely unladylike, or that he was remembering the morning he found me on that very beach.

"No," he said, gently taking my hand. "I think that we should do that on our own. Swimming at night, I mean," he said, a smile teasing the corners of his lips.

"Javier, I…"

He stepped closer to me. "Zara." He placed my hand against his chest. I felt his heart, pounding beneath my fingertips. "Do you feel what you are doing to my heart, my sweet?" He swallowed hard, and I found myself staring at the strong muscles of his neck, extending down to his collarbone, the breeze teasing his shirt slightly open. His skin—so copper-brown and smooth—urged me to reach up and touch it.

"Zara," he whispered again.

"No," I muttered, beginning to pull away. I felt his grip tighten, urging me to stay in place. "No," I said more firmly, now wrenching out of his grasp, aware that he'd had a hand behind my waist. "We can't do this, Javier! We can't!" I cried.

"Zara," he said, following after me, step for step. "Forgive me! I forgot myself," he pleaded. "It's only that—"

"No," I said, shaking my head, continuing to retreat. "You don't understand. I want to kiss you, I do. It's just that…Javier, I'm not from here. Not from your world." My momentum with this partial-truth strengthened me, clarified my thoughts, bringing me back to earth when he threatened to cast me into orbit. "I'm a common girl, a worker in a restaurant," I said, hoping *that* reminder would anchor him in thoughts about why we, together, were all wrong. "You are the ranchero, head of this vast, beautiful, amazing land, with big responsibilities. You need a woman from a fine family, not a girl given to swims in the ocean at night." I added weight to that last word, as if it was the most scandalous thing possible. "What would people say?"

"I do not care what they say," he said, shaking his head. "I've never cared how the tongues wag among people who have nothing better to do than gossip."

"But your mother does," I tried desperately, aware that he was getting closer to me again, wearing me down. And I'd backed into a small cleft in the rocks.

"My mother thinks that you're a perfect match for me," he said.

"She doesn't know me. Know where I came from. I don't know myself!"

"She recognizes something unique within you, Zara Ruiz," he said, lifting a hand above me to the rock, leaning closer, "something that I keep discovering myself." He put his other hand on the rock above me, on the other side. "Here I am, Zara. Vulnerable to you. I know what you could do to me, in this position, legs akimbo," he said with a slight, teasing smile. "But I want you to know I shall not harm you, just as I trust you shall not…harm… me," he whispered, his hot breath on my ear sending shivers down my neck.

There was nothing in his action that made me fear for my body—only my heart. I stared up at him, waiting for him to straighten and meet my gaze, wondering how much pain he'd feel when I left him, for my own time. "Javier, please. Don't do this."

"Do what?" he said, leaning closer again, his lips so close to my cheek that I could feel them pass by, slowly, a whisper away.

I closed my eyes, feeling frozen between what I wanted—to accept him—and the distant call to run.

His lips hovered over mine, slightly parted.

Waiting.

And then I was lifting my chin, unable to deny him any longer.

I wanted this.

I wanted Javier to hold me.

Even if it did cost me a piece of my heart when I left.

CHAPTER 11

"Javier! Zara!" cried a voice at the mouth of this small canyon.

My eyes sprang open.

Javier dropped his hands, storm clouds of emotion visible on his face. Giving me one last anxious stare, he forced himself to turn away.

"Javier!" cried another voice.

It was Jacinto and Estrella. "Please, Javier!" Estrella cried. "You must come quickly!"

Grim-faced, Javier glanced at me and offered his hand, and we scurried down the rocks just as the children rode up to us. "What is it?" Javier growled.

"It's Mamá and Adalia," Estrella said, plainly having been crying. "They're arguing. Adalia is saying she wants to go home to her own family. She's going to take the baby!"

I swallowed hard. Had I influenced her when we talked? Set this plan in motion? I thought of the young woman's deep grief, of her talk about just not being whole anymore, and her warning to me. And hadn't I just about kissed Javier? What was I *doing*?

"She's having the maids pack their trunks," Jacinto affirmed glumly. "Mamá sent us after you. She wants you to talk some sense into Adalia."

I thought about the quiet girl with the eyes that missed nothing. Of the deep grief within her, obviously longing for her husband even while surrounded by his family. Maybe that made it harder, being with them all, constant, living reminders of the man she'd loved. He might even have looked like one of them—or all of them.

Javier helped me down from the rocks and back into my saddle, giving me a rueful look. But I evaded his gaze because while a part of me *so* wanted to know what it would be like to have him kiss me, the rest of me knew it would be the worst possible thing. The dude was already taking over my mind 24/7. The last thing I needed was to actually fall in love with him. Because where would that leave me? Stuck in 1840. And while living in the Wild West was somewhat intriguing, I didn't know if I could do it forever. I just didn't think I had it in me.

Still, I watched as he moved to his little brother and patted his leg, then went and spoke quietly to Estie, handing her a handkerchief. She nodded, apparently reassured by him, and sniffed one last time. Then we all headed out of the canyon, back to the villa.

I imagined the babe wailing in his mother's arms and the women screaming at each other. But it was worse. Doña Elena stood in the library, staring out the window, hands clenched in front of her waist, looking grief-stricken but keeping utterly silent. Adalia had retreated to her room, Francesca presumably with her. "I'll go and try and talk some sense into Adalia," Javier said. "Might you try and bring some comfort to my mother?"

I gazed, doubtfully, in her direction, then shrugged. "I can try."

He gave me a tiny, grateful smile, and I turned away, suddenly glad for the task ahead. Better to focus on the tough old lady than Mr. Hottie.

I tentatively moved into the room, and Doña Elena faced me for a sec. "Ahh, Zara," she said, eyes sweeping past me to the empty doorway, as if hoping Adalia would reappear. "How was your ride?"

"Lovely," I said, coming to stand beside her, looking out. I'd heard that the vaqueros were gathering a hundred head of cattle for us to take to the charreada—to sell—as well as neighbors' cattle that had wandered onto Ventura land. In the distance, I could see them driving a group south, whips curling in the air, a cloud of dust behind them. Men on horses cut left and right, disappearing into the dust for moments before reappearing on the far side. "We came back because the children said you and Adalia were…at odds?"

"She wishes to leave us," Doña Elena said dully, the pain evident in her voice. "After all Dante did for her, all we've done for her. She wishes to 'go home to her own.' And she intends to take my grandson with her." The last of this came out of her mouth tinged with grief and bitterness.

I swallowed hard. "Sometimes, no matter how good things are someplace new, we are pulled home."

She narrowed her eyes at me and crossed her arms before turning back to the window. "To make the most out of our lives, Zara, we must embrace what is, rather than what was." She let out a mirthless laugh, and she lifted a hand. "I was born and raised in España. Do you think I did not often wish I could return? Of course I did! But my place was with my husband, in Mexico. And then when we came here, when we started with nothing but a sod hut fifty miles from the last town, do you think I did not hunger for Mexico? Of course! Of course," she repeated, more softly.

"But Doña Elena," I said gently, "you had your husband. Adalia, she still mourns Dante."

"Life is as full of death as it is of birth," she said, brushing past me to pace a bit, then returned to my side. "I have lost a husband, a son, and two daughters as tiny babes. We must take full advantage of *life*, every moment we have, Zara, to combat *death*. Otherwise, we drown in the darkness. I fear…I fear that Adalia is running, thinking that if she leaves here, she will leave behind her grief over Dante as well. But I think she will only find more of it, without the comforts of his home and his family around her."

"Maybe she only needs to try it for a time, to discover that for herself," I said gently. "She and Álvaro might return to you later, and be more settled, once she has had the chance to find out."

She stared at me and nodded, but her heart wasn't in it. She wrung her hands and looked again to the window. "I've treated her as a daughter. Loved her as a daughter. And now she…" She brought up a hand to her nose, blinking rapidly.

I put a hand on her shoulder. "If you do not leave the choice to her, if Adalia has to decide against you rather than feeling your permission to leave or stay as she wishes, she might consider the door to your home shut to them forever."

She stared at me for a long moment. Outside, the vaqueros were getting closer with the cattle. A shirtless boy opened a gate for them in a corral, while a small girl did the same on another. Each then hurriedly climbed up the fence, clearly worried about getting trampled. Doña Elena stared in silence as we watched the men drive the cattle in, neatly turning them in an arc toward the open gate. Perhaps the older woman was thinking about what I'd said, perhaps not.

At last she moved, and I thought she might leave without another word to me. But she paused in the doorway, looking back over her shoulder at me. "Thank you, Zara."

"Of course, Doña Elena," I said.

But I wondered if she'd be thanking me if she knew about my earlier conversation with Adalia.

CHAPTER 12

So it was that we were a somber crew at dinner and retired early to our rooms soon after, given that we were to leave at sunrise. I think we used it as an excuse to escape the tension that clouded every room Doña Elena entered. I hadn't seen Adalia or her baby since I'd returned, and I guessed they remained hidden away in their rooms.

Estie and Jacinto were both wide-eyed and worried, looking back and forth between Javier and their mother. I thought it sweet of Javier when he finally pushed aside his half-eaten meal, rose, and touched Estrella's shoulders, then Jacinto's, and then gestured for the younger children to come with him. "Come, you two, I need your help in the stables to prepare for our ride tomorrow."

They waited for their mother's nod of dismissal from the table before scampering off to take their big brother's hands. Javier gave me a soft smile before leaving, but he said no more. I felt both grateful for it and a little sorry for myself. Could he not have invited me, too, away from this table? I wanted to be with him, I admitted. Especially if there were little sibs to keep us at arm's length from each other. That was what I'd have to finagle on our trip tomorrow and the days that followed. Company. Constant company. No more rides alone. No way.

So as soon as I could, I went to my room.

And that's when I found it. A perfect scallop shell fossil,

carefully cut from a rock like those we'd seen today, with a note underneath. I unfolded the paper and took in Javier's perfect, elegant script, swirling across the page.

22 May 1840

My dear Zara,

Our sojourn might have been brief, but I wanted you to have a piece of it to keep. This was a fossil that Dante and I found as boys, one of two. He always had one and I the other. I wish for you to have mine now, and I will keep Dante's, so that we might remember those brief moments we shared.

I look forward to escorting you to town tomorrow and pray that you might save me a dance. And, at some point, a kiss. For as much as Adalia's decision has distracted my family, I confess that I cannot free my mind of anything but you, Zara.

Yours,

Javier

I smiled and reread it, trying to decipher deeper meanings—everything from "My dear Zara" to the fact that he was giving away his own fossil, something clearly very close to his heart, a treasured memory with his brother. And the thought of dancing with him…or kissing him…my heart did a double-flip.

I sighed, squirmed out of my gown, slipped on my shift, and climbed into bed. Then, still holding the fossil, running my fingers across the scalloped edges that made me think of a fairy's gown, I went to sleep.

The trip south was not bad. It was horrible.

Three hours into the ride, my butt and legs had passed from ache to total numbness, which made me afraid of stopping, because I had no idea how I was going to get down. But there was no way around it. We stopped when we neared a spring, to allow everyone the chance to fill up canteens and a water barrel in the back of the wagon, and for the women to trade out rides. Everyone seemed to wander off as soon as we came to a stop, and it was only my own painful bladder that made me realize what they were after—a bit of privacy among the tall, swaying grasses or behind trees and bushes. But I honestly didn't know how I was going to see to any of that. *I'll just have to pee my bloomers*, I thought glumly, *and pray no one notices*.

But then Javier was there, walking his mare toward me, looking almost shy, as if curiosity pressed him to approach. I'd noticed him keeping his distance all morning, busying himself with correcting his brother's riding form, shouting at the vaqueros to keep a sharper eye on the cattle trailing behind us. But as we settled into a decent pace, I felt his eyes slip to me again and again.

I did my best to pretend I didn't notice. I chatted with Estrella, riding beside me, and then Maria, slightly behind us, one of six ladies' maids who would attend our party.

Now here he was, and I couldn't very well look away or pretend I didn't see him. "Zara?" he asked. "Are you not wishing for a chance to stretch your legs at least? Or trade out with Frani in the wagon for a while?"

I sighed heavily. "I'd like nothing more than that. It's only that— You see, I've never ridden this far before…"

A small smile tugged at his lips. "And you can't feel your legs?"

"Yes," I admitted, feeling my face flame.

His smile broadened. "Happened to me too, the first time my father took us on a long trail ride." He sobered, all business. "Come. I'll see to you."

"No, I…oh…" I began to protest, but he was already taking firm hold of my front leg and pulling it free from the hook. Then he slipped my back boot out of the stirrup and reached up. "Come, Zara. Trust me," he said.

I had little choice. I knew all of this was already drawing attention. The longer I hesitated, the more they would all stare. I leaned over, and he took my waist and brought me down to the ground, but my deadened legs folded beneath me.

"Whoa," he said, catching me as I collapsed, sweeping me up in his arms. "Forgive me," he said, with a devilish grin. "It is far worse than I thought."

"Why do I doubt that?" I asked. But I could hardly demand he put me down. My legs and rear end were on fire with a thousand pinpricks. Which was probably a good sign. He carried me over to a boulder and gently set me down, ignoring all the faces beyond him, pretty much gaping at us. If this were happening in my own time, they all would have had their smart phones out, taking video to post later. You would've thought we were a couple of giraffes rather than the ranchero and his guest.

"I'll fetch you some water," he said and straightened.

But Maria was already there, offering me a metal canteen.

"Rub your legs and wiggle your toes," Javier said to me. "It will get the blood flowing again."

After drinking deeply from the canteen, I handed it to Maria and set about following his instruction, wincing a bit as I did so. Doña Elena came by, watching me with some dismay. "So you are unused to the saddle, truly? Not only the sidesaddle, but riding at all?"

"I'd say that's right," I said. "I guess I'm from a town, more likely to walk than ride."

"Hmph," she sniffed, moving on, as if this was distressing, disappointing news. I supposed if she wanted to marry me off to her son, she hoped I'd be decent at this frontier stuff. And I was clearly failing on the horse-girl count, big-time.

"Do not mind her," Javier said with a laugh, sitting down beside me and pulling his own canteen to his lips. "She was always a fine horsewoman, and she expects nothing less of everyone she meets. It is hardly fair. Especially if it is as you say—that you grew up in a town and are more accustomed to walking."

I nodded. "Do you think I might have a turn in the wagon?"

"Of course," he said, rising. "Frani can ride your gelding for a time." He offered his hand, and I took it, grateful that the strength was returning to my lower extremities at last. But it felt oddly intimate, both of us standing there thinking about my legs, and I hurriedly dropped his hand. I moved away from him, hesitant at first, then striding faster. "If you'll excuse me," I said, when he moved to follow, as if worried that I'd fall, "I need a bit of privacy."

That brought him up short, and he nodded quickly. "Of course, of course," he said, gesturing me forward. I found my place behind some brush, warily looking in all directions before squatting. But no one came near.

The trail was long and dusty, and I soon wondered why I'd bothered with a bath at all this week. At this rate, we'd all arrive covered in dust and stinking in our sweaty clothes. I bounced along in the back of the wagon beside Adalia, who absently patted her sleeping child's body. I had no idea how the toddler could sleep, tossed about as we were, and I soon wondered if it was simply a different sort of torture than the saddle, the only consolation being that I *felt* the pain in my backside rather than the dulling paralysis that I'd experienced earlier. Still, the others seemed well used to it, and I was determined not to complain, especially with Doña Elena riding alongside.

When the grand old lady finally edged away, I had a moment alone with Adalia at last. "So…you are returning to your own family."

"Yes," she said, a wave of sorrow crossing her face as her dark, almond-shaped eyes flicked over Jacinto and Estrella, on the seat in the front of the wagon. She repositioned herself on her sack of dried beans. "It was no easy decision for me. But I think it for the best. Ever since Dante died…" She paused, swallowed hard, and blinked before beginning again. "Ever since, I've felt so adrift. And I wonder…I'm hoping that in going home, I might find my anchor again. Not in another man," she said, leaning toward me, as if sharing a secret. "Something that can never be taken from me," she added, patting her chest. "Here."

I nodded, remembering our conversation. "I understand," I said. "Sometimes we have to do the thing that no one else wants us to do, in order to do what we feel led to do. And you know what else?" I said, leaning toward her, offering my hands when little Álvaro stirred irritably in his mother's arms, agitated by the sweat and dust and bouncing. "You can always return," I said in her ear. "There will be an open door for you at Rancho Ventura, no matter how sad and angry they seem." All morning I had watched them all, and no one but the servants and Estrella had spoken to Adalia. No one had reached for the baby—a child they'd all doted upon. "They're just trying to prepare their hearts for your farewell," I said, gesturing at the children and at Doña Elena, all carefully avoiding our gaze. "No one willingly welcomes pain. They're simply trying to steel themselves so they can get through it."

Adalia nodded and blinked back tears as she handed me her son. "Thank you, Zara. That helps me."

"I'm glad."

I held Álvaro until he pooped his pants, then watched in some amazement as Adalia managed to change him, cleaning him up the best she could, in the back of the bouncing wagon. By nightfall, we'd covered more than half the distance to Santa Barbara, and I was just wondering how I would sleep, in the middle of so many people, when I drifted off under stars I recognized as my own, even if they were in a different century. And somehow that gave me just the comfort I needed.

CHAPTER 13

The next afternoon, we arrived on the edge of Santa Barbara weary and more than a little trail-sore. My body screamed for an Advil—or ten—but the best I was going to get was a change of clothes, a hot meal, and some tea. Happily, we paused on the edge of town, and the men and women divided up. I was wondering why when we came to a glen with a small pond at the center. It took everything in me not to shriek and tear off the wretched riding habit, but I managed to keep myself together as servants brought our trunks and offered us towels and soap. The women and girls all went to the mossy-edged pond, undressing behind prickly bushes that did a neat job of holding our clothes, like we were in some sort of early-California locker room. Then we slipped into the sun-warmed, murky waters, and I honestly thought I'd never felt anything as good in my entire life. It was almost as if the wear and tear of the trail had been worth it in order for me to feel this…this…*glory*.

Estrella moved behind me, soap suds on her hands, and passed me the bar. We ran the soap through our hair and over our skin and played and dunked until Doña Elena announced it was time to get dressed again, leaving the pool for the men. Apparently this was the routine—the way to reach the gathering not looking like filthy cast members on the set of *Mad Max*.

Maria, her own straight hair dripping, offered me a fresh petticoat and corset and the brown day dress—a blessed break from the tight riding habit. I slipped the dress on, and then after she'd combed out my hair, I crunched it with my fingers, encouraging the curls to form. I stopped her when she came at me, armed with pins and hairnet. "Please," I said, "would it be all right to leave it down?"

She frowned in confusion but then shrugged and moved on to Estrella. We ate a bit of dried beef and tortillas, waiting at a distance as the men bathed, and once they were finished and had a bit to eat, we set off again.

When we arrived at the gathering place, just north of town, I stared in bewilderment. Before us were thousands of cattle—and our vaqueros drove the cattle we'd brought into the mix. Beside us, lines of tents formed a virtual town, and people from Rancho Ventura began pulling bundles from the backs of mules and the wagons to add our own section. Visions of a cozy frontier hotel vanished from my head as I realized that this was it. This was no trip to a charming, historical version of the Santa Barbara I had known in the future; this was a camping expedition on her outskirts.

I sighed and accepted a servant's help in dismounting, Javier having gone somewhere with his men. I handed my reins to the man, gripped my skirts, and ascended a nearby knoll to check out the scene. After a short hike, I arrived and looked down to the gathering herd, watching as men moved through them on horses, pointing at one or another. To sell? To purchase? I had no idea. They'd erected ten corrals, perhaps for sorting or bronco riding or whatever they did at rodeos in this era.

There were a good fifty tents pitched already, with about fifteen campfires already sending up smoke. The smell of roasting meat blended with the sea air. In the distance, I could see the curve of the coastline and the bright white of a few buildings in the town proper, as well as the warm adobe and cross of the mission.

Around the edge of the tents, I spied six men in black and white uniform, with white Xs across their chests, following a leader with gold epaulets on his shoulders and a sharp, black hat. They approached a cluster of six men—with younger men hovering about—and I saw Javier at the center. Perhaps they were the rancheros, all gathered together. I thought I'd made out Mateo hovering close by them.

They stood there stiffly, listening to whatever the head X-man dude had to say. I stifled a giggle at my own internal joke, but managed to keep my composure. Then Javier gestured to the right, clearly inviting them to stay but with no enthusiasm. Mr. Blackcoat nodded once, and the men set out, riding directly beneath where I stood, where Mr. Blackcoat caught sight of me and smiled, touching his hat as he nodded in my direction. I pretended to smile back. He was about thirty, a big but homely man, and he and his men appeared to be the remaining Mexican military contingent from the presidio—the ones Javier seemed to so thoroughly resent.

We'd eaten our supper around the campfire, alongside Rafael Vasquez, his sister, Patricio, and a friend, when Javier rose, went to the wagon, opened the lid of a trunk, and brought back his father's guitar. He handed it to me as the group around us fell silent. His mother began with stiff agitation, "Javier, this is not the place—"

But he shushed her with a wave of his hand, only looking at me. "The charreada is a time of celebration. I would like it very much if you might gift all of us with a song, Zara."

I hesitated, glancing at Doña Elena and Adalia, who both bore warning expressions, but the rest were all encouragement and curiosity. And what was the harm, truly? Vanity won out; I felt the need to show them all just what I could do with the strings of a guitar, even if I was a lousy horsewoman. I shifted on my rock-seat to better balance the instrument and considered what I might play. I settled on "El Pomponderano," the first song I'd learned via YouTube, with its intriguing blend of plucked notes along the strings, with the tapping the body of the guitar as a sort of mild drumbeat, and then building in tempo and complexity.

It began slowly, and I felt sweat beginning to bead on my forehead, aware that every single person was staring at me. I could hear others at neighboring campfires still talking and laughing, the occasional shout and the lowing of the cattle, but gradually centered in on only my song. My fingers, connecting lightly with the strings, were poised for the speed of the piece ahead. I closed my eyes and felt the rhythm, smiling as I heard someone begin to clap expertly—almost like another instrument, and then a second, picking up additional beats, at once making the song familiar to me but also giving it new life. My smile grew, but I kept my eyes closed, hearing the song build from the old guitar into something I knew I'd remember the rest of my life. Being here, in such a pretty place, on the edge of one of California's earliest rodeos, and playing in a mariachi version of jazz? I had to admit, it was pretty cool, and I was going to relish every minute of it.

But when the song came to a close and I opened my eyes, I was aware that neighboring sounds had stopped—other than from the animals—and that our group had grown. People stood three-deep all around us, and children squatted in a posse all around me, staring up in rapt attention. Javier rose, grinning from ear to ear and applauding.

"Brava!" he cried, urging the others to similar accolades. "Brava!"

I smiled with him, offering the guitar back to him, when I saw his face fall and followed his gaze. "Señor de la Ventura." It was the lead X-man, coming closer, followed by his squad. But his eyes were only on me. "So this new rose is your guest? Why was I not introduced the last time I came to your rancho?"

"She had not yet arrived," Javier said, the muscles at his cheek tightening.

I stood, now grateful I was still holding the guitar. I could sense the danger in this one—the entire group around me reflected it—and the guitar gave my hands something to do.

Javier edged in beside me. "Lieutenant de Leon, this is our guest, Señorita Zara Ruiz. Señorita Ruiz, Lieutenant de Leon."

He took off his tall hat and tucked it under his arm, then bowed over my hand, low enough that his long, greasy black curls brushed the top of my wrist. But he did not kiss it. "I am your servant, Señorita Ruiz," he said, his eyes lingering on my face and down to my chest and back up again. *My servant. Right.* He did not release my hand but covered it with his other. "Now you must tell me," he said with a smile, tearing his eyes from me to Javier a moment, "where did your lovely guest come from, Ventura? A musician of such caliber?"

"I was actually hoping you might be of some assistance to her, Lieutenant," Javier said flatly. "Señorita Ruiz survived a most harrowing blow to her head, resulting in a fall from a ship along my shore. She made land along Pirata Cove. Have you heard of any ships passing southward, with tales of a woman lost?"

I could hear the murmurs of other newcomers in the crowd around us. It wouldn't take long for everyone encamped here to know my story.

"Indeed not," the soldier said. I slipped my hand from his at last, and he frowned as if a fish had just spit out his hook. He turned to a man behind him. "Gutierrez, have you gotten wind of any such story at the harbor house?"

The man shook his head too, staring at me, mouth agape.

"But you have sent word to her family?" the lieutenant asked.

"No. I fear Señorita Ruiz remembers precious little, other than her name."

"Well, thank God she remembers how to play that guitar!" the man said, with a bark of a laugh. Uneasy, forced laughter followed him.

"Yes," Javier said. "Well, we—Señorita Ruiz and my family would greatly appreciate your sending word if you hear anything relevant at the presidio."

"Of course, of course," said the man, looking down at me as if I'd just become a hundred times more intriguing. "Perhaps with a rose such as this in my midst, I can ignore the rather thorny issue that we have yet to receive your quarterly taxes, Ventura." His dark eyes moved to meet Javier's, who stiffened. "I assume you brought it with you? Surely it was only an oversight, you not sending it by messenger last month."

"I have it with me," Javier said, measuring each word. He didn't promise to give it to him.

Doña Elena rose to her feet and, spying an ally, Lieutenant de Leon turned to her, fawning over her and the girls. Francesca smiled shyly, but Estrella didn't seem too pleased with his attention. I supposed it was the age…I remembered just starting to notice at about Francesca's age that I was capturing attention of the male sort and the strange power that accompanied it.

Javier stood there as if enduring the scene. Clearly, he did not have a lot of love for these dudes. I remembered his comments about their tax demands and the lack of return for that investment. But was it any different here and now than it was in my own day? Back home, the old people talked about a lack of medical care; delivery drivers bellowed about the potholes in the streets; teachers and students griped about the constantly broken air conditioner at school. But here, there was an obvious threat in the soldiers' body language that I'd never seen among the police or politicians of my day. Plainly, they were nothing more than bullies.

Adalia gestured toward me, and we went to the tent we were to share. "We're to dress for the dance," she said quietly, setting little Álvaro down on a makeshift cot. "You've already drawn the lieutenant's attention. He'll surely require a turn around the floor."

I hesitated, noticing the distinctly pinched look around her lips. She didn't like this. Because she was jealous? Surely she didn't think that guy was cute…

"I…uh, I won't be dancing tonight," I said, forcing a smile. "Too saddle-sore to do more than turn in, I'm afraid." That was true. I didn't know if I could walk a mile, let alone dance this night.

"Nonsense," she said softly. "You must come. Everyone will be there. Including Javier." Her eyes slid to me.

"Maybe that's the best reason of all to stay away." I sighed as I sat down on my cot and shrugged. "I'm like you. Leaving soon. The closer Javier and I get, the harder that will be."

She sat down across from me, looking impossibly fresh and beautiful in her shift. Suddenly younger. Like maybe she was only a year or two older than I was. But she was frowning. "Where will you go, if you cannot remember where you came from?"

"I…I don't know. I just know I have to be ready when the time comes. And Javier…" I gazed over at her, feeling helpless to describe it.

She gave me an understanding smile. "Javier and Dante…" She looked to her son, as if to distract herself, holding on to his hand as he struggled to his feet, wavering on the lumpy cot and falling into her arms. "They have always been wonderful. I was the envy of every girl from here to the border when Dante professed his love to me. And then it was…gone."

"How did he die, Adalia?" I asked quietly.

"Steer-wrestling," she said bitterly, shaking her head. "Here at the rodeo, last year."

"Oh," I said, startled. Maybe this was what pushed her over the edge. Returning to where her future with her husband had abruptly ended. "I'm so sorry."

She stared at me, obviously confused by my phrase, but she understood the look of compassion on my face and softened, looking for a moment as if she might cry, but then carefully regaining control. "You will see Javier wrestle tomorrow. He and his brother had no rival other than each other. But last year, as Dante brought his steer down, one horn pierced his belly."

I swallowed hard, feeling a bit sick. I imagined what that must have been like—the horrible pain for Dante, the lack of medical care, what had to be a long, drawn-out death.

"I had always liked Javier, but it was Dante who held my heart," she went on, unbuttoning her son's small shirt, even amid his squirming. "I awaited his return, thinking he might do his duty and take his brother's place."

"But Javier did," I said, puzzled. "Didn't he?"

Her dark eyes met mine. "I mean, in taking me as his bride."

"Oh," I breathed, for the second time. Apparently this was A Thing. Stepping in for Big Bro. In *all* ways. "Oh," I repeated, feeling totally lame, but lost for something to say. "So, uh… So then…you and Javier…"

"Javier and I have always been friends," she said. "It simply became clear that it would never be more, even before you arrived." She set down her son and watched a moment as he maneuvered along the edge of the cot to the end. "And honestly, Zara, I don't know how I might have…adjusted." She reached out and took my hand. "Once a Ventura captures your heart, I doubt another can ever compare. Even if it is his brother."

I swallowed hard. I'd been thinking about that a lot on the ride down here. About Javier's note. And wondering if I'd ever find a guy like him in my own time. "So were you disappointed? Or relieved? When things didn't work out between you and Javier?"

"I…" She paused, fiddling with the edge of her blanket. "I felt nothing," she said with a shrug. "It is as if my heart is not only halved, but numb. I'm hoping that in returning home, I'll begin to feel something again—anything."

I reached out and took her hand, smiling a little. "If my backside can begin to feel anything after that ride, your heart can begin to feel again too."

She laughed at that, pulling back her hand to cover her mouth as if embarrassed. But then she continued to laugh, so hard that it made me giggle too. She covered her mouth with both hands, but tears streamed from her eyes as she looked over at me. "Oh, Zara," she said finally, wiping her eyes, "I can see why Javier is falling in love with you."

I pulled back. "What?"

She studied me, sobering. "Surely you know."

I stared at her.

"He is falling in love," she said, more firmly this time. "As you are, for him. Despite my warning." She leaned closer and nudged me, as if in on the most delicious secret. "I know. A man like that…a man who can love you to your very soul, is impossible to turn away, once they set their eyes on you."

"What?" I breathed, knowing the truth of her words, despite my desire to deny them. "It can't be. I've never been in love. And Javier does not yet know me!"

She pulled back, examining every inch of my face, assessing. "He knows enough, as do you," she said. "The heart recognizes its mate before the head does. I think it was happening even before I warned you to watch out."

"No," I said, slowly shaking my head back and forth. "No."

She leaned forward, taking my hand in hers again. "Yes."

"No," I whispered. "It can't happen. Not now."

"Love happens where it ought. It happened for me and Dante, even though ours was a much more…*arranged* union than yours might be with Javier. I always knew Javier's heart would be stolen only by a girl who could surprise him."

"No," I said, pulling my hand from hers and shaking my head. "You don't understand."

"I do," she said lightly, rising, as if I were just thickheaded. She went to my trunk and lifted the lid, then pulled out my green and black gown, the gift from Captain Worthington. She laid it on the cot beside me. "Wear this to the dance tonight. I think Javier was in love with you even before you showed up at the ranch in it. But this will remind him."

"I...I don't want to remind him. I mean...if what you say is true. I don't want to remind him! I have to leave soon, Adalia. Go home, as you are doing!"

She turned to me, now reaching for her own gown. "Oh Zara," she said. "Where is that?"

I swallowed hard. "I-I don't know."

"But doesn't that leave you free to accept all the Venturas offer you? A fine home. A loving family. And...Javier?"

CHAPTER 14

She left me there, sitting on the cot, clutching my gown, wondering over her words.

A fine home. A loving family. And...Javier.

A loving family, I repeated silently. *My big Wish Número Uno...*

Weren't the Venturas everything I'd always wished for? What Abuela had wished for too?

But it couldn't be. It just couldn't.

Yes, there just might be love starting to simmer between me and Javier. Wish *Número Dos.* I was brave enough to admit that—that there just might be the kind of love I'd always hoped for, in time. And his family...they represented everything I'd imagined, good and bad. Life was way simpler with just me and Abuela. But hadn't I hungered for the kind of varied personalities that Rancho Ventura held, from Doña Elena on down to little Álvaro?

And yet Wish Número *Tres...Ay caramba.* This was far more adventure than I'd ever hoped for. Abuela had said that sometimes adventure was closer at hand than I might've imagined, but this... this was ridiculous. Totally ridiculous. Here in the Wild West, there were all kinds of ways to die. Wasn't Adalia's story of Dante evidence of that? I'd wanted Weather-Channel adventure. Measured, "check all the forecasts and decide" sort of adventure.

Not a spin of the reality wheel in which my life might be at risk.

Or a spin of my heart.

No, combining all the Family and Love and Adventure wishes had never been a part of the deal. *You hear me on that, Lord?* I asked silently, staring up at the central post of the tent. *I didn't ask for a combination of family, love, and adventure.*

But you didn't specify that they had to be distinct, did you, Zara?

Numbly, I pulled off my drab brown dress and slipped on the black and green over my petticoat. Then I pulled back the top of my hair, leaving the rest curling around my shoulders, brushed out my skirts, and left the tent. The campground had been transformed with nightfall. Kerosene lamps swung at intervals down the row, as if leading the way. In the distance, I could hear music, laughter, cheering.

But Javier was there, looking like something of a matador. Tight black pants that tucked into perfectly polished boots; above that, a short, tailored jacket, embellished with silver thread embroidery, over an immaculate, white shirt that made his teeth seem brighter when he smiled at me. His hair was pulled back with a band. I'd never seen him look so…buttoned-up. Back home he was always more relaxed in some way: either his hair was flopping down over one eye, or his shirt flapped open over that broad chest…

He leaned toward me. "You look beautiful, Zara," he said. "Will you do me the pleasure of accompanying me to the dance?"

"Yes," I breathed. We turned to walk down the dusty path, picking our way around bigger rocks. "Javier, I…I cannot dance tonight."

"No?" he said, sounding so disappointed it surprised me. The only guys I'd ever known who were into dancing were a couple at school who had learned that getting good at salsa meant insta-access to a girl's heart. Players. Maybe that was his game… "Why not?" he asked.

"Well, I'm terribly sore from the ride," I said ruefully. "And I fear I've forgotten. I don't remember dancing."

He rested his gloved fingers on top of mine. "There is no reason to fear. I taught my sisters. I shall simply teach you. It will all come back to you soon after we begin." We were close to the others, and the music and conversation began to envelop us. Others must have arrived in the last hours of the day; there were more than a hundred people now as I looked around, maybe a hundred and fifty.

"People come from town and farther for our rodeo," Javier explained. "They like the dancing, the roping, the horsemanship."

"The roping?" I inquired.

"Tomorrow. Every man will be on his horse while the women and children watch from up there," he said, gesturing toward the rocks above. "We find our own cattle that have mixed with others over the last month, separate them from the rest, rope them and get them to our corral. The first rancho to gather all its lost cattle is honored, of course."

"So it is a game, of sorts."

"Of sorts." His dark eyes narrowed as he stared at an obviously wealthy family across the relatively flat area of the makeshift dance floor. "But I can tell you already that we're missing at least fifty head. And I would wager they're not lost among the hills, as the Vargases might claim."

I followed his gaze to the family, clearly friendly with Lieutenant de Leon and his men. Two young women hung on the arms of two of the soldiers, while the lieutenant lifted a mug in a toast with the gray-bearded man in the fine black coat. A younger man, just a little older than Javier, looked over at him in sly, subtle challenge and then at me. He said something out of the corner of his mouth to the lieutenant, and that man, in turn, looked to me and answered him. They laughed, and I felt Javier stiffen beside me.

"They took my cattle," he said. "The vaqueros had them on land along our southern border. Come morning, they'd disappeared from the valley."

"How do you steal fifty head of cattle?" I asked, thinking it was pretty hard to hide that many cows.

"You steal them and slaughter them before your neighbors can come looking. Especially when the *Guadiana* is anchored off the coast."

"That was why you gambled with those men that night? Because you were bent on getting back at them?"

He gave me a little smile, half-victorious, half-bitter. "She and her sister ship had plenty of fresh meat that night. I was only intent on obtaining a portion of the payment I was due."

"But you couldn't prove anything? Go to the authorities?" I knew the folly of what I'd just asked even before he looked my way.

"No. In many ways, we have to see to our own justice in Alta California. Because those who are here to 'protect' us fail, utterly. It kindles no love for the mother country, or those who remain true."

Those who remain true...Was he no longer a loyalist? I said nothing more, because he seemed eager to put it behind him and adopt the festive mood of the party ahead. But, as he led me deeper into the mingling crowd, I wondered if we were to divide all who attended into two parties—those loyal to Mexico and those looking to the States—where exactly the line would fall.

The children were running around, carrying what looked like bits of honeycomb in handkerchiefs, their faces glistening with honey around their mouths. Patricio arrived, carrying six mugs—three in each hand—and gladly passed them out to other men, and one to me.

Thirsty, I took a tentative sip and discovered it was a sort of ginger beer.

That was when the music began, and my heart lurched. I was only so-so at dancing in my own day. I had no idea how these 1840s peeps did it. Was it square dancing? We'd done a bit of that at school…

But as the players in the band—two guitars, two trumpets and a *vihuela*—came together in their first song, I smiled a little in recognition. They weren't great, but they were decent, and it sounded a bit like really old mariachi music.

"You'd better get your girl out on that floor," Patricio said, nudging Javier forward, "before someone else does."

It took me a sec to realize he meant me. So I was Javier's "girl" now? When did that happen? And I was just trying to phrase the right way to turn him down when he took my hand, bowed with his other arm behind his back, and looked up at me through those luscious, black lashes… "Trust me, Zara," he said softly. "I will show you the steps."

We were one of many couples who swirled into the clearing. Patricio escorted Doña Elena—who barely hid her distaste—and a woman I didn't know was on tall, elegant Rafael's arm. Francesca came too, looking flustered but pleased beside a boy a little older than she. More entered around them. Apparently, this wasn't like the high school dances of my day; everyone seemed eager to take part. Even little kids stood around, holding hands, watching and mimicking the adults' actions.

It was a lot of action. But on the edge of all of it, Javier and I stood, and I felt like he saw or heard none of it. Only me. My entire body felt electrified, so close to him. "You could teach them some of your music," he said, giving me a smile as he gestured with his head toward the band.

"I don't know," I said shyly. "I think they're doing well enough."

"Well enough to dance," he said, seeming to remember why we were there. "Now…you don't remember anything at all?"

I shook my head.

"Well, all right," he said, straightening a bit, even as he set his feet slightly apart and squared his hips. "Place your left hand here, on my shoulder, and your right here, in my hand."

I did as he asked, and we were instantly closer than before. I stared at the pearl button at his throat, not daring to look up as he put his wide, warm hand against my lower back.

"I will use this hand," he said, pressing inward and then from one side to the other, "to help guide you. If you give in to following my lead," he said, leaning a little closer to my ear, "you'll find it rather simple." He then moved on to show me the basic square pattern of the steps. "That's it," he said, as the song came to an end. "Do you wish to try now?"

"I, uh…I suppose, yes."

He didn't wait for a firmer reply but just moved me gently out and into the center of the dancing couples. He was quietly counting with me in time to the music, half as fast as the others were moving, not caring about their wondering glances, only caring about me. I felt that tender, thoughtful care from my toes to my scalp and back again. I had a hard time thinking about anything but how we seemed to fit together—how his hand felt beneath mine, how his shoulder was so wide and strong, how his other hand guided me. Never had a first dance been easier for me. But it didn't seem to matter that it was new. In Javier's arms, I simply melded into his lifelong knowledge, his lead, his steps.

I relaxed as the next song began, and Javier smiled, feeling my joy lap my fear. "Trust me," he said, suddenly pulling away and twirling me under his arm and bringing me back against his chest. We both laughed when I came in a little hard, but he had me back in place and back in step in seconds.

"May I cut in, Señor Ventura?" asked a voice behind me.

Javier's smile disappeared into defiance. "I think not. Señorita Ruiz is just learning our steps. Her amnesia has made her forget."

"And yet under your tutelage, she appears to have remembered quite well," Lieutenant de Leon said, as I turned slightly toward him.

I could feel the line etching in the dust between the men and didn't want it to build into something that would ruin the high mood of the party. "Just one dance," I said, more to Javier than the lieutenant.

Jaw clenched, Javier bowed. "As you wish, Señorita. I'll be back at the end of the song."

"Just one song? So miserly, Ventura," Leon chided as he took me in his arms, pulling me a bit too close. "You'd think letting me dance with this girl was as painful as paying your taxes!"

He smiled at his own joke and then lurched me through the steps of the dance. He was tall and strong, and he was a skilled dancer, just not quite as graceful and intuitive as Javier. Trying to follow his lead felt more like a guessing game—always a second behind—than what it had been with Javier. It was as if he decided and pushed and pulled me on, rather than anticipating the next steps and leading me.

At one point, I stepped on his toe, and he frowned a little. "You truly do not know this dance?" he asked, turning me in a tight circle, bringing me closer to him.

"I do not. My head injury…it's left me with few memories."

"Hmm," he said. "The mysterious castaway, who can remember

songs on the guitar but not steps to a simple dance. The thing that troubles me, Señorita, is that women do not wash up on shores in these parts without someone looking for them. Being the officer in charge in Santa Barbara, I would hear of such a matter. Unless…someone did not wish it to be known."

"What do you mean, Lieutenant?" I asked, frowning up at him.

He lifted a brow. "I mean that there could be two explanations. One, you are more than an acquaintance to that vile traitor, Patricio Casales," he hissed, eying the man as he went by, a cute girl in his arms. "And you are joining forces with him to woo Javier into his treasonous cause for the Union."

I bit back a retort. "Or?"

"Or you were the mistress of a sea captain who found you on the streets of Mexico, convinced you to come along on his voyage, grew tired of you, and thought the most expedient way to end it was to toss you overboard." He grinned at that and pulled me a bit closer even as I tried to squirm away. "If *that* is the truth, Señorita, there are other ways for you to find room and board…when your host discovers it too. Do not fear, pretty girl. As either a spy or whore, there is always a dollar to be made. You only need take care where you make your bed."

Mercifully, the song came to an end, and he finally allowed me to step away. I stared at the lieutenant as I felt Javier join me on one side, Rafael on the other. This Leon was nothing but a bully. A snake, trying to get under my skin. Making guesses in an era when women really didn't have many options other than what he'd laid out.

"Or Lieutenant, there is a third option. I am a lady, lost at sea, innocent of either of your charges," I said, my fingernails digging into my palms. I longed to ram my hand up and into that big, bulbous nose…

"Of course, of course," he said, as if he and I were sharing a private joke. "Thank you for the dance, Señorita," he said and turned on his heel, heading directly toward another woman and asking her to dance next.

"What did he say to you?" Javier growled, offering his arm. "Were you trying to get away from him?" He shook his head at a vaquero coming in our direction, visibly hoping for a dance but backing away when Javier's expression made it clear that the next was his and his alone.

"It was nothing," I said, gratefully taking Javier's arm, forcing myself to breathe, hoping he wouldn't feel me trembling. I was angry, and that made me want to cry. "He is making idle guesses about me. Trying to figure out my story—as everyone else is," I added wearily. "Including me."

He lifted my chin as I blinked away tears. "It will come back to you, Zara, in time. I know it will."

And as he swept me into the next dance, I thought about his turn of phrase. *It will come back to you in time.*

Sí, claro. Sure it would. If I bopped on back to the twenty-first-century sort of time, all would slip back in place.

Except I'd be without Javier…and his family…

CHAPTER 15

The next morning, as we stood on the knoll, a man shot a gun into the air, and all the rest scattered into motion around the massive herd of mixed cattle. I gaped in admiration. Most of them appeared to guide their mounts with their feet and legs more than with the reins—leaving them more ready to divide and chase cattle to their respective corrals. In minutes, the hillside below us was a dusty mass of activity, but I had a hard time looking away from Javier.

Women and children were clapping and cheering, each for their own rancho, but I could see the Ventura crew was pulling ahead. Javier led a fourth cow into the corral, a vaquero quickly opening and closing the gate behind her. Fifteen others were moving at a similar rate, including young Mateo. Jacinto was up with us, clearly itching to take part but far too young to risk in the crazy mosh pit below us.

Carried away by the excitement, I cheered too, knowing that Javier couldn't hear me, not over all the bellowing of the cattle. Their bovine complaints made me think they were all seriously stressed. And no wonder…there were so many vaqueros moving around them, identifying brands, dividing their own from the rest, that it was pure chaos. But within twenty minutes, Javier was waving his hat to the judge, up with us, along with the rest of the crew from Rancho Ventura, all surrounding the corral as others continued to cut and drag their own cattle "home."

The judge acknowledged him—and the Herreras soon after—but we had to wait until every cow was claimed and corralled before the victor was announced. I held my breath, tense, worried that one of the last twenty cows below might have been marked with a V—the Ventura brand—but missed. I knew now that would mean instant disqualification. But Javier just sat confidently on his mount, looking up at the judge, awaiting what he clearly knew would be his.

And it was. "De la Ventura!" shouted the judge, when the last cow was claimed.

Doña Elena laughed softly, a welcome sound I hadn't heard from her. I turned to her, and she said proudly, "There. You have seen my boy in his element. Never has this territory had such horsemen as my Dante and Javier. Mateo and Jacinto shall be the same."

"And perhaps Estrella and Francesca too?" I added hopefully.

She gave me a puzzled smile. "What a thing to say!"

"Well, why not? Your girls were born to you and your husband, were they not? What keeps them from having the same gifts?"

She let out a scoffing laugh and drew herself up again. "No daughter of mine will ever be among the men, down there," she said. "They are ladies."

Oh, right, I thought, my gaze turning back to the men, all slapping one another on the back in congratulations. Because I knew that if I was good enough on the back of my horse, that's exactly where I'd want to be. Javier looked over his cattle, an expression of growing dissatisfaction on his face, now that the competition was over. I knew he was thinking again of those unaccounted for….and who might have stolen them.

Fortunately, the group immediately moved toward another corral where five men took turns showing off their skills at *calla de caballo,* a complex display of cantering, galloping, slide stopping, spins and more. It was tough for me to figure out the point system—but I couldn't help but grin with Rafael Vasquez when he was honored as the winning *charro.*

Then we were on to *jineteo de yegua*, which I found somewhat stunning, observing one man after another cling to the back of a mare desperate to unseat him, my teeth hurting from just watching the repeated, jarring impact for each rider. Javier was last, and I held my breath as he came out, holding on to the rope and leaning back, taking each landing with a roll, as if absorbing the jump and letting it wash through him. He held on through five or six increasingly high jumps when the mare actually stood so high—front hooves waving in the air—that Javier's weight pulled her backward.

They seemed suspended in midair as Francesca and others screamed, men cried out, and my heart pretty much thudded to a halt. But Javier somehow somersaulted and landed partially on his feet, then back on his rear, narrowly falling away before the horse fell right in front of him and fortunately rolled in the other direction.

I remembered to breathe as Javier grinned, rose, and picked up his hat, dusting it off. The people cheered wildly, and, while Javier was apparently disqualified for not dismounting and landing on his feet, people congratulated him as if he had won. He came to me, dust still in his dark hair and lashes, happier than I'd ever seen him. "A kiss for the almost-winner?" he whispered, leading me on to the next event.

"Be serious, Javier," I teased, looking at him as if the thought disgusted me. "With so much dirt between your teeth?"

He laughed under his breath, but it didn't escape me that, as he moved away to get ready for the next event, he appeared to be running his tongue across his teeth. I hid a smile.

The crowd now approached a pen holding six big steers with ominously curved horns, all about the same size. Warily, I looked around for Adalia, but she'd clearly left the group, likely headed back to the tents. Every one of the Ventura family seemed to slow in their walk toward the pen—and others, remembering, seemed to hold back too. Javier went to his mother and kissed her cheek, and she whispered something to him, putting on a brave smile. I remained beside her, wondering why he couldn't sit this one out—especially after just losing his brother the year before—but there seemed to be a collective attitude that this had to be done, as if doing so would make things right again. *Back in the saddle* and all of that silliness. It made me angry. After watching the bronco riding, what would *this* be like? And why must they do it? To prove something?

The six men who intended to compete went to their horses, and I saw, then, that the pen that held the steers led into the larger corral before us. It was around that bigger, longer corral that we congregated. An older man offered each man, now mounted, a stick held in his round fist. Each drew one, determining the order in which they'd compete. Javier was last. He lifted his head to the sky and sighed, as if groaning, and the Vargas son, also competing, laughed. I supposed that since he had gone last for the bronco riding, he didn't like waiting until the end again.

The first man, the eldest Herrera, took his place in the corral before us. Another man on horseback hovered near. When Herrera nodded, the pen was opened, allowing one steer to bolt forward. The crowd began to chant together, "*Uno, dos, tres*," counting the time as Herrera chased down the steer. At *seis*, Herrera dismounted at a full gallop, taking but one step as he grabbed hold of the running steer's horns and twisted, using his full body weight to bring the animal down just as we got to *diez, once, doce* in our counting.

I shook my head. Twelve seconds to wrestle a young animal to the ground. And I could too readily see how Dante had been gored. If a man didn't get just the right grip on the horns, in the act of bringing him down, he could easily be impaled.

Lieutenant de Leon pushed his way to my side. I pretended not to notice him. Vargas went next, bringing his steer down in ten seconds. Leon grinned and turned, accepting a coin from another soldier behind him, obviously winning his bet. The third, a Fuentes, judging by his family's excitement as he took his place, took eighteen seconds when the steer abruptly stopped and switched course. You would have thought that the family had suffered a mortal blow, so glum were they. The fourth and fifth men went next, the last struggling to pin the steer's head to the ground because he didn't have quite the right grip on his horns.

And then it was Javier's turn. He came into the corral, and narrowed his eyes at Leon when he saw he stood beside me. Leon chuckled quietly and seemed to lean toward me as if to taunt him, but I only wanted Javier to concentrate on what he had to do right now. Nothing else. "Come on, Ventura!" I cried, clapping along with the rest. "Show them how it's done!"

I bit my lip as Javier wrenched his gaze from me to the man atop the gate, focusing, nodding once. His eyes never left the monstrous black steer as it tore out into the corral. Indeed, his mare was already in motion, galloping alongside the young animal. As Javier swung his leg over to dismount, I could see the steer seem to sense his progress, and he swerved away. Javier leaped more than jumped, aware that he had to cover more distance if this was going to work.

And then he was twisting, wrenching the animal's head to one side, forcing him down to the ground, just as the crowd counted *nueve*. Nine seconds. He'd won it. Again, the crowd cheered. With the competition over, everyone turned to slap or pat another's back, as if it had been our collective win, rather than Javier's. All around me, men were shaking hands and kissing the nearest woman.

I was just taking in this exuberant response, turning and glimpsing Javier coming my way through the well-wishers, when I felt Lieutenant de Leon's hand around my neck, eagerly forcing his mouth toward mine. Clearly, he wanted to take advantage of the moment—within Javier's view. But I wrenched back. "No!"

His leering grin turned into a sneer, and he took hold of my neck with *both* his meaty hands then, forcing me toward him. Setting my feet, I acted on instinct. I thrust my hands upward, between his arms, then pressed my forearms outward, breaking his grasp. Then I rammed upward, into his nose with the palm of my fist, giving it all I had. I heard a satisfying crack and saw blood fly in an arc, unfortunately landing across young Señorita Vargas's pristine yellow gown. The crowd instantly quieted, split, and backed away from us in collective shock.

The big soldier turned back to me, humiliated rage in his eyes. "Why, you little…"

I was getting my feet set, raising my fists, preparing for his advance, when Patricio and Rafael intervened. Rafael patted Leon on the arm, while Patricio wrapped his arm around my shoulders, each of them subtly easing us apart. "Ho!" Patricio cried, grinning as if this was a planned part of the festivities. "¡Ay caramba! It looks like our champion steer wrestler has picked a girl with similar courage! Imagine! A girl with the power to resist Lieutenant de Leon! Fortunately for us, *la República's* servant would never force himself on any young woman, would he? Of course not! He is a man of honor, sent here to keep the peace!"

My cheeks burned now, as I felt Javier arrive, panting, and I saw that the crowd had surged around Leon, all forcing laughs and shouting, trying to restore the festive mood and separate him further from me. "Zara…" Javier whispered, gazing over his shoulder and then back to me, trying to figure out what had happened.

"No, I think it's all right," I said, still watching Leon as he disappeared among women offering him clean handkerchiefs and crooning words and men patting his back.

Patricio let go of my shoulders. "I'd get her out of sight for a bit," he said softly, all trace of humor gone from his face. "Leon will swallow his rage, given his need for public favor, but it won't take much to set him off again. I'll send a couple of your men to watch over you."

"Right," Javier said, leading me away, in the opposite direction from the crowd, heading back to camp. "Zara, what happened?" he asked, turning to face me but still glancing over his shoulder as if worried someone was coming after us.

"You didn't see any of it?"

"No. I was coming your way, saw that the lieutenant was turning toward you, but then others blocked my view. By the time I reached you, they were leading him away. Bloody?"

My legs trembled, the adrenaline now morphing into slick oil in my veins, making me feel weak and wobbly. "I…I'm afraid I just made things worse for you, Javier. I just made the lieutenant a bigger enemy than before."

Javier smiled. "I gathered that much." He pulled me into his arms, hugging me to his chest and tenderly stroking my hair.

"Now tell me everything."

"I think I broke his nose."

"You *what*?" He pulled away from me, looking into my face. "Truly? Why?"

"I'm sorry, Javier. But he…well, he tried to kiss me," I said, giving him a rueful smile. "When everyone was celebrating after your win."

Javier laughed, his handsome, dust-covered face splitting into a glorious grin. He pulled me to his chest again, laughter still rumbling in his chest. "Oh, you marvelous, darling girl. You wondrous, mysterious woman. If that's the case, you simply saved me the trouble of breaking his nose myself. Because if I haven't had the chance to kiss you," he whispered, "it would've driven me mad seeing *him* do so."

He squeezed me tight. But then his demeanor softened, warmed. His hands moved across my back a moment and then to my arms, pulling away a bit.

I dared to look up at him, then, his features half in shadow.

"Zara," he whispered. "May I kiss you? Just once?"

And I don't know what it was. Suddenly I was weary, so weary of holding up my guard. Of keeping everyone at bay. Especially him. *Oh, especially him.*

I bit my lip and gave him a little nod.

He reached up to tilt my chin, bending slowly to meet my lips. And then he kissed me, slowly, softly, reverently, his hands wrapping around my back to press me to him for a moment.

Then he lifted his head, giving me a little smile as he stared into my eyes. "I've wanted to do that since the moment we were together in the stables."

"Not on the beach when we met?" I said, giving him a teasing, puzzled frown.

"No, at that point, I fairly wanted to throttle you."

Fair enough, I thought. I had wounded him and stolen his horse, after all. But there was no bitterness in his tone, only humor.

He wrapped me in his arms again, and I rested my head on his chest, thinking I'd never been kissed the way he'd just kissed me. The most action I'd ever gotten was an awkward encounter after a high school dance. I'd never let a guy get close to me since.

But this? This thing between Javier de la Ventura and me?

This was an entirely different school of dance.

CHAPTER 16

There was no dance that second night of the rodeo—only a feast. Everyone wore their finest clothing and brought their best food. It was like a girl's coming-of-age *quinceañera* party, with a full-on festive atmosphere. Food like I'd never seen since I'd arrived was served as we sat around in rings surrounding bonfires. *Queso fundido*—melted cheese with strips of *poblano chilis* on top—was served alongside platters of grilled *cabrito*, baby goat. Other platters held steaming *minilla de pescado*, a shredded fish dish with olives and capers. Piles of *tamales de pollo* came around, with a pitcher of *verde* sauce to pour over them. Black licorice and more chunks of honeycomb were in most of the children's hands, and adults poured themselves generous amounts from casks of wine.

I spotted Francesca in a group of girls her age, talking to some new arrivals—sailors, from the looks of them—and watched as one captain grandly introduced himself to each one, much to the consternation of the mothers, who diplomatically eased each of them away. It didn't take long to figure out why; the captain was apparently British, and a staunch USA-fan, even as he took advantage of his Mexican hosts' hospitality. But still Francesca stood there, talking to the man—twice her age—and smiling coquettishly, blushing. *Where is Doña Elena?* I thought with agitation. I realized Frani was pretty, on the brink of womanhood, but my blood boiled as if I was her older sister, realizing that this dude was moving in on a girl who was… vulnerable.

I thought about intervening but knew it wasn't my place. Not yet.

Not yet. I checked myself.

Did I think there would be a time when it *would* be my place?

The thought took my breath away.

Once more I looked around but saw Javier break away from Patricio and Rafael—both clearly a few mugs into the wine—grab Mateo, and head toward his sister, clearly intent on intervening. I breathed a sigh of relief.

Estrella came up beside me then, holding Jacinto's hand. Despite the festive mood, the two looked positively grief-stricken. "Oh!" I cried, leaning over and looking into their faces. "What is it, Estie? Jacinto?"

"It…it's Adalia," said Estrella, dissolving into tears and clinging to me. "Her…her family is here."

"They're going to take Álvaro with them!" cried Jacinto, wrapping his arms around my waist from the opposite side of his sister.

"Oh!" I cried, tearing up. So it was happening, really happening. I leaned down, taking each of them in my arms. "I'm so sorry, my friends. I know this hurts so much. But listen. Listen to me." I waited while they tried to get their sniffles under control. I put one hand on Estie's cheek and the other under Jacinto's chin, waiting for them to meet my gaze. "Adalia needs to go for a while. But I don't think she'll be gone forever. She just needs time to be with her own family. It will help her remember how much each of you means to her too. She's…lost her place. But she's about to find it again. And she needs this time to find herself. Can you trust God to restore her and your nephew to you in time?"

They both stared at me, big brown eyes streaming tears.

Helpless, I passed my handkerchief from one to the other. Their grief at this impending separation made my own rise up fresh, and the tears rose in my eyes too as I took my turn with the cloth. It was disgusting, but what could I do?

A fresh handkerchief appeared, with the initials AV on the corner. I looked up, and there was Adalia, with twin tracks of tears streaming down her face. "Oh my dears," she said to Estie and Jacinto, "I couldn't have worded it better myself." She hugged each of the children. "We are not gone from you forever," she pledged. "Just for a time. And isn't it sweet of the Lord to bring you Zara in my absence? She will be your friend when you are missing me."

I swallowed hard. The girl was making promises I wasn't sure I could keep. But hadn't I just done the same for her? I felt my future spinning out of my hands and into the star-strewn sky.

"We shall see you at the fall rodeo, come rain or shine," Adalia promised, brushing her fingers beneath each of the children's chins. "Now go and say your farewells to Álvaro. But don't say farewell, will you? Just hug and kiss him and say good night, mind you?"

The two nodded miserably, then moved away.

But I thought there was a bit more hope in their stride as they left to do as she bid. She turned and put her hands on my shoulders. "Now, Zara. You see to yourself in my absence, won't you? Your arrival has been a gift to the Ventura family, a gift they're still unwrapping." She turned to the right, as if sensing his presence. And I saw him then. Javier. Watching this whole thing go down.

I swallowed hard and forced myself to look at Adalia, when she continued to speak. "The children need someone…gentler, in their lives. Doña Elena…since her husband's and Dante's passing…the children need love. Laughter. Joy. I see that in you," she said tenderly, making my eyes prick with tears. "And I will see it again," she pledged. "I look forward to our paths crossing soon. Take close care of our family in my absence."

I nodded, too strangled with words that longed to pour out—*not so fast…I'm not so sure about that…I, uh…don't think so…*

And her words, *our family,* rang in my ears.

But I remained silent because what Adalia needed most right now was permission to leave. And somehow, some way, my arrival had given her that space. Something told me it was right. The knowledge of it was almost…holy.

Into that circle came Javier, taking my hand briefly and then Adalia's. He wrapped his sister-in-law into his arms. "We shall miss you, with every heartbeat," he murmured, making me weep more. Who *said* such things? Especially a guy? "Know that you forever have a home with us, sister. You and Álvaro. Send word, and we'll come for you. Arrive on our doorstep, and your rooms will be ready. We are forever your kin, as much as when Dante walked this earth alongside us." When I saw that he was crying too, I really lost it.

"I miss him," he said, cradling her even closer and kissing her temple. "But I know you are doing what you must. Go, with my blessing. But sister, come back to us. Often, if you cannot come to us forever."

Then, seeing me crying over his sister-in-law's shoulder, he wrapped us both into his big, warm hug. Holding on to Adalia's hand, he turned to walk sedately over to his mother, took little Álvaro from her—a tiny replica of his uncle—kissed him on both cheeks—softly, so as not as to alarm the child—and then gently handed him to Adalia. He kept a firm arm around his mother's shoulders and looked at his sister-in-law. "Until we see you again," he said. "*Vaya con Dios.*"

Go with God.

Then he turned his mother around and led her toward our tents, with me following behind, holding Estrella and Jacinto's hands. Mateo hovered nearby. Where was Frani? I hadn't seen her since she was talking with that captain.

I looked over my shoulder at Adalia, with her brother and parents gathering around her. Then, cradling her sleepy toddler, she turned and moved through groups of curious onlookers, into the dark, away from us.

And the curious thing for me, as a girl who'd only met this family a week before…was that I felt her parting as a tearing. As surely as she and Álvaro were my own blood kin. I shook my head.

I was just empathizing with the Venturas, wishing they didn't have to go through this fresh pain.

Wasn't I?

We were nearing our tents, Doña Elena now surrounded by friends crooning to her and offering her fresh handkerchiefs as she wept, Francesca finally arriving and leading her younger siblings away, when Mateo growled a warning to his older brother. Two black-coated soldiers joined me and Javier from either side, walking amiably beside us.

"It's a shame, watching your family divide," the one I thought was named Gutierrez said. Leon's aide? "I hope the Venturas don't suffer any further calamities this year."

"Such as?" Javier asked.

"Oh, I don't know, Ranchero," he said, his tone falsely caring.

"All sorts of maladies can befall a rancho. Cattle rustlers. Kidnappers. Fires in the storehouses."

Javier abruptly turned to face him. "Are you threatening me, Captain?"

The other blackcoat stood beside Gutierrez, and Mateo silently stepped up beside his brother, his hands clenching into fists. He was young but scrappy.

"Threatening you, a Mexican loyalist?" Gutierrez said, casting him a wry smile. But his eyes held no merriment. "Why would I do that? With you running the most successful rancho in Alta California and paying your taxes…" His words fell away, as if he'd just remembered. "Oh, it slipped my mind. You *haven't* paid your taxes. Let us settle up right now, shall we? It'd be terrible if we had to come to you in order to collect. No, that might require further taxation for our trouble." His eyes swept over first Mateo and then me.

Javier stepped between me and the captain. "I am a loyal son of Mexico. But you and your contingent do nothing but damage our nation's reputation. You skim from shipments bound toward the ranchos and call it further 'taxes.' You do nothing to chase down pirates that prowl the waters of your citizens. You allow the presidio to fall into disrepair. You build neither piers nor storehouses of your own, taking cattle and goats and fruit from us as if you are holy men in need, not soldiers, paid agents of our country. You are leeches," he finished, leaning toward the captain. "So that is why I am *tardy* with my taxes, because I am reluctant to hand a *leech* a bowl of *blood*."

Gutierrez didn't flinch, but I saw his hand tighten around the hilt of his sword, as did the other man's. Javier and Mateo were unarmed. "I'd be careful, Don Javier, if I were you. Your girl attacked one of our soldiers. We have just cause to take her into custody. And if we do not have your gold this very night, we shall do that *and* pay your rancho that visit." He seemed to remember himself and straightened, smoothing down his coat. "It is our duty to take an equal share of their profits from every citizen. It would not be fair to your neighbors if I collected their taxes and not yours, would it?"

"No," Javier said. "It would not be equitable. But how do I know that my gold will actually go to the capital, rather than line each of your pockets?" He crossed his arms and eyed the others.

Gutierrez gave him a small smile. "You must trust us, as fellow loyalists," he said, lifting his hands. "Unless you are no longer truly a loyalist." His eyes narrowed and turned toward me. "Perhaps your reluctance to pay is due to this mysterious girl's presence, and why she behaved so inappropriately with the lieutenant? Is she truly a spy, Don Ventura, bent on sowing seeds of division among our peace-loving people?" He reached for me, and I shied away, clenching my fists. He smirked at me and turned back to Javier. "Perhaps we *do* need to take her into custody and question her thoroughly. Patricio Casales, too, as well as others in this gathering. It seems a shame to put a damper on the festivities, but…"

Javier's jaw muscles tensed, and he swallowed hard. "Come with me," he spat out and strode away. The two blackcoats followed behind him, sharing a triumphant glance, and Mateo took my arm as we trailed after them. I glanced at the younger teen, grateful. It was clear to me that being taken into custody by the soldiers would be very bad indeed. A shiver ran down my back, thinking of being locked in a cell with jackals like these holding the keys…

We followed them straight to a Ventura wagon, still loaded with barrels and crates of food, a guard sitting on either end holding a musket. Javier threw back a blanket, pushed aside a crate, and lifted out a small, heavy chest about the size of a football.

He set it on the open end of the wagon's gate and lifted the lid. "I assume that our taxes, now paid in full, will make your lieutenant more mindful of his actions in the future, and I trust that none of you shall further press me, Señorita Ruiz, Señor Casales—nor any of my family."

Gutierrez and the other soldier crowded in, glee in their eyes. The captain reached in and took a handful of heavy, golden coins and let them fall back to the pile beneath with a satisfying metallic sound. He grinned. "I believe that will be true," he said, snapping the lid shut and sliding the lock into place. He lifted the chest and handed it to the other man. "Good evening, Don Javier, Mateo—Señorita," he said with a cordial bow. "We wish you a safe journey home."

They left us then, and I went to Javier and wrapped my hand around the crook of his elbow, wanting to give him some comfort. It had clearly burned him to hand over that money. "Is it not simply part of living here, Javier? A necessary evil?"

He shook his head and then rubbed the back of his neck with his other hand. "A necessary evil. That is a good way to put it." He gave me a rueful smile. "And at least I do not need to deal with that particular evil for another year."

CHAPTER 17

I'd thought that after all that had happened, Doña Elena would forget that she ever wanted to take me to the beach and see where I'd found the lamp. I prayed about it all the way home, over the two days it took us to make the trek back to Rancho Ventura, and every time I felt her inquisitive gaze upon me. I thought that, with all that had transpired... with the grief over Adalia and little Álvaro, with the heady joy of the rodeo...there'd be plenty to occupy her mind, other than me.

But it was as if glimpsing her own stretch of coastline had reminded the older woman of the task. I happened to be riding near her, and she edged her mare closer to me. "Soon, my girl. Soon you must take me to where Javier discovered you and tell me what you can remember."

"Oh, certainly," I said, as if I had no qualms about it at all. But inwardly, I cringed. Clearly she just wanted to make sure I wasn't a spy. Having that British captain show up at the charreada, plus Gutierrez tossing out the suggestion, seemed to stir up anti-American sentiment all over again for the loyalists. But really... what exactly did she or anyone else think I could accomplish here at the ranch? What would a spy even do in this day and age? Report on the number of cattle? Trade rates? Would that really be worthwhile? But even Javier had worried about it...

Javier.

I sighed, admitting it to myself. She saw what everyone else did… Javier and me getting closer, day by day. And as much as this Mexican mama had declared I might be the perfect bride for him, she obviously wanted to make sure I was as perfect as she had hoped.

That night, I was so road-weary, I fell into bed, sure I'd be asleep before my head hit the pillow. But thoughts of Doña Elena, Javier, our kiss, the gold coins he'd had to pay in taxes…all of it swirled in my mind until I finally sat up again.

Javier had been gone since we arrived home, apparently seeing to rancho business, the storehouse by the harbor—I wasn't sure what all he was up to. But I hadn't seen him for hours. He had helped me to dismount, asked me if my legs were numb with a teasing smile, and then he was off. And throughout those hours I'd missed him.

Missed him.

I frowned at that thought. I shouldn't have ever let him kiss me. He was in my head, weaving his way into my heart, far too quickly. And it would just make it all the harder when it was time for me to leave this place. I didn't need some crazy-hot, tall, Mexican man in my head as The One when I got back. Who was ever going to live up to him, back in the twenty-first century? I rubbed my face.

It didn't matter. I was going back for *me*, to accomplish *my* dreams. I would find my way to school and through it. Become somebody. Establish a career with my own income, my own house, a wardrobe—yeah, a news station would probably give me a stipend for clothes so I'd look decent on camera. I'd have adventure, and eventually fall in love—I swallowed hard, shoving Javier out of my mind again—

and family.

It would all come together. I was not even eighteen yet. I had time to find love again. Lots of time. It didn't all have to happen here, back in 1840, where there weren't equal rights for girls, or modern medicine that could save a man after a rodeo accident, or even a decent road, for that matter. I winced and rubbed my lower back, still so sore after our long ride.

The house seemed deadly still, and I thought I might go fetch a mug of too-thick milk and play a little guitar to get my mind off everything. I threw on my brown dress and padded down the hall and stairs, but a light in the library drew me.

It was Mateo, looking startlingly like his older brother for a moment, in the solitary, low light of a single candle.

"You couldn't sleep either?" I said, leaning against the frame of the doorway.

He looked up at me, startled. He'd been playing solitaire at the big desk. "No," he said. "I wanted to go with Javier to the harbor, but he refused." I walked closer, and observed the frustration in every play of his cards.

"You can put your red eight on the nine," I said, pointing.

He nodded and made the move, then two others.

"Why wouldn't Javier take you?"

"He said I was too young. That he was to play cards, and I wasn't yet of age."

"To play *cards*?"

He paused as I sat down across from him. "To play poker. The trouble is that when he was my age, he played. He and Dante learned about the same time. But my brother…He treats me as if I am still but a boy. Too young to learn. As if I am Jacinto's age!"

I swallowed hard, determined not to smile. He *was* a boy, but I could see why he'd be frustrated, because while he was only as old as a freshman, he behaved more like a senior, in my day. They just grew up faster, back in the 1800s, I decided. "Javier was away for a time," I said. "He hasn't yet had much of a chance to see you as a man."

"He hasn't *given* me the chance," Mateo said, slapping down his hand in frustration when he got stuck for good, and he rubbed his head in irritation. The guy was such a gentle sort, I knew that he was really worked up.

"So…what if I taught you how to play?" I asked, gathering the cards together.

It was his turn to gape at me in surprise. "*You* play?"

"A little," I said, cutting the deck, shuffling, and then using a bridge to neatly fold them back together like some sort of Vegas cardsharp—a trick my abuela had taught me. I shuffled again.

"Yes. I'd be most grateful," he said, eyes wide with hope and surprise.

And so we began. I taught him about pairs, and three-of-a-kind, full houses and straights. About how to watch what others picked up and discarded, making calculations about the odds of having this or that. "You'll be good about keeping a poker face," I said, as we started our fifth round. "You're a quiet sort, so use that, not betraying if your hand is good or bad. And watch for it in others—but be aware that they may be bluffing, making you think what they have is good or bad. Watch them, learn their 'tells'—things about the way they move their fingers, their lips, their eyes, before you're even playing cards with them."

By the seventh hand, he'd won, fair and square. By the tenth, he had won two more. I smiled at him and shook my head, yawning.

"There it is…the fruits of your poker face and a keen mind. You didn't need a teacher. You only needed the opportunity to play."

"Thank you," he said, with a pleased little smile, "for giving me one."

"Of course," I said, rising. "Now, I think I can sleep. And you?"

"Yes." He gathered the worn cards together and placed them in a wooden box, beside another deck. "Will you teach me how do that thing while shuffling, sometime?"

"The bridge?" I asked. "Of course. By the time Javier finally gives you a chance to play, he won't recognize his baby brother."

He grinned at that, and we turned to go—just as Javier was coming through the front door. He looked up at us in surprise, took off his hat, hung it on a peg, and his cape beneath it. "You two are up rather late," he said, obviously waiting for an explanation.

"Yes," Mateo said, turning to follow me up the stairs. "I'm not as young as I used to be, brother."

"We'll see if you say that tomorrow when it's time to rise and see to your studies," Javier said. But his eyes were on me, clearly wishing I'd stay behind.

Instead, I hurried up several more stairs, widening our distance. I didn't need time with him. I needed to steer clear of him, because the more time we spent together, the harder our separation would be. And if we found ourselves alone…and he kissed me again… No, I'd let things go too far.

And soon, I'd have to set it all straight.

The next day, as soon as breakfast was done and Javier and the latest guests headed toward Bonita Harbor, Doña Elena requested a stable boy bring around two saddled horses and called for two armed men to accompany us on our ride. "Request that Hector and Ignacio attend us." Her eyes moved to me. "My dear, are you ready?"

I nodded. Perhaps if I had this conversation with her at last, she could help me convince Javier to let me have my lamp back. To try and get back to my own time. Panic was building in my chest, as day by day these people were weaving me more deeply into their lives, making me forget where—and when—I truly belonged. Even last night, with Mateo, had made me feel more at home!

"May we go with you, Mamá?" Estrella asked eagerly, the first note of hope in her tone I'd heard since seeing her baby cousin depart.

"No, my dear. You and Francesca must stay here and see to your correspondence; there is much that requires your attention after our absence."

"But Mamá," the girl said, "that will only take—"

"This is a ride that Señorita Ruiz and I must take on our own," the grand lady replied firmly.

Estrella clamped her lips shut, saying nothing more, although her big brown eyes radiated disappointment. Francesca, standing behind her, had a measure of resentment in her eyes. But Doña Elena, ignoring them, turned toward the doorway and looked to me. "Come, my dear. Let us change into our riding habits. We shall meet momentarily in the front hall, yes? It's a pretty day for a ride."

"Yes, yes," I mumbled, barely glancing to the window. My breakfast roiled in my stomach. How was I supposed to deal with this formidable woman? Tell her enough truth to satisfy whatever curiosity was driving her, and yet not too much?

Upstairs, Maria was waiting on me, with items of clothing splayed across the bed behind her: the freshly washed, ruby colored, long-sleeved fitted coat; long skirt; and tiny top hat with veil. She had the cursed corset back in her hands. "Forgive me, Señorita," she said, glancing aside in embarrassment.

Yeah, yeah. I sighed and reached for the top button on my brown day dress. I'd made it all the way to Santa Barbara and back in the cursed riding habit and corset—what would one more day be? Maria swiftly saw to the other buttons, I slipped it off, and she wrapped the corset around my chest and belly. In seconds, it seemed, she had it laced up the back again, like an old…*friend.*

That was it. I just needed to make peace with the awful thing, and I wouldn't resent it so much. That's what I told myself anyway.

Doña Elena awaited me in the foyer, looking fresh and smart in her own all-black riding habit and not the least out of breath. In fact, she looked totally pumped up for this adventure ahead. *That makes one of us.* After the trek south and back, I was over riding in such a contraption. *So* over it.

"Ready, my dear?" she asked.

"As ready as I'll ever be," I muttered, passing by her through the door a servant had opened. I blinked in the bright sunshine, again thankful for the slight shielding of the veil on the hat. *Sunglasses, version 1.8.4.0.*

Doña Elena paused behind me a moment and then followed, mounted and looking prim and perfect. Her silver hair was in a neat bun at the nape of her neck, her black hat pinned at a jaunty angle. With a glance back at me, sitting more confidently on my gelding today, despite my sore butt screaming to get back off, she set off at a trot.

Sighing heavily, I followed, just wanting to get it over with now.

Our two armed guardians fell into line behind me, their rifles across their laps. But they seemed relaxed, not really concerned at all. "So are the armed guards really necessary?" I asked the woman, when she settled her mare back to a walk, and I could come alongside.

Guards had been with us all the way to Santa Barbara and back, of course, just more…subdued. Today they were all Secret-Servicey. Because I went with Doña Elena alone? Maybe the grand old lady demanded extra protection. Maybe she was more at risk, a bigger target, like the First Lady or something. I hid a smile, thinking of Hector or Ignacio with ear pieces and black sunglasses, speaking into a microphone at their wrists. *"Lady Hawk is on the move. I repeat, Lady Hawk is on the move."*

She glanced at me, and her dark eyes flicked back to the men behind me. "You were not the only one who saw the heavy taxes Javier paid at the charreada. To be seen without them would be to invite dark thoughts among our enemies, no? Many might suppose that if the rancho had that much gold to pay, there must be much more available to pay a ransom…Javier and I are determined not to give them such an opportunity."

My mind flicked back through all the people we'd met up with. Who would dare to truly threaten them? The Vargases? Lieutenant de Leon? But wasn't she a fan of that guy, given that he was clearly a Mexican loyalist? Maybe she referred to Patricio… "You have far more friends than enemies, from what I've seen," I said.

"And yet it only takes one," she said, turning away from me.

I thought about having enemies in my own time. Guys I knew sometimes had enemies, mostly those in gangs, or the football players with their chief rivals. Girls at school did too, when they got sucked into Stupid-Girl politics or love triangles. But I couldn't think of one person I'd call an *enemy*.

Did the Venturas have true enemies, really? I thought back on the rodeo, the Vargases, and the nameless sea captain with Francesca, making them all tense.

"Why do you have enemies?" I dared to press.

Her shoulders stiffened, as if irritated by my questioning, but she looked back to me again. "We have money and position, which others envy and would like to make their own. We are against those who lobby for statehood. This is Mexican territory," she said with a firm nod. "We shall defend her with everything we have against the aggressions of the States, or Russia, or anyone else who dares to trespass."

"Oh," was all I could manage. *That's gonna be a problem, Lady… because in about nine years, the forty-niners will be arriving up north.*

She waved a hand in irritation. "That Patricio comes calling and fills Javier's mind with all sorts of intrigue. My boy has more than enough to manage here on the rancho; he need not take on the concerns of foreign politics."

I filed that away in my brain, wondering if that played into Javier's desire to keep watch over his family 24/7, with guards, if he couldn't be present himself. With so many coming in and out of the harbor… Again, I recalled his first thought when we met—to accuse me of being a spy. Just what did he fear I might discover? That he had more cowhides than he claimed? A secret stash of tallow? What could a ranchero in the middle of nowhere have to hide?

We spent the rest of the ride in silence, and my heart continued to beat faster and faster, the closer we got to the cove. What was I to tell her? The only thing I came back to, again and again, was the truth.

Lord, I prayed, *give me something else. Something she'll believe.*

But the only thing I got back again was *Truth. Tell her the truth.*

Yeah. That would never work.

I forced myself to inhale and exhale as best I could. With my heart racing as I faced this confrontation, my breathing constricted, and the corset squeezing the life out of me, I was getting more scared by the minute. I figured I'd likely keel over, off the saddle, leg brace or no. At least it'd be a soft landing in the sand…

We were churning through the dunes, up and down, the sound of waves now in our ears, the scent of saltwater filling our nostrils. And then it sprawled before us, that big, beautiful turquoise Pacific that I recognized as my own, yet felt like I was seeing anew at the same time. Again, I looked around, wondering if I might discover the shadows or ghostlike outlines of businesses I knew, set right about here along the PCH…hidden just behind the veil of time. But as I lifted my *literal* veil, I saw nothing but pristine coastline, and behind us, the vast acreage of Rancho Ventura.

"Where does your property end?" I managed to ask Doña Elena as we reached the first damp sand, evidence of the morning's high tide.

"About two miles southward," she said, gesturing down the coast. "There is a rocky jetty there that marks the beginning of Vargas land."

"What is their rancho called?" I went on, trying to buy time. The two guards split up and stayed high on the crest of the hill, where they could keep watch over us and yet also see any trouble coming from any direction.

"Rancho Vargas, of course," she said, eying me a moment. We looked along the cove, from the big lava boulders on the left, to the shipwreck, and up to George Point on the right. Or was it known as Punta Jorge in 1840? "Where did my son discover you?"

she asked.

"Down there," I said, nodding toward the rocks. "I had fallen asleep."

"And were you anywhere else that day?" she asked softly.

"Up there," I said, gesturing toward the north part of the cove. "At low tide."

She frowned slightly. "Show me."

With a sigh, I led the way, my mount growing less labored, the closer we were to the water, as the wet sand became firmer beneath his hooves. We passed the big bones of the old shipwreck, and I paused, right above the place I figured the pools would be in a century or two. "It was here that it all began," I said.

Her dark eyes moved to the wash of the waves upon the smooth sand and back to me. She unhooked her leg and slid from the saddle, holding on to the horn in a graceful move that set her to rights in a moment. Blinking, I followed suit, but my skirt slid up to my thighs as I did so, and I landed heavily, almost falling over.

Her eyes widened in surprise as I attempted to straighten and pretend that hadn't just happened. She stepped forward. "Who are you, girl? Who are you really? You are educated, but you have none of our social graces." She lifted a hand toward my horse. "You appear never to have ridden sidesaddle before. Your Spanish is neither common Mexican nor Castilian in accent. Your education is…remarkable. And you play the guitar? No woman I have ever met plays the guitar."

I stared back at her. "If I could tell you, I would," I said, again choosing honesty.

She sniffed and looked down the length of the cove. "You said you found the golden lamp in tide pools here?"

"Yes," I said. "There were so many starfish with it, they practically covered it up. But then a wave passed and they moved, and I saw it. I fished it out from the very center of a pool."

She eyed me from the side, hands clasped before her waist. "I have come here often. Truthfully, it is one of my very favorite coves, and my husband and I used to picnic here. But I have never seen tide pools, no matter the time of day." She turned to face me. Reached out and took my hand. "There is something you wish to tell me. Something you're holding back," she whispered. "Dare to tell me the truth, girl. I like to think of myself as a fair-minded person."

I cleared my throat, searching the wrinkled lines of her face, the deep pools of her eyes, wondering if I truly dared to do so. I wished I had that lamp in my hands right then. I wished I could tear down the beach, into the water, wishing, wishing to go back. I had simply done something wrong that day I came here, slipped through a portal I was never meant to go through…

"Zara," she said, squeezing my hand. "The pools," I said urgently, "they were here. *Right here.* I swear it. There were orange and purple starfish. More than I'd ever seen before. A fisherman pointed me toward it. I'd never seen him before…"

"A man," she repeated. "Fishing along the shore? Perhaps one of our men?"

But she was clearly more intent upon me than discovering the identity of the man.

"I do not wish to be a burden to you, Doña Elena," I said. "More than anything, I wish I could go home." I pulled my hand from hers and lifted it to my forehead, itching where the veil blew against my skin.

"You are anxious to return home. But you cannot. Even the tide pools that gave you the golden lamp are not where you last saw them.

They've disappeared, further blocking your path home."

I searched her profile, still pretty, but with strong, almost masculine lines, puzzling over her words. "Yes," I faltered. "Exactly. How…how could you know that?"

There was something in her tone that told me she knew. She *knew* what I was saying. *Believed* me.

She paused there, her distinct profile a silhouette against the sand dunes behind her. And then she turned to me, as if weighing her answer. "Because I, too, came to this family in a similar manner."

CHAPTER 18

It felt like every ounce of oxygen had been squeezed from my lungs. I had to remind myself to breathe and then breathe again.

"Pardon me?" I managed to squeak out. "What did you say?"

"You understood me," she said solemnly. "It was your golden lamp that brought me to Carlos, Javier's father, in España. I was but a girl, longing for something more, something to move my heart, when I stumbled upon that lamp in a marketplace, very far from here."

I held my breath, staring at her. "You…found the lamp. *My* lamp. In a market." I lifted my veil, wanting nothing between us.

"Yes, Zara," she said, staring into my eyes. "I was facing spinsterhood, almost thirty. And it was the year of our Lord, 1741."

We were silent and still for a moment. Then two.

"It was 1741," I dragged out, when I could manage it. About a hundred years prior to our current day.

There was no way this woman was older than fifty-five or sixty, despite her silver hair. "And you were transported to the year…"

"I arrived in 1810," she said, turning to look at the valley before us. "I was the same, from head to toe, but I was in a different era than my own, far more advanced. With young men sailing to the colony of Mexico and others north from there…"

"So you went f-forward almost eighty years," I stammered. "I—" I hesitated, wondering if she was really ready to take this in. "I seem to have gone *back* almost a hundred and eighty."

"A *hundred* and eighty," she breathed, her brows rising. "That must be quite…disorienting."

"Quite," was all I could manage to respond. But although she'd mentioned disorientation, I hadn't felt any disorientation within her at all.

Long moments went by, both of us lost in our own thoughts.

"So how did you come across the lamp?" she asked gently. "Can you tell me more?"

"As I said…I found it in a tide pool. Those tide pools, as near as I can figure, are buried by about fifty feet of sand, right here below us. In my time," I rushed on, "the beach is far narrower, the sand eroded. The shipwreck is gone. There are houses all in a line, right up there…"

Her face sparked with alarm. I figured I'd better stick to the bare facts.

"The morning after my abuela died—my only family left to me," I went on, the story now spilling from me. If she had slipped through time too, maybe she knew the way to return! "I went for a walk on the beach. Abuela always loved starfish, and I went down to the beach and saw so many…That fisherman told me there were more in a pool just a bit farther out, so I went out among the rocks. And, after a wave passed, I saw the lamp. I climbed down into the pool and grabbed it."

"And then?" she prompted softly, as if half-remembering her own experience.

"Then I was back on the beach, studying it, wondering what it might be and where it came from…thinking back on my last conversation with my grandmother." I shook my head as if to bring myself back. "There was a loud pop, a bright light, I felt sick to my stomach and, and…I was here."

She nodded, her own black eyes now wide and distant, the lines of her mouth drawn.

"And you…Doña Elena, tell me, please. How did you come to find that lamp?"

"It was sold to me in a *suk* in Marrakesh," she said. "I lived in España and was traveling with my father, a merchant. The dealer said it would bring me love," she said, arching a brow my way. "My father said if it would make me a wife rather than an aging spinster daughter, he would buy it for me."

"And he did?"

"He did," she said.

I was holding my breath, making me light-headed. Was it the corset or our conversation? *Probably both.* I forced myself to inhale, exhale. *Marrakesh.* That was in Morocco, I thought, which explained the odd writing on the lamp. "And then what happened?"

"I was on my father's ship, and we were just docking at home—in Valencia," she added, looking my way to see if I knew of it, "and I was holding the lamp and thinking about what I wanted in the future."

Thinking about what I wanted in the future.

"And then?" I prompted, when she fell silent, staring again toward the horizon.

"And then I was still in Valencia, but in a very different time than my own." She lifted her fingers and snapped. "A pop, a flash of light, the nausea, as you described, and my papá, his ship, the men…they were gone." She blinked several times, as if reliving it. "Forever," she added, in a whisper.

She stepped forward, toward the water, head held high, shoulders back, the epitome of Spanish grace and gentility.

"What did you do?" I whispered, stepping up beside her. "What did you say? How did you explain yourself?"

"I didn't," she said, turning toward me partway, half with me, half in that moment. "And in time it didn't matter. Because I'd found what I'd wanted in that future, right there in *that* time, where Carlos found me. Love."

I met her gaze. "Carlos found you there? He was the one to discover you, help you?"

"Yes." She took my hand. "And a year ago, when I tossed that same golden lamp out to the sea here, I prayed for you, dear girl. For a woman who might capture my wayward son's heart. Captivate his mind. Intrigue him and anchor him into the destiny that is his for the taking. Making a life here, where his father worked so hard to establish a—"

"W-wait," I said, pulling away in confusion. "You threw the lamp back into the sea? Like… *bait* for a fish?"

"I didn't think of it in such a way," she said. "It was a prayer, a wish. For someone seeking us with a similar prayer or wish." She lifted her hands, brows arching together. "And here you are! God be praised!" Her face faltered. "You are not quite what I imagined, but if the blessed Father has ordained this, who am I to—"

"No. Hold on." Anger stirring in me, I lifted a finger and waved it back and forth. "I didn't want this. I didn't want to leave my own *time*."

"I understand. You wanted something bigger, more important than even your own time." She matched every step I took away from her. "Something your heart wanted."

"Did you not try to get back? To your own time?" I asked, lifting my hands to my head.

"I tried, yes. But don't you see? My wish was already coming true!"

I shook my head and walked away from her. Here I had feared she'd think me crazy. But she was the crazy one. And she'd pulled me into her weird time warp!

"Zara," she said, striding after me, trying to take my arm.

"No!" I said, wrenching away from her grasp. "Leave me alone!"

But she didn't, following me step for step, waiting for me to slow and face her again. The danged corset was working against me. In minutes, I was gasping for breath and sat down heavily in the sand, not caring if I harmed her precious old riding habit. Surprisingly, she sank to the sand beside me.

"You're angry," she said simply.

"Yes, I'm angry!" I spat out. "You…you trapped me!"

"Trapped? Or gave you just the right invitation?"

"What does it matter? You pulled me here, into your time and out of my own! Now what am I supposed to do?" I cried.

She shrugged. "Allow your new destiny to unfold. If it is half as grand as my own, you will not regret it."

I shook my head. My hat flapped on my head, and I angrily pulled the pins out and sent it flying behind me. *Just what I'd like to do to her…*

We sat in silence for a bit, staring at the waves cresting, washing over the beach, and receding. Then she dared, "May I ask what you wished for, Zara?"

I frowned. I didn't want to tell her. I didn't ever want to speak to her again. If I could possibly get away, I would've. But there wasn't exactly a bus stop up the road…there wasn't even a stagecoach coming through. I rubbed my face and watched the waves, willing myself back to calm. I had to think this through. Find my way. Strangling the woman who brought me here probably wouldn't do the trick.

"I wished for adventure," I muttered, feeling like an idiot. "To see the world and meet others from different cultures and ways of life." Why had I ever shared something so intimate with Abuela? If I hadn't, I wouldn't have been thinking back to that conversation, right when I was holding the cursed lamp…

"You did not have much adventure in your life," she said tentatively, "in your own time?"

"No," I said. "We never went anywhere. There was never enough money or opportunity for such things." I arched a brow at her. "I am no fine lady from a fine family, as you have guessed. My abuela ran a *restaurant*."

"I see," she said gently. "But I think your abuela must have been a very fine lady indeed, no matter where you lived. I can see it in you, Zara, despite our…differences. What else?" she asked, after silence settled between us.

"Love," I admitted. "Real love. Apparently the curse of every girl who slips through time?" We shared a brief, wry smile before I recovered my anger again, remembering that she wasn't my confidante. She was the one who made me come here. And she feared kidnappings! This was the Mother of all Kidnappings, wasn't it?

"Anything else?" she prodded.

What was the harm? I thought wearily. I'd already told her the rest. "Family," I said with a sigh, knowing I'd played right into her hands. I closed my eyes and shook my head. "Back home, in my own time, it was just the two of us. And after Abuela died—"

"You had no one," she finished softly. "But don't you see, Zara? You have the potential of claiming *everything*. Here. With us. This adventurous life you seek, learning about others, perhaps even traveling—maybe even as far as Monterey or Mexico. And love?" Her lips quirked. "Family? My children already are taken with you. *All* of my children."

"No," I said, rising, shaking my head in anger. "I want to claim all of that at home, in my *own* time."

"But why must you go back?" she pressed, standing up too. "Who is waiting on you? You said yourself that it was only you and your grandmother…"

"I have friends! Employees at the restaurant who are counting on me! Probably looking for me right now!"

She blinked and wrinkled her brow at me in confusion. "Employees?"

"Yes!" I didn't want to explain any further. I was out of patience. "You listen to me, Doña Elena," I said, shaking my finger at her. "You got me here. Now you need to get me *home*."

She stared back at me, lifting her chin, and I faltered. It was the practiced move of every Mexican matriarch I knew, designed to instill terror in everyone younger. And most of the older ones too.

"You listen to me, *girl*," she said sternly. "You have been granted every wish your heart cried out for. But you are too foolish to recognize it yet. I have great faith in the One who brought me to Carlos and you to Javier, so I shall pray that your foolishness will diminish in time." She waved her hand grandly.

"Javier? What if I was brought here to meet one of the Vargases? Or Captain Worthington? Or—I don't know…someone else? What makes you so sure it was *Javier* who was to claim my heart?"

"Because he found you first, just as Carlos found me." She looked down her regal nose at me.

"That doesn't mean anything. It's just what you choose to believe."

"You are here to stay, Zara. The sooner you accept it, the happier you will be."

I let out a cry of rage then, clenching my fists and narrowly stifling my desire to tackle her to the sand and fill her mouth with it. "Leave me! Go home! I just want to be alone!"

She stood there, stunned a moment. Maybe no one had spoken to her in such a way for a very long time, if ever. "We shall speak again of this," she said curtly, pivoting to walk back toward her horse. "And I shall teach you more of the social graces of our own time, to help you adjust."

"The only instruction I want from you is how to find my way out of here!" I yelled after her.

She ignored me as if I were nothing more than a spoiled toddler throwing a tantrum.

And then I sat back down on the sand and practically did just that.

CHAPTER 19

I saw her when my tears finally seemed spent, and I was breathing in that hiccupping sort of way after a Big Cry. That wolf-dog, coming around the point, sitting down for a second, checking out the whole beach, and then turning back to me. I looked up the hill, worried that one of the guards was still there, ready to shoot at it, but Doña Elena had apparently given my custody over to whatever fates had brought us both here, to this place and this time, and honored my request to be alone.

Who knew? Maybe after the last of that conversation, she'd decided to go and fetch the lamp from the safe after all, eager to send me home. Or maybe she was hoping a kidnapper would swoop in and take me away…

The dog was a welcome distraction. At least I thought she was a dog. She had to be a blend, since she was too small to be fully wolf and too big to be fully dog. I couldn't have said why I didn't fear her. She just seemed tame, a guardian of sorts for me. She paused about thirty feet away, sidling back and forth, lifting her nose to the air to smell me, I supposed. My gelding, a quarter mile beyond, caught the wolf-dog's scent and whinnied nervously, ears perked forward, but the dog didn't seem to be on the hunt.

She was looking at me. "Come here, sweet pup," I crooned, lifting my hand, palm up. "Come, my *centinela*," I said, making a sound of invitation with my lips, wishing I had a treat of some sort to offer her. My guardian, my sentinel. "Centinela," I repeated to myself. "Shall I call you that?"

She moved ten feet closer, then sat down on her haunches, again lifting her nose to the air.

"Come, sweet girl. You're so pretty," I said, getting up.

My movement sent her skittering away again. She loped back and forth in an arc, keeping distant. I knelt again, lifting my hand, palm up. After a moment, she ventured closer. Twenty feet away. Fifteen. Ten.

She was beautiful. Gray and white with patches of black and the brightest blue eyes. "Hello, Centinela," I said softly. "Did you sense I needed a friend right now?"

She took another step, and then another. Just five feet away from me now, close enough that I could see sand clinging to her furry legs.

Three feet. Two. Her nose twitched. Then those bright blue eyes cast beyond me. The wolf-dog tore off, back up the beach toward George Point, and as I glanced back, the first gunshot rent the air.

"No! Stop!" I cried.

It was Javier, sliding from his saddle, aiming with his revolver across his forearm this time, even as he judged the growing distance between him and his prey. He squeezed off a second shot.

"Javier! No!" I screamed, holding my breath until I saw he had missed again.

He shoved his revolver in his holster and turned toward me, his face a mask of fury. He trudged down the sandy dune. "What were you thinking, Zara? That animal is dangerous!"

"No, she's not!" I said, picking up my skirts and making my way toward him as fast as he was coming toward me. "She's tame! A pet for someone!"

"Well, she'd better get off my land before she becomes a *pelt* to trade."

"You wouldn't!"

"I would!"

We stood there, face to face for a moment, both panting.

"What happened here?" he finally asked. "Hector came riding for me. Said you and my mother had some sort of spat, and she left you behind?"

"Yes," I said. "By my request. I was fine! Fine," I repeated. I turned away from him, back toward the sea. Doña Elena's little top hat rolled across the sand toward us, as if begging me to put it back on. "I didn't need you to ride out here for me."

"Obviously you did," he said, coming around me to enter my line of vision again. His white shirt was unbuttoned one more than usual, flapping a little open, giving me a generous view of the smooth, golden-brown expanse of his chest. I hurriedly looked to the water. "Because if I hadn't," he went on, "that wolf would've been having you for supper!"

"Wolves don't attack people," I muttered tiredly. "That's a myth."

"Oh no? They have no trouble attacking my sheep and cattle."

"Well, that one wasn't going to attack. We were becoming...friends."

He let out a wondering laugh and came further around to face me. "Who are you, Zara? A girl who just appears on my shore, who plays the guitar like an angel, breaks the noses of her attackers, and charms wolves—"

"Dogs," I corrected. "I think she's a dog."

"So be it!" he said, lifting a hand in exasperation. "Charms *wolf-dogs* to eat from her hand." He stared at me, as if he couldn't decide whether to throttle the truth out of me or take me into his arms.

"Who are you?" he whispered, lifting a hand as if to touch my face.

"I'm no one," I muttered, stepping away from him. "Just a traveler making her way through. I'm sorry I upset your mother. As soon as I can find other accommodations, I will—"

"Wait, I was not suggesting that you needed to *leave*." He grabbed my arm, turning me gently back toward him. But there was no threat in his action, only concern. "You've been weeping," he said, a little shocked. He lifted his hand to my cheek, gently urging me to look up at him. "What made you cry? My mother?"

I met his eyes. "There's just so much, Javier. So much I cannot tell you."

"Cannot, because you don't know?" he asked, gentling his tone. "Or cannot because you do not wish to?"

"Both," I whispered.

He leaned closer to me, his thumb tracing the curve of my cheek. "So all of your past is not truly forgotten. Some of what you hold back is a secret. Do you not yet trust me?"

"Yes," I whispered. "But I cannot tell you, Javier. I simply cannot. I'd understand if you need me to go."

"No, that can't be the answer," he said huskily. "All I know is that you are unlike any woman I have ever met, Zara Ruiz." He shook his head slightly, as if in wonder. "And I hate it that my mother made you cry. What was it? What tore such a terrible rift between you? Did she guess your secret?"

I wanted to tell him then. Just let it all spill out. But it was one thing to share my secret and another to expose his mother's too.

I cast about for what I *could* say. "Your mother…believes I shouldn't try to return to my own home. It's as if…it matters not to her. She thinks I should only be content to be here, with y-your family."

His handsome eyes lit up with surprise and a flash of bitterness. "It was not her place, Zara, to say such things. Of course you must wish to regain your memory. It must drive you nearly mad to not remember." He paused. "But would it be so awful, truly? To remain here with…us?"

I sighed and looked down to the sand then back into his eyes. "We argued about that, Javier. It's not the right…*time* for me to be here. With you."

His hands dropped away from me, and he stepped back as if he'd been struck. He swallowed hard. "I see."

Part of me silently screamed *no*, aware that I'd hurt him. But part of me was relieved. When he was touching me, looking so caring and concerned for me…that was a sort of pull I didn't need right now, when I was thinking about how to get home. I'd gotten caught up—so caught up in this time, with these people, that I'd started to forget that I didn't belong here at all.

He rubbed the back of his neck and stared at me with big puppy-dog eyes, making him look all kinds of sexy. I hurriedly glanced to the waves again.

"So that is what made her angry?" he asked. "Angry enough to leave you and take both guards with her? Because you refused her? Refused…us?"

"No. I asked her to leave," I muttered. "I wanted to be alone."

He huffed a laugh. "Except for your wolf-dog."

I smiled and glanced sidelong at him. "Yes, except for Centinela," I said. "*She* was welcome."

He shook his head, silently chiding me for going so far as to name her. "And then I intruded."

"Yes," I said softly, crossing my arms, wanting to forget that moment he touched my face so tenderly.

I could feel him staring at me. "But that still doesn't explain your tears."

"I was angry," I said with a shrug. "Sometimes I cry when I'm angry." *Like when I want to kill someone.*

"That is an odd reaction," he mused.

"Is it?" I asked. I'd cried when I was angry for as long as I could remember, which invariably made me angrier, because I didn't want to cry. It had been especially bad in elementary school. The bullies always thought they had the upper hand. It was part of why I'd agreed to learn self-defense, I mused, wanting to know how to take someone down if they were attacking me. Now I was confident that I could face anyone in a dark alley and not dissolve into tears. But when someone wasn't physically attacking me, if I was just emotionally angry…I dissolved into tears, nine times out of ten.

I almost itched for a physical fight now, and my knife. My Krav Maga instructor had taught me how to use my pocket knife well—how to disarm someone threatening me with one. I wished I'd taken it that night I'd gone to the beach. A bit more of home, my past, to remember it by. A bit more protection in a land, a time, in which I felt crazy-vulnerable.

"I will try not to make you angry," Javier said beside me, bringing me back to the present. "I don't like to see a woman cry." He sighed. "Did I make you want to cry the other day when I said I'd keep your golden lamp?"

"Yes."

"You cried?"

"A little. But mostly I plotted how to break into your safe."

He laughed at that. "Did you try?" He turned to face me, a look of wonder etched into his expression again.

"I haven't had the chance yet. But I will."

His smile broadened. "I suppose that next you'll remember that you're a bank robber and have never met a safe you couldn't crack."

"Why, yes," I said. "That is indeed my next surprise for you."

He reached up to tuck a strand of my hair behind my ear. "You're not really a bank robber, are you? That isn't your secret?"

I smiled. Was that a hint of true fear in his eyes? "No," I said. "That's not on my list of talents, as much as I wish it were." I reached out to take his big hand in both of mine. "Please, Javier. Will you please give me my lamp back?"

"Why? Why do you need it? Unless you are leaving..." Concern tightened the muscles at his cheek and jawline.

"I'm not leaving. Not yet. It just would make me feel better, having it in my room. Please?"

"Just as soon as you tell me your secret," he said, tipping up my chin and looking over my face as if he meant to sketch it later. "That's when I shall give you back your golden lamp."

I swallowed hard, feeling angry tears prick behind my eyes. "Javier..."

"Zara," he returned, leaning closer, "those are my terms. Are you ready?"

He leaned closer still, searching my eyes. *Ready for another kiss?* I thought madly. *Or for me to tell him?*

"I can't, Javier, I just can't." I said, wrenching aside and striding angrily away to grab the little hat. Why did he have to press me on it? Why did he have to make me feel all that I was feeling for him, confusing the issue?

I might've been sent here for some weird reason, but I wasn't a foolish, googly-eyed, romantic chica, ready to accept some crazy fairy tale that it was for love. I was smarter than Doña Elena on this front. Wiser.

I was a self-made woman. Making my way through a somewhat challenging life. Fairy tales didn't come around for girls like me. They came to girls who grew up in Beverly Hills or Palos Verdes. Girls who got a shiny new BMW on their sixteenth birthday, girls who had handsome boys hanging around them all the time, not just when they *flew through time*.

I trudged up to my gelding, lifted my hand, and smiled again as he turned to me for a good scratch of his long nose before I grabbed hold of the reins. But then, as I studied the stirrup, I bit my lip. I'd never mounted a horse in a corset without help; I could barely breathe, let alone move well enough to attempt it.

"May I assist you?" Javier asked, leading his mare up to me.

My first instinct was to say no, to find a way on my own. But I knew that would be idiotic. I might be trying until sundown and have to walk all the way home. And he would never leave me alone. He'd stand back and watch me flounder in the fallout of my own stubborn pride.

"Yes," I said primly. "Thank you."

He bent to offer me his interlaced hands. I lifted my skirts slightly, set one boot in his hands, and reached for the saddle horn with the other.

"Ready?" he asked.

"Ready," I said.

"Up you go," he said, lifting me neatly into place.

I busied myself with arranging my skirts, trying to ignore his warm hand as he settled my boot in a stirrup and then looked up at me. "Good?"

"Yes, thank you," I said, taking the reins from him.

His mouth twitched, as if he held back a smile, wanting to keep toying with me. As we set off for home, I wondered just how long I'd be able to hold out against Javier and his longing looks and angsty questions.

I have to get that lamp and get the heck out of here, I thought. *I just have to.*

Because day by day, I was falling deeper and deeper, like the tide pools buried by the sands of time.

CHAPTER 20

The next day at the ranch was pretty tense. I managed to avoid Doña Elena and Javier most of the day after breakfast, and I convinced Maria to bring me my lunch, claiming illness.

Because I *was* sick in a way. Sick at heart, sick with grief, sick with worry. That was how I justified it anyway.

When I didn't show up for supper, Francesca came to check on me, carrying a tray of tea and *churros*, looking perfectly put together, as usual. Like a mini-Elena. "May I join you for a moment? Or are you convalescing?" she asked.

No, no, I thought, staring out my window. *I'm flat-out spent on the "convalescing" front. I just don't want to go out there to face Doña Elena. Or your brother.* "Come in," I said.

She set the tray on my table and glanced at me. "Well, I must say that you look well," she said. "Your color is high. Or is that a fever? Should you not be in bed?"

"No, I don't think I have a fever," I said. "Please, sit, Francesca. Stay with me for a while."

"Are you certain?" she asked, her delicate, dark brows arcing together. "I will not tax you?"

"I'm certain," I said, gesturing toward the chair.

She took a seat by the table and poured me a cup of tea. "I take it you are not ill?"

"No. I just needed…to be alone."

"Ah," she said, wise eyes scanning mine. "Is it my older brother or my mother who has caused this? Or Jacinto, begging you for that game of backgammon? Or Estie, wanting to braid your hair?"

I matched her gentle smile. "No, none of them. Or, well… maybe all of them."

Francesca's smile faded, though, as she set down her cup. "Zara, I needed to ask you about something. I heard Mamá and Javier arguing…"

Noise downstairs made us look up, then to each other. The front door opened and closed. Then we heard Javier say, "What a surprise, to see you here," his tone tight, displeased.

Frani rose. "Do you mind?" she asked, gesturing toward the door, clearly more interested in the newcomers than me now.

I followed her out into the hall but held back, peeking over the edge of the railing toward the front door below as Frani paused partway down the stairs.

"Miss Ventura!" cried a low voice in an English accent. I saw the sweep of a hat and a dark head bob in a bow. "How is it possible that you are even prettier than when we met at the rodeo?"

Frani giggled and hurried down the rest of the stairs. I moved left, trying to see a bit better…

There, I thought, peeking around a column. The man had two others behind him. Doña Elena stood a few paces away, clearly unhappy. Javier, not much better. Only the children looked delighted at the prospect of visitors.

"Madame Ventura," the man said grandly, taking her reluctant hand in his and kissing it. "It has been far too long." He went on to kiss Frani's hand like a proper gentleman and then shook Jacinto's hand in grave, ceremonious fashion, which moved him more clearly into my line of vision. Mateo and Estie were next. "Ah, you are all here," he said. "But what of the mysterious guest I've heard so much about? She is the talk of the entire Alta California coast! I was so disappointed not to meet her at the rodeo."

Now I knew him. The one Frani had flirted with at the rodeo—the man twice her age. The reason why her eyes were so bright, a blush at her cheeks.

"Señorita Ruiz has taken ill today, Captain Craig," Javier said, now sounding oddly stressed. "Perhaps you can make her acquaintance at a later date."

Just then Captain Craig glanced up, and his hazel eyes met mine before I could duck away. "Perhaps," he said, with a secretive glint to his smile.

Javier started to follow his gaze upward, but I moved safely out of sight. I felt childish and silly, but I deeply desired to know what all the fuss was about. Why Doña Elena didn't like this guy. Why Frani did. Why Javier seemed to be hanging back, not the normal gracious host he'd been with every other captain who came to visit.

I needed the distraction. To think of anything but me, the Venturas, and my time-slip conundrum.

I took a deep breath and let it out. I couldn't hide away for days at a time, could I? No matter how uncomfortable I might be in Doña Elena's company, wasn't it sensible to make the most of every hour I had here until it was time for me to head home?

As the group moved into the library, I went to my room, combed out my hair, swept it up into some sort of messy bun—I didn't bother to look—pinned it, and then headed down the stairs.

I found Doña Elena and Javier arguing in hushed tones in the foyer outside the library. "We do not entertain those of his ilk, Javier," she whispered. "Send him on his way. If Lieutenant de Leon heard that we'd entertained him, here on Mexican soil…"

"I cannot simply toss him out the door, Mamá," Javier returned, so quietly I barely heard him. "And he was on 'Mexican soil,' at the rodeo, right under Leon's nose. There is no law against that."

"That is far different than having a *Unionist* here, in our very home!"

Javier took a long, deep breath and pinched his nose. "We need to conduct business with him and others like him. It is unwise to turn him away."

"Unwise? Or have you welcomed him because you want to hear more of his treasonous—" She broke off when she finally saw me, and she gave me a tentative smile. "Why, Zara, my dear. You are feeling better, I see."

"Indeed," I said. "I heard that we had guests, and thought it might be the perfect medicine for what ailed me."

Javier and Doña Elena both frowned at me in confusion.

"Ahh, there she is! I take it this is your mysterious Miss Zara Ruiz?" Captain Craig appeared in the library doorway, as if he'd been standing just inside, listening.

We all turned in surprise to face the man as well as the three others with him, each dressed immaculately in crisp white shirts, long blue jackets with brass buttons above tight-fitting trousers and polished boots.

Javier was immediately at my side, his actions conveying protective-ness and caution. And yet his words were nothing but genteel. "Captain Craig," he said, "may I introduce our guest, Señorita Zara Ruiz?"

"So lovely to meet you, Señorita Ruiz," the captain said in admiration, taking my hand in his and hovering so close to it that I could feel the warm breath from his nostrils. "I've been hearing the most fascinating stories about you." He kissed my knuckles then, his lips warm and dry.

Captain Craig was a few inches shorter than Javier, and yet still had a few on me. And while he was trim, I imagined he was quite fit under that uniform, like the high school baseball players at home versus the football players. Except, you know, about ten years older. And the English accent…I had to admit it. While I loved the sultry nature of my native Spanish, the crisp allure of a proper man's English…well, it could make a modern-day girl swoon.

I turned to greet the others, who were his first mate, Abraham, his steward and his cook. Abraham said, "We are pleased to make your acquaintance, Miss Ruiz."

The captain boomed, "You do know you're the talk of Alta California, do you not? Tell me, Miss Ruiz," he said, clapping Javier's shoulder as he turned his face but didn't release me from his gaze, "how did this lucky dog happen to have you wash up on his shores?"

"Because," I began, searching for the answer that would appeal most to this sort of man, "some sea captain keeps a less-than-perfect account of his passengers. Trust me when I say that when I catch up with him, there will be a dire reckoning."

Captain Craig's eyebrows shot up at the center, his face alight. "Quite right, quite right," he said with a laugh, clapping Javier on the shoulder again. Javier did not look half as amused. "And I've heard you are quite an accomplished musician," he said, offering me his arm. "I was sorely disappointed to miss your performance at the rodeo—perhaps you would indulge me now with a song?"

Javier took a step forward. "I do not think that Señorita Ruiz should tax herself."

"What?" Craig asked, looking at me with wry surprise. "Since when is music taxing? I've always found it quite therapeutic. Do you agree, Miss Ruiz?"

"Why, yes," I said.

He smiled, his grin a fine display of even, white teeth. He wasn't as handsome as Javier, but he was plenty cute. And that accent. That *accent.* I could see why Frani had her crush. Not that he could compete with Javier.

I glanced over his shoulder and saw that Abraham, the first mate, was now offering his arm to the young girl. The two went over to the big oil painting above Javier's desk, as if he'd inquired about its history. Doña Elena, catching sight of the action, bustled in after them to chaperone. She paused to dismiss the younger children from their map puzzle and send them upstairs. Mateo and Frani were apparently allowed to stay behind, though her expression told me that she'd rather sequester the whole lot, keeping them away from the evil presence of this Captain Craig.

"I'll make a bargain with you, Miss Ruiz. Play one song," Craig lifted a finger, shushing Javier's obvious next step to intervene, "one song for us, and we shall be on our way. In *addition*, I shall host you and the Venturas for dinner aboard my ship on the morrow. It appears that Madame Ventura would be far more at ease there than with us here."

"I'm afraid we cannot," Doña Elena intervened, pausing in her herding of children up the stairs. "We must always be ready to host other guests here. We are never certain when another ship might arrive." She cast a look to her glowering son and faltered.

"Perhaps Javier can meet you there, if he must," she sniffed.

"Indeed," Javier said smoothly to his mother. What was this? Did he want to meet with this Craig, just not under the nose of his mother?

"I understand that you have a great deal to look after here, Madame Ventura," Craig said with a level tone and gaze, as if he could see through her lie. "Perhaps, Javier," he said, turning toward his host, "you would like to bring along your enchanting younger sister, and this fine young man, Mateo. And your guest, Miss Ruiz?" His eyes slid to me with a charming grin.

"Oh yes, please, Mamá," Frani begged, instantly at her arm, fairly bobbing in excitement.

Elena's head whipped toward her child, instantly shushing her, then glanced at Javier, but he evaded her gaze. Why? Because he wished to go? Clearly, he was far more open to this Unionist than his mother was…

She paused for a breath and then, spreading her hands, said, "I am grateful for your kind offer, Captain. But I fear a ship is no place for my children. I cannot speak, of course, for Señorita Ruiz, but—"

"Oh, but I would love to accept," I interrupted smoothly. If Javier was going, I wanted to see just what he was up to.

"And Mateo is of age too," Javier said, ignoring his mother's look full of daggers. So he wanted his little brother in on this…

"Excellent," Captain Craig said. "We shall serve a fine meal for you all to enjoy. And if you change your mind, Madame Ventura, you and the others are more than welcome," he said with a genteel bow.

"Thank you, Captain Craig," she managed to reply. Jacinto, Estie, and Frani looked totally depressed at this turn, and I felt a little guilty. At least quiet Mateo looked jubilant.

"Very good! Well, we do not wish to divest you of further hospitality this night, arriving here unannounced, but I did wonder…."

Staring down her nose at him, but also seeing an opportunity to get rid of them sooner than later, Elena bit. "What is it, Captain? We'll see to it at once so you can be on your way."

His smile grew, catlike. "It's that song we hoped to hear from Miss Ruiz…"

She glanced at me, clearly caught.

"Of course," I interceded. "Let me fetch an instrument, and I'll join you in the library. The music room only has a few seats."

"It would be my pleasure to escort you," Captain Craig said, firmly taking my elbow.

"Zara hardly has a need for an escort down our *hall*," Javier said, lifting a confused brow and waving behind him. "Señorita Ruiz knows the way to our music room and back."

"So miserly of you, friend, not to accept my feigned excuse," Craig said good-naturedly, patting him on the chest. "Now stand aside. I have no desire to steal your girl. I only wish to see what other fine instruments your villa holds. I'm a musician myself," he said, with a nod toward Elena, "and I might not have another opportunity to see this room."

He took my elbow and pulled me aside, before Javier could protest further. I caught Javier's puzzled expression, as well as a hint of warning as we passed. What was that supposed to mean? Did he like this guy or not? It was impossible to tell.

Together we walked down the tiled hallway. The captain dropped my elbow and tucked his hands behind his back, assuming the most benign, gentlemanly escort stance possible, which made me feel more relaxed. Perhaps he'd missed my playing but had seen or heard what happened to Lieutenant de Leon at the rodeo…

"Ah, splendid," the captain said, as we entered the music room and he gazed around at the various instruments. He went immediately to the harpsichord and sat down, playing a classical tune so lightly and prettily that I had no choice but to smile with him. "Come, Miss Ruiz," he said, patting the bench beside him before immediately continuing on. "Do you play the harpsichord too? Perhaps we can play a duet. It's a fine instrument."

"Oh, I'm sorry. I do not play the harpsichord. Only guitar."

"Ahh," he said, hands still dancing over the keys. "Pity, that. But I would like to know," he said, so quietly that I had to come around the corner of it to hear him better over the music, "who sent you here, my dear? Are your loyalties with the Mexicans or the Americans? Or are you simply a clever, pretty girl, angling for a wedding ring?"

"I…I'm an American," I said, opting for the closest thing to the truth. "And I did not come here for any reason you have imagined. Now if you will excuse me." I turned and went to the wall, pulling down the guitar. He abruptly left his song and slid from the bench.

I was turning around when I found him right beside me. "An *American*, you say," he said, giving me a penetrating look. "Does that mean you stand for the Unionist cause?"

I frowned. "All I know is that the United States is what is most familiar to me," I said. "Perhaps I lived in one of those United States? My amnesia," I said, putting my hand to my head, "keeps me from saying more."

"Indeed! Such a *mystery* you are, you delightful little minx. Perhaps a convenient little miracle too," he said in a whisper. "I've been trying to woo the Venturas for years. Maybe all I needed was a pretty girl to seal the deal." He touched my chin as if I were already in on his plan.

I narrowed my eyes and edged away from him in confusion. "Shall we go back to the library, Captain?" I asked tightly.

"Indeed," he said, gesturing grandly toward the door. I hurried along, passing Frani, who stood in a small alcove worrying a hangnail, clearly waiting for Captain Craig to come out again. She cast me a jealous, angry look, and I rolled my eyes as I walked on, leaving the two alone to chat. She wanted that dude? Fine! I was hardly in competition for him.

I hurried down the hall, hearing the sailors' laughter in the big room now, and saw Javier waiting for me ahead. I took a breath, relieved to even have him in sight. But when I reached him, he took my arm and pulled me around a big column.

"Ow!" I said. "Javier, what—"

"What do you think you are doing?" he interrupted, shaking me once.

I frowned up at him in confusion. "Entertaining your guest!"

He seemed to catch himself and lifted his head, eased his grip. "Be cautious around him, Zara. He is not all he seems to be."

"I understand. He seems to think I might be willing to assist him in his work of wooing you to the Unionist cause." I left out the fact that he also suspected me of trying to get Javier to propose.

He let out a sigh and took a step away as if to begin pacing, chin in hand. He looked worried. Seriously worried.

I lifted a brow. "Javier, is he…a threat to you?" I thought this was just a tiff between Doña Elena and Craig, with Javier somewhere in the middle.

He let out a humorless laugh, hands on his hips, and shook his head. "Yes. And no. There are things you don't yet understand—about how it is here, what it is to be in my place, the decisions I must make."

"No, I don't. Not really," I said.

"Do me a favor?"

I waited.

"Don't allow him to get you alone again? Always have an escort?"

"It's not me you should be worried about, Javier. It's your little sis. You saw her flirting with him at the rodeo—well, just now she was waiting for us outside the music room in that little alcove."

"Wh-what?" he said, his head snapping in that direction.

"Go," I said, even as he was already in motion.

Taking a firmer grip on the neck of the guitar, I turned and entered the library, forcing a smile as others all around welcomed me with anticipation. Doña Elena sat in the corner, back ramrod-straight, hands clasped in her lap, Mateo at her side. Abraham, the first mate, continued to chat with the other two sailors, doing their best to ignore their silent hostess. I reached for a stool someone had placed in the center of the room, as Captain Craig entered, Frani on his arm, Javier directly behind them.

I didn't look at Doña Elena then. It had to be the last thing she wanted to see.

I sank to my seat, settled the guitar on my lap, placed my fingers over the strings, and wondered, *What would be right? Perfect for this moment?* I had no idea if the songs I knew had been written before 1840, or if I was stealing a future artist's idea. But what choice did I have? I knew what I knew.

As soon as the song came into my head, I didn't question—I set to it, strumming fast, my fingers wildly flying over the chords of the verse, then slowing, quieting. My fingers strummed through the following chorus, then swiftly plucked out each note of the verse. The acoustics of the library were wonderful—I briefly wondered why this wasn't the music room—and then I was lost again in the song. I remembered, distantly, that it was about a torrential love affair that was halted, then rediscovered in time. Belatedly, I felt the heat of my blush as I wondered if these people knew this song… and its context.

But as I opened my eyes and dared to look around, the men exploded into applause. I smiled, laughing under my breath, surprised by the flood of appreciation. Every face glowed with *delight*. That was the only way I could describe it. Well, except for Doña Elena. She looked…*tight*. So did Frani.

I tried to lift my guitar and set it aside, but Captain Craig half rose out of his seat, pulling pleading hands to his chest. "One more, Señorita Ruiz. I beg of you."

Javier nodded, giving me his okay. "One more," he said. "And then we must bid you farewell, Captain."

"Agreed, agreed," he said easily, settling back into the corner of the settee.

I didn't dare to look toward the Ventura women. I could feel their tension from ten feet away, both with their own reasons to dislike this. But I didn't see that I had any other options. I closed my eyes, considering. And this time I remembered something far more subtle. A gentle ballad. I hummed along, in time, the chorus irresistible.

Captain Craig urged me to sing, but I smiled and demurely shook my head as I continued to play. At the end, as the last note hung in the air, I looked around at all those rapt faces. They appeared dumbstruck, as if they'd never heard anything like it in all their lives. And perhaps they hadn't.

Captain Craig began applauding first, and then the rest joined in. "Brava, Miss Ruiz, brava. Would you be so kind as to bring your guitar tomorrow? The men of my ship would appreciate a few songs."

"Certainly."

"*Enchanté,* Miss Ruiz."

"It was so nice to meet you," I returned, having no idea if that was the thing to do. Probably not.

Javier stood, looking even tighter. "Until tomorrow at sundown, Captain?" He shook each of their hands and saw them to the door. As he did so, I slipped up the stairs, instinctively feeling that I'd made things somehow more complicated. Best to become scarce, I thought. Somehow I was in hot water with Javier, his mom, and Frani, all for different reasons.

The guests were out the door before I reached the top of the stairs. I practically raced for my room, hearing Javier behind me, taking the stairs two at a time, his mother calling his name. I was just closing my door when he pressed it back open and marched in.

"What?" I said. "What are you doing?"

"What were *you* doing?" he asked, moving toward me. "You hid away all day in here, and when he comes? Him? *Then* you come out?"

I shook my head, wondering what fueled his rage. Fear or jealousy? "Who is he? I don't know! I was only…curious." I dropped the last word, suddenly ashamed, wondering what harm I'd caused. Captain Craig seemed harmless. A charmer, for sure. But all lights and show, no true stage. And Javier seemed to have a handle on his particular brand of politics…

"*Curious,*" Javier said, taking my arm. "That is a man to be carefully managed," he said. "Every interaction I have with him is a poker match, not a frivolous game."

"You gamble with him?"

"In a way," he said, running his hands through his hair and

over his face. "It is all far too complicated for you, Zara."

"You might be surprised," I said, disliking his patronizing tone.

"No, it is not that I doubt you," he said, reaching out to run his hands down my shoulders to my elbows. "It is that I have yet to uncover all of Alistair Craig's motivations. And I don't wish for you to be in the middle. It may very well be dangerous, because a man like that would not hesitate to use every angle he could to bring me into his fold, including my feelings for you."

I swallowed hard. He had feelings for me. Serious feelings.

He shook his head back and forth, as if he couldn't decide what to do. And then he pulled me roughly against his chest, cradling my head right beneath his. "Saints, woman, what you do to me… Zara, you've practically turned me inside out. Not seeing you all day… Forgive me. I've overreacted, over Craig. It's only that…Oh, Zara. How could I have missed you so much these last hours?"

I could feel his heart pounding as I stood there, certain my own was pounding at a similar staccato beat. He was hugging me, and oh, it felt so good to be in his arms. Warm and welcoming and…

He moved slightly away from me, and he cupped my neck with one hand. Then he caressed my cheek with the other, our faces just a foot apart. "Zara," he breathed, leaning closer. "May I kiss you? Please give me permission to kiss you. Not seeing you all day, and then…And now…Please. May I simply kiss you? Just once?"

I nodded, transfixed; his intoxicating mix of need and frustration mirrored my own. I lifted my lips as he lowered his own to mine, and he began softly, searchingly, as I hesitantly yielded. Then he tugged me deeper and deeper, until we were both gasping for breath.

He stepped away suddenly, leaving me slightly dizzy.

We stared at each other for a long moment.

"There is something between us, yet. Tell me what you must," he whispered. "Tell me your secret, Zara."

"You have secrets of your own," I said, stepping toward him, placing my hand over his heart. "There is something happening—something that involves Captain Craig?—that you don't want me to know either. Perhaps we best both keep our secrets for another day," I breathed, moving even closer. "And just concentrate on this..."

He abruptly stepped away from me, as if trying to regain his composure. "It *can't* wait another day. I must know, Zara, this very night. Who are you?" he repeated, looking pained this time as he said it. "You seem to entrance everyone you meet. Patricio, Rafael, Captain Craig..." He shook his head, winding his fingers through his dark curls and then releasing them. "My family. Even my mother, before yesterday," he said pointedly.

I ignored this last jibe and remained silent for a moment. "Who are *you*?" I asked, half-desperate to get him off this track. We couldn't have this conversation, not now. It would ruin everything! "No one has made me feel the way you do in all my life. No one."

He stepped toward me without hesitation. Took my hips in both of his hands, and bent to rest his forehead against mine. "I am Javier de la Ventura. Do you not yet know me?" he whispered, and *oh*, the look in his eyes...the *look*. "Is there not yet a part of you," he went on, "that has *always* known me, as I've known you?"

He kissed me again, softly.

It was my turn to push him gently away, feeling dazed. "Javier."

"Zara," he breathed, moving in again.

"Javier," I said, more firmly, holding him away with both hands.

He stood there, looking hurt, then chastised. "Forgive me,"

he said, lifting his hands. "I only wanted to—"

"No," I said, raising my hands now, first to stop his speech and then to drop them in conciliatory fashion. "It's all right. I did too," I said softly, smiling as his eyebrows rose in hope. "It's just we can't keep kissing. Not when…" I glanced out my open doorway to the hallway, hoping against hope that none of his family had seen any part of that make-out session. "Not when I haven't told you what I must. There are things you need to know…things that might change everything."

And make you want to never kiss me again…

He lifted his chin, his jaw clenching, his brow lowering. Then he sat down heavily on my stool, and took a long, deep breath. It was as if he fought to bring his attention back to what mattered, rather than the crazy pull between us.

I sank down to the edge of my bed, three feet away.

His dark eyes met mine. "Tell me, Zara. What you must. Quickly."

I stared at him. Waffled. Wondered.

He leaned forward, resting his arms on his legs. "Is it as I feared? Are you a spy?"

I blinked. We were back to that again?

"For the Union? Did Captain Craig leave you on my shores? Was he here to check on you? Was that why he insisted on escorting you to the music—"

"I'm no spy, Javier," I blurted out, shaking my head. "I'm… I'm from the future."

"What?" His full lips quirked to the side, as if he thought he'd misheard me.

"It's true. That golden lamp I came with? It brought me here, almost a hundred and eighty years back in time."

His dark eyes shifted back and forth, and a frown came and went as if some things now made sense, but then he dismissed it, shaking his head. "That's impossible." He rose, reaching for me. "It must be your head injury, making you believe something so fanciful. You—"

"No," I said, standing in turn and putting up a hand, warning him not to come closer. "It's the truth. The *truth*, Javier."

He stared at me. "How is that possible?"

"I don't know. All I know is that I was on that beach and I found that lamp and I was thinking about what I wanted in life, and the next moment, I was here."

"Here," he said slowly. "As in, *now*."

"Yes."

He shook his head again. "Zara, what you're saying is impossible. You're saying that that old lamp is some sort of fantastical device, capable of transporting a person from one time to *another*?" His last words came out in a scoff, making me defensive.

"Yes. That's exactly what I'm saying."

"You're unwell," he said, lifting a hand, his face awash with concern. "Not in your right mind."

"I wish that was the case, truly. It'd be easier to accept, in a way. But no, this is the truth, Javier. I am from the future."

He frowned and shook his head slowly. "No."

"Yes," I said, matching his tone.

"This is far worse than anything I feared, Zara. I'm telling you, you're unwell. That blow you took to your head…We will seek a doctor. I will take you to Monterey. Or to the East, if necessary."

"There was no blow to my head, Javier. No blood, no bruising, because—"

"Perhaps we can secure passage with John, to Panama. Get you to the East. They have better doctors there."

"Javier…I am from the future. I am completely in my right mind. I know it sounds crazy."

"He should return in the next couple of weeks. He'd be more than—"

"Listen to me!" I cried, leaning forward too. "I am telling you the truth!"

He gave me an incredulous look and paused, gathering himself. "You want me to believe that you are from the future," he said tonelessly. "Almost two centuries distant."

"Yes."

"Forgive me," he said, shaking his head. "I do not."

It was my turn to pause. Somehow, I hadn't expected his outright disbelief. Anger flashed through me. Tears pricked behind my eyes. "Ask your mother, Javier. Ask *her* if what I say is true."

His lips clamped into a line. "My mother. I don't think it wise that we bring her into this sort of hysteria."

"It isn't *hysteria*," I said, frowning and wiping away my hot tears. "It is the truth, and she knows it."

He shook his head sorrowfully and reached for my hand. "Zara, I didn't mean to make you cry."

"Listen to me," I whispered urgently, taking his hand in both of mine. "Your mother knows I speak the truth because I am not the only one here who has travelled through time. I came *back* in time. A hundred and eighty years back. But she went to her *future*, where she met your father."

He pulled back at that, brows lowering, and shook his head slowly, as if he felt *sorry* for me. Perhaps sorry for himself too, falling for a mental patient. "It's not true." He folded his arms.

"It's not true, Zara."

I sighed and squeezed my temples between thumb and finger, closing my eyes a moment before staring into his again. "Ask her if you don't believe me, Javier. Ask her why she's always been so certain I am to be your *wife*, a girl she *just* met. A girl who doesn't live up to her expectations for a hundred different reasons! It's why I was so furious with her after our ride to the beach yesterday. That's when she told me."

"Told you what?" he asked faintly.

"Javier, she *tossed* that lamp into the sea, that lamp that brought her to her future—she tossed it back in and prayed it would bring you a wife."

He stared at me for a long moment. Squinted at me, as if doubting again, then opening his eyes wide, as if pieces of a puzzle were falling into place for him.

"It's why I couldn't tell you where I'm from," I said. "Because I'm from *here*, Javier. Right here. Or, well, right by Pirata Cove. *Tainter Cove*, in my time. It's why my accent is different than yours. Why I play the guitar when no other girls do. Why I cook and helped my abuela in a restaurant. It's why I didn't know how to ride sidesaddle, but can defend myself. Because in my time… well, things are much different. In a thousand ways, they are different."

He searched my eyes, my face, for a trace of lie. On and on he searched. Finding none, he licked his lips, looking dazed, and stood. "Thank you," he muttered, shoving out a hand as he turned to go. "For telling me at last."

"Javier…" I began. I walked on trembling legs behind him, going to the door, clinging to the jamb. It could *not* be as simple as that. There was *no way* it could be as simple as that. He just…believed me now? Or had he decided I just believed my own whacked version of the truth?

He was staggering along the hallway as if drunk, although I knew he hadn't had any wine. He glanced back at me, eyes wide and wondering—as if I were an apparition in his dreams, the Ghost of Christmas Yet-to-Come—and then reached for the railing to steady himself, still moving away. It was as if I'd wounded him, shot him with an arrow that both cursed his dreams and resolved all his wonderings.

Both torture and treatment.

I shoved the door closed and leaned my head against it, unable to watch his pain any longer or bear that pain of the soul. Things were falling into place in his mind and heart, as perfectly as a long-sought puzzle piece finally slipping into its uniquely cut hole.

All I could think was *What have I done?*

Because I'd finally told him what I had to.

But I'd also just outed Doña Elena.

Big-time.

CHAPTER 24

I later heard the low, urgent tones of the escalating argument downstairs, in the music room, but could not make out any of their words from my hiding place beside the column. At last Javier stalked out, strode through the front door, and slammed it behind him. Minutes later, Doña Elena came out, stopped in the front hall, and looked up in my direction. I quickly ducked backward. She looked shaken, her hands clenched in a ball, her face wan. I dared to peek out at her again; she stared at the front door as if she feared Javier had left and would never return.

He didn't. At least all night.

I was up for most of it, alert to every sound, keeping my window wide to listen for his horse, waiting for the front door to open again. As morning dawned, I sat up and rubbed my face. I'd gotten maybe a couple hours of sleep, dozing off and on. Might he have slipped in while I was out?

I'd ruined things here—caused a rift in this big, wonderful family. Why hadn't I found a way to leave before I'd done such damage?

I moved to the green and black dress Captain Worthington had given me, something I could put on by myself, and then paused. I turned toward the chest and fished out my maxiskirt and cami, bundling them inside Abuela's shawl.

I had to get back to a time when a cami and maxiskirt were cool, not this crazy costume from a Western set in Hollywood.

I had to get home to my own time, before I destroyed everyone I was coming to care for.

Let the Venturas—these people who had so quickly wormed their way into my heart—get back to their normal life, before I screwed things up even more.

That thought brought me up short. I was coming to care for them, I admitted to myself. Every one of the Venturas. Javier. Each of his siblings. Adalia and little Álvaro. Even Doña Elena.

That wasn't good. It wasn't good at all. Surely that would tie me here to this time all the more securely, making it more difficult to get back. The beginnings of love? Family?

I shook my head and sighed, running my fingers through my curly mop, pushing it up into another messy bun. Doña Elena wouldn't approve, but I was about to get out of her hair shortly. I just had to get into that safe…

I slipped on my socks and boots, opened a drawer to grab the fossil and Javier's note, reached for my clothes bundled in Abuela's shawl, and hurried down the stairs and into the library. No one was about, the house curiously quiet, other than servants chatting and laughing back in the kitchen. Maybe everyone was exhausted after entertaining the guests so late the night before. I moved behind Javier's massive desk, slid the chair to one side, and then cautiously opened the huge oil painting that covered the safe like a door. It squeaked on the hinges, but thankfully, no one came to check out the noise.

I stared in relief at the smooth, black surface. It was here, right where I assumed it was. One hurdle crossed. But now…

There was a lock on the metal door. With an opening for a

sizable key. I tried the handle, on the crazy-lucky chance that Javier had left it unlocked. But it didn't move. My eyes went back to the keyhole. At least it wasn't a combination lock. Where would he keep the key? I opened his desk drawers, starting at the bottom, checking for false bottoms or sides.

"What are you doing, Zara?" Doña Elena barked, striding through the door. She came straight to the desk.

I rose, startled, feeling the blush of guilt on my cheeks.

"I'm searching for the key to the safe. I-I need that lamp. Javier put it in here. I need to try to get home."

Her dark eyes pierced mine. "You are home, Zara. Where you are meant to be."

"I need to try and get back to my own home in my own time, Doña Elena. This was a mistake. Such a big mistake. I will find what I wished for there and not divide your family any farther."

I took a deep breath and moved around the desk. "Please forgive me for telling Javier your secret. I had no right. It was only that he didn't believe me, not totally. Only when I told him about the lamp, and how you tossed it into the sea, did things seem to make sense to him. But I'm sorry. Truly."

She stiffened, glanced to the window, then back to me. "I supposed it was a matter of time, with your arrival. I'd only thought that I would be the one to tell him."

"You should've been. Forgive me. I was angry and frustrated, and it simply came out. I had no right. Did…Carlos ever know?"

She nodded and looked to the window and back. "He did."

"Did he know you were throwing the lamp back out to sea? For me?"

She shook her head "No. It was after he was gone. He would not have approved. He thought it…unsettling how I came to him. He loved me, with a great, deep love, but he preferred to forget how our love began."

"That's understandable."

She looked into my eyes. "Zara, Javier responded in a similar manner to his father. But I can see it in him. My son and you can share the sort of love his father and I did. I feel it in my bones." She reached out to take my hand. "In my soul. I know it as utter *truth*. It would be a grave mistake to leave him."

To leave us, her eyes told me.

I stared at her and gently pulled my hand from hers. "Your son is undeniably wonderful, Doña Elena, but I can't help feeling that this is wrong, as much as it is right."

"That will ease in time."

"No, I don't think so. I'm leaving, Doña Elena. Going back to my own time. Javier will find the love you wish for him. With a woman of *this* time and place. It will be better. You'll see."

She shook her eyes sadly. "No. My boy needs the extraordinary. Someone different than the girls here. Don't you see? I had to bring him home from university, from a future he greatly desired. The only way to keep him here was to bring him a love that makes this place, in this time, the thing he desires most. Otherwise, he'll forever be lost in dreams about the future."

"I'm sorry," I whispered. "I cannot be that person for you. I'll throw the lamp into the sea when I get back and pray that it brings you the daughter-in-law you deserve. The girl who *wishes* to be here, in this time, as well as for love and family."

She swallowed hard, waited a moment, then a moment more, as if thinking I'd change my mind. Then she moved around the desk, removed a book from a shelf, fetched a key from its center, put it in the lock and turned it, and pressed the lever to one side. The heavy door creaked open. Inside were stacks of gold and paper dollars, but my eyes were on the older, more brassy gold of the lamp. She took hold of it with both hands, bent her head in prayer, and then turned to me. "Go," she said. "Go, if God and the future will allow you to return. And if not, return to us, Zara. Embrace this as His good gift to you."

"Thank you," I muttered, taking it from her and wrapping it tenderly in Abuela's shawl with my clothes, intent on keeping it hidden from anyone I met on the way. I glanced back through the open doorway. "Say good-bye for me? To the children, to Javier? To…everyone?"

She nodded, once, and I turned to go. In the doorway I stopped and looked back to her sad face again. "Thank you, Doña Elena. For welcoming me. Believing that I could be…what you prayed for. It was an honor."

She didn't answer, and I slipped out the front door as quietly as possible. I didn't take a horse this time. I'd walk the several miles to the beach, because I didn't want to leave one of the Venturas' horses there to find her way home—or get caught by blackcoats or the Vargases. And without a corset to keep me from breathing well, I figured it was doable, even in the laced-up boots that were as far from Nikes as a girl could get.

I trudged down the road, ignoring the calls of the guards above the house, ignoring the curious gazes of the workers in the vineyard on one side and fields on the other. I even ignored the snuffling horses that came to the fence as I passed the farthest corral, as if I might have a carrot or sugar beet in my pocket. I was going home. Back to my own time. To our apartment and a fresh change of clothes every day. To showers and buses and cell phones. To the restaurant and student loans and college with a program for meteorologist-wannabes.

To the future I'd always thought I'd have.

I looked up to the skies, where gathering clouds dotted the horizon, indicating moisture in the atmosphere, a possible approaching storm. It felt a little cooler today, cool enough that I was glad I'd brought Abuela's shawl. I switched the lamp to my other arm and forced myself to forget how warm and welcoming the villa had been. How I'd loved living with a family and gradually feeling a part of them.

I paused a moment—actually stopped short in the road—thinking of Abuela's empty apartment.

Of the urn, full of ashes, sitting on the kitchen counter, waiting for me to do something about it.

I forced myself to move on, telling myself I'd figure that out soon. Maybe I'd scatter her ashes at George Point, near the tide pools and starfish she'd loved.

I had to go back. Had to, had to, had to.

It was my place, my time. Not here, not now.

In less than an hour, I was trudging along the crest above Tainter Cove, looking in relief at the big boulders to my left, the shipwreck below me, and George Point to the right. The last time I'd tried to go back, I'd sat near those stones, thinking it was where I was when I came to this time. Maybe the trick was to get as close as I could to the tide pools, where I'd found it in the first place. I trudged down the bank of sand, sinking so low that it crept over and into the edges of my high boots. But it didn't matter. Soon I'd be kicking them off, so I could leave them behind.

The wolf-dog raced past me, startling me and then making me laugh. I shifted left, and she shifted right, turning in a wide circle along the waves' edge, then loped back toward me, as if seriously happy to see me. I smiled. "Centinela," I greeted her.

I knelt and waited for her to approach, again crooning to her when she hesitated, sniffed the air, then backed away. It took several long minutes, but at last she nosed my open palm and allowed me to scratch her chin, her cheek, her ears. Then she ran away along the water, acting as if she was playing a game with the wash of it, nipping at the foam, tossing her head in the air.

I shook my head. I'd never unravel the mystery of where she came from and why. But at least I'd managed to save her life. Twice. And she'd made me smile when I needed a smile most. I'd always be grateful for that.

I sank down to the sand, as close as I could get to where I believed the tide pools would someday emerge, unlaced my boots and yanked them off, and stuffed the socks inside. My toes dug into the sand, and already I felt a little closer to home.

I set about trying to wish my way back. I thought about all the wishes I had in my old-present. Tried thinking about them in different combinations.

But after several hours, it hadn't worked.

Eventually the wolf-dog came to sit beside me, and I rubbed her back. She turned to look at me and whined a little.

"What is it, girl? Do you not want me to go? Well, I have to. I have to."

I rose and walked down to the water, letting the waves wash around my feet and climb up my skirts. I was thirsty. I hadn't thought to bring a canteen; I hadn't thought I'd be here that long, now that I was ready, *really* ready to get back to my own time and had the lamp in hand. I set off down the beach toward the shipwreck.

Centinela paused and lifted her head, staring up the dunes, growling quietly. I turned.

And there he was again. Javier.

He didn't hold a gun this time. He just stared down at me with such a mix of frustration and fear and relief that it made me catch my breath. He eased his mare down the dune, swaying in the saddle, and when he reached my side, Centinela loped off down the beach, as if she didn't want to intrude.

I found myself wishing she had stayed.

Javier lifted his far leg over the saddle and slipped to the ground. Then he turned back, pulled a slightly rumpled red rose from his bag, and brought it over to me. "A farewell present," he said softly, lifting my hair and tucking the fat bud behind my ear. "I thought you could press it, if it survived the trip. Something to remember me by."

I looked up into his eyes. "I don't think I could ever forget you, Javier. Ever."

He glanced down to the lamp tucked in the crook of my arm and took a slight step away. "So there it is. You can open locked safes as easily as you seem to do everything else."

"I wish," I said, smiling up at him. "Your mother opened it for me. When it became clear that I only wanted this—to return here, and try and get home."

"My mother…wants the best for people. But clearly, she goes too far at times."

"Isn't that the way of every mother you know?"

He sighed. "Mine is more overbearing than most," he said. "Zara, I'm sorry. I'm sorry that you feel trapped here. That you were pulled back into a time and place you did not want. Into a…into our world. It wasn't fair of her. I can see why you were angry with her. Even though such a…*transition* proved to be a boon for her, she should not have assumed it would prove a boon for another."

The frustration, the hurt on his face, mingled with the heavy, magnetic draw between us, made me want to cry. I lifted a hand to his cheek. "It's terrible, Javier. This. It's not because of you. I swear it isn't you. You are…wonderful. So is your family. Even your mamá. But I don't *belong* here."

He swallowed hard and ran a hand through his curls, pushing them back, then letting them fall exactly back where they'd been. "So…have you tried?"

I nodded, frowning. "So far, no luck." I gestured down the beach. "I tried there, first. As near as I could get to where I found the lamp. You know, back in my own time."

My eyes met his as he nodded. He seemed to have accepted it as truth, strange and fantastic as it might be. It was as if we were both trying to make our way through this strange dream, so that we could both wake up and move on with our lives.

"May I stay with you, until you go?" he asked.

I shrugged and moved on down the beach, back to the big boulders again. Maybe it'd help, having him here, as it seemed he was one of the touchstones that pulled me to this time. *Love.*

I shoved away the word, tried to swallow, but found my mouth dry. "Do you have any water?" I managed.

"Yes," he said, turning to his saddle. He fished out his tin canteen and handed it to me. I drank deeply, and then he took a drink too, before popping on the cork and returning it to his bag. We moved on, back to the rocks.

"I was about here," I said, pointing to the sand and looking up at the rock. "When you first saw me, right?"

"That's right," he whispered, sorrow etching each syllable.

"Javier?" I asked.

He looked at me, and I swear to God, he had tears in his big, brown eyes.

"Javier?"

He shook his head, angrily wiped his eyes, and stood there, hands on hips, staring at the ground a moment before looking my way again. "I don't know, Zara. This feels so wrong to me. As if I should do anything I can to stop you from leaving." He moved toward me and I backed away, up against the rock. "Perhaps if I told you—"

"No, Javier," I begged. "Please, don't say anything more. This is hard enough…"

"I will not say anything," he whispered huskily, still advancing. He pulled me to him, almost angry as he kissed me, kissed me harder and deeper and for longer than I'd ever been kissed before…as if he *willed* me to understand how deep his feelings for me ran, if I wouldn't let him tell me. My hands slipped up his shoulders, to his hair—his glorious hair—rubbing his scalp, pulling his head down closer to mine.

We paused after a while, panting, our breath intermingling before our faces, his nose rubbing my cheek. And those moments were almost more passionate than kissing, that intimacy, standing so close. "Javier—"

"Zara. Please. Please don't go. Let us see what this is between us. Let us explore it, determine if it's the love we both most want."

"No," I said, half moaning, "no," and I shoved him back a step.

"No," I repeated a final time.

He blinked again, looking at me with such hurt hound dog eyes that I had to turn away, toward the sea. "I need to go back, Javier. As much as it pains me to do so."

He wrapped his big hands around the curve of my bare shoulders and gently pulled, until my back rested against his chest. He wrapped his arms across my chest and over my shoulders, lowering his face down beside mine. I held on to his forearms, my nose against his sleeves, trying to memorize his scent of leather and salt and sweat and sage. "Are you certain, Zara?" he whispered.

Was I certain? Truly? Because right now, I couldn't imagine anywhere, any *time*, I'd rather be than right now, here, in his arms.

"Are you certain you aren't about to do something that we'll regret forever?" he went on, tightening his grip, as if he intended to never let me go.

"No, I'm not," I said, twisting in his arms to face him. "But I think I have to, Javier. If it's wrong when I get back, don't you think I could just sit down and wish those same three wishes again and return to you?"

He took my face in his hands. "Or is it a one-time opportunity? A hand of cards that might never be dealt again?"

"How do I know?" I said, with a humorless huff of a laugh.

"What *do* you know?" he whispered, nuzzling my cheek, my ear, hovering close and yet not allowing himself to get any closer. It was an agony. A sweet agony. "Zara, tell me what you know for certain."

"That's not fair," I whispered back, closing my eyes, feeling it all as pain now, a tearing, as if my torso were being ripped in two. Half of me was called to go; half of me shouted to remain. He wanted to hear about the part that shouted. He wanted to hear that I was falling in love, just as surely as he was.

"You know what I know?" he said, wrapping me back in his arms, cradling my head to his chest. "I know my heart cries out to fall to my knees and beg you to remain. To profess the words in my heart that you do not want to hear. But, Zara, I was forced to return to this place. I will not do the same to you. I care for you too much to ever force anything on you but what your own heart desires."

I swallowed hard and nodded. "I think I must try," I said, forcing myself to look him in the eye. He had to know that I was feeling the same kind of pain as he was over this. "If I didn't, I think I'd always wonder. Wonder if this was a mistake, me being here at all."

He pinched my chin between thumb and forefinger and looked into my eyes. Then he bent to kiss my lips softly. "You will try," he said, "and if the Lord doesn't send you back, you will be satisfied? To remain here with me in this time?"

I nodded. That seemed right. It wasn't up to me, not really. I didn't have the power to send myself to one era or another. That had to be all God, all the way. There was no other explanation for it. Some weird portal wrapped up in an ancient golden lamp, a highway that transcended time.

Javier sat down in the sand, legs sprawled. He patted the sand in front of him. "Come here, future-girl. Sit with me. I will have you as close to me as I can, until you are wrenched from my grasp, if that is to be the way of it."

I smiled sadly at him and sat down between his legs. I unwrapped my bundle that contained the lamp; he looked over my shoulder at what else it contained, nestled in the folds of my clothing and the shawl.

"You are taking the fossil? And my note?"

I gazed down at them sadly, then picked up the fossil, settling back against his chest. "It will always remind me of our day together. I needed something, to show me this all wasn't some vivid dream."

He was silent a moment. "And the lamp? It's the same one my mother had?" he asked. "You both are certain?"

"It is the one that brought me here," I said. "She seemed to think it was the same."

"It is all so very strange. I have never heard of such a thing. Have you?"

"Time travel? Only in books. Movies," I said.

"What are movies?"

"Something from the future," I mused. "Pictures, in sequence, action. It's hard to explain…"

"I scraped off the growth," he said, a moment later, touching the lamp between my fingers, running a finger over the odd lettering.

"I see that."

"Do you think that might have harmed its power?"

"I don't think so," I said. "Whatever animates this thing is bigger than a few shells. And your mother didn't pause over it—as if when she received it from the merchant in Morocco, it wasn't perfect then either."

His hands left the lamp, and he pulled back my hair, lifting it to his face? His lips? A shiver ran down my back. "Do what you must, Zara," he said softly, moving his hands down my bare arms, entwining his fingers between my knuckles, still covering the lamp. "I cannot bear this for long. But I am ready. Do what you must. God brought you to us. If he wills it, you shall go. I will trust him, no matter what happens."

I didn't hesitate. I closed my eyes and wished. Wished with everything in me. For this kind of love, just sparking between Javier and me, back home, in my own time. For family like Javier's, for little brothers and sisters who could become like my own. For a mother like I'd never had. Men who would be like fathers. For adventure…

On and on, I wished, waiting for the pop, the flash of light. Bracing myself for the comforting warmth of Javier's body to disappear from my back. For the sounds of cars and shrieking children and a distant train along the tracks. For the smell of asphalt and tar to mingle with the salty sea on my nose…

Again and again, I tried.

For hours more.

Until I was spent and weeping, cradled in Javier's arms, and gave way to exhaustion…

The rumble of my stomach woke me, and I found I was lying beside Javier, snoring softly. We'd fallen asleep on our sides at some point, him curved behind me, the wolf-dog curled up before me. The dog smelled of wind and grass and sea salt and musk. Javier's arm, under my cheek, smelled of leather and oranges and sagebrush. And for a moment, I just lay there, unmoving, trying on this reality for size.

I was apparently in 1840 to stay.

Relief flooded through me, making me want to shout and cry at the same time. I shuddered. My skin felt hot and tears coursed down my cheeks before I even realized I was weeping.

"Zara?" Behind me, Javier stirred, eased his arm from beneath my head, and rose up on his elbow to look down at me. "You are here," he whispered, his own eyes welling up as he gently wiped away my tears. "But you are crying. Because you are angry?"

"No," I said, shaking my head. "Because I'm relieved. Because I feel like I just made a terrible decision, but was spared. Because I'm *here*. With *you*." I reached up and caressed his face, staring into his eyes. "And Javier, there is no place I'd rather be."

He took one of my hands and kissed the knuckles, staring back at me all the while. "I am so grateful, Zara. So grateful," he repeated, swallowing hard. "What I wanted to tell you before was—"

"Shhh," I said, lifting two fingers to his lips. "I know," I whispered. "I know. I want to hear those words, in time. But today…Today… it's been nearly more than I can handle. Do you understand?"

"I do," he said, gently pushing a coil of hair from my eye. "And I shall abide by your wishes. Only if you allow me to tell you some day, and the day after that. And the day after that…"

He bent to gently kiss me on the lips, then on my eyes, then pulled me into his arms for a long hug. He sighed, rose, brushed the sand from his trousers and reached out a hand to help me up. "Sadly, *mi corazón*, we must go. There is a storm gathering," he said, eyeing the gray skies, heavy with rain, "but I think we have time to get there in time."

"Get where?" I asked blankly, brushing off the skirt of my dress, but mostly thinking that he'd just called me his *heart*. It made my own beat double-time.

"Where?" he asked me in confusion. "You thought you'd be gone," he said a moment later, understanding washing over his face as he tucked my hand in the crook of his elbow and we began the climb up the sand dune. "Remember Captain Craig's invitation? He awaits us. And happily, I shall have the prettiest woman in all of Alta California on my arm when I arrive. I confess I did not enjoy the thought of arriving alone, and trying to explain your…absence.

Only my mother would have understood."

"Your mother!" I said. "Do you think she will forgive me? For trying to leave?"

He nodded and lifted my hand again to his lips. "I wager she already has. She…*feels* for you, Zara. As my entire family does. Me, most of all."

"Careful," I said in mock warning, even as I smiled, aware of the L-word he was trying to avoid, feeling the ache, the glory of it in my own heart too. But it had been enough this day, all we'd said, all we'd experienced. And there was a ship captain to meet and a dinner to make it through before I slept this night.

And when I went to sleep, I knew I'd rest deeply, at peace in a home that was already becoming my own, among a family that I was eager to claim forever. To figure out just what this L-thing with Javier would look like, and discover what adventures were ahead of us, hand in hand.

Because I'd already begun to see my wishes fully granted.

My future begin to unfold.

In this great, distant past.

A SNEAK PEEK AT THE UPCOMING SEQUEL TO *THREE WISHES*...

FOUR WINDS

RELEASING FALL 2016

CHAPTER 4

Javier laughed and shook his head as we reached the top of the sand dune, Centinela loping in a wide circle around us. "I do not know if I can court a girl from the future and have a pet wolf. That is a lot to ask of one man."

I gave him a half-smile, not yet ready to admit it—that I might be his girlfriend, that I might be here to stay, even if I knew it was totally, unavoidably true.

He reached for the reins of his hobbled gelding and peered toward the setting sun, barely visible behind a dark, gray cloud bank. "We need to hurry if we're to get to the harbor before that rain lets loose."

Javier reached down to help lift me to the back of his horse. "What is it about Captain Craig, Javier?" I asked in Spanish. "What must I know about him?"

He looked back at me, suddenly wary.

"If I am to remain here, be a part of life at Rancho Ventura, doesn't it make sense for me to understand what concerns you and your mother about him? What your secret is?"

"He is a nationalist," Javier said, mounting ahead of me. "A lobbyist, bent on making Alta California the newest of the United States. And he does not fear a potential war with Mexico in order to accomplish what he wishes."

"I gathered that much from your mother's clear distaste."

"Refusing to receive him…" Javier began over his shoulder, as I wrapped my arms around him. His big, broad hand covered my own as he seemed to forget what he was about to say and turned to look at me. "Zara, the feel of your arms around me…Coming here this day, I feared I'd never experience that again."

I gave him a gentle smile. "But God had other plans."

He released my arm to lift a fist and his chin to the sky. "May He be forever praised!" he shouted.

I grinned and laughed under my breath. "You were saying… Refusing to receive him…"

"Craig could set up a barrier, keeping ships from entering Bonita Harbor. Convince others not to trade with us. Upset all we have built. As a ranchero, I must keep good relations with both sides of this political wall, regardless of what my mother wants. You've seen that the soldiers of the presidio do little to intervene, other than collect what they deem due. And yet I trade with Spanish and Mexican ships too. So if they learned that I'd become a traitor—regardless of the disarray of our mother country in the hands of General Santa Anna—we could be swiftly cut off by either side. So I continue to gamble, playing my cards on both tables."

"And what do you want, Javier? For Alta California?"

"I think it is only a matter of time, before the United States turns her eyes upon this beautiful land. And Mexico has all but abandoned us, lost in constant uprisings and poorly managed wars. Her treasury is empty, so they gladly take our taxes, but do they send patrols to help keep cattle rustlers in check? Do they sail our coast, keeping alert to those—like Captain Craig—who might block our trade, holding us captive? No," he said bitterly. "They think they can occupy this territory, but at no cost. They do not realize that the power is slipping from their grasp."

He pulled up on the reins suddenly, and turned toward me again, his face aglow. "But you…you know what transpires here. You know!" he cried, his face splitting into a beatific grin, his eyebrows arcing in wonder. He squeezed my arm. "Tell me, Zara. In your time, is it Mexican or American rule? Or perhaps Russian? They have some northern holdings and are most interested in pelts…"

I stared at him. Was I supposed to tell him such things? Would it interrupt the space-time continuum or something? Might I…change the future?

"I…I need to think about that, Javier. Maybe I shouldn't tell you what happens. Maybe what is meant to happen will unfold because you make wise decisions."

He gazed at me, his brow lowering. "But you will tell me, if I choose wrongly?" he asked. "Would you do that much for me?"

I studied his handsome, earnest face. "I don't know, Javier. Let me think about it, please?"

Centinela whined then, her ears pricking forward as she raised her head. I thought her action spooked Javier's horse, making her shy and whinny.

Javier yanked the gelding's reins back and stroked her neck. "Whoa, whoa," he said.

But a second later, we heard what had upset both animals. A low boom reached our ears, and then another, identical to the first.

"What was *that*?" I asked.

Javier was already mounting ahead of me. "Cannon fire," he said grimly. "And from the sounds of it, coming from Bonita Harbor. Hold on."

I clung to Javier all the way to the harbor, about a mile-and-a-half distant from Tainter Cove. By the time we reached it, my arms and legs were trembling from the effort to hold on, even with Javier's firm grip on my hands in a knot at his sternum. I'd forced him to wait so that I could switch to riding astride, at least—not caring how it might chafe or how it might look, only wishing to stay seated.

We reached the harbor and saw a newly arrived three-masted ship, right beside Captain Craig's damaged, listing *Heron*. Her deck was crowded with men, all in hand-to-hand combat with their attackers. We could see smoke rising from a fire below decks and a second massive hole in her deck, visible even from the beach.

"Who is that?" I cried.

"Pirates," Javier grit out. He was off the horse before we'd completely reached a stop and quickly handed me the reins. "Get in the saddle, quickly!"

I did what he asked without thinking, trying to shove my boots in the stirrups. But they were too long for me.

"You go!" he demanded. "Ride to the villa! You will be safest there!"

"No, Javier, I—"

With a quick touch behind her shoulder, Javier turned the mare's head in the direction of the villa and then slapped her on the rump, sending her skittering ahead. Uncertain after such rash action from her master, she surged into a mad gallop. I rode up and over several hills before I pulled up on the reins in horror.

Because there I found Mateo's mount and two villa guards lying dead on the ground. I swallowed hard and looked to Craig's burning ship again, only her mast visible from this angle.

"No, no, no…" Mateo had clearly been taken captive. I glanced toward the rancho, thinking that others must have heard the cannon fire, as we had. How long until reinforcements arrived?

I circled around, understanding what I must do.

If Javier de la Ventura was wading into that fight, a fight that might save his brother's life, I was determined to be by his side.

CHAPTER 2

I left Javier's mare on the landward side of the dunes, hobbling her just out of sight from the shore. I grabbed his long, curved knife from the saddlebag. Then I crouched over and scurried to the edge to peer down at the warehouse. There were no guards in sight, no sounds of bullets fired or men fighting. I could only hear the crash of waves, swollen by the approaching storm.

Pirates were launching one rowboat after another, loaded with crates and barrels and bundles, systematically removing every bit of the rancho's treasured exports that had been stored here. Stacks and stacks of hides—which I'd heard sailors call "California dollars"—two freshly butchered sides of beef, coils of tanned leather and rope, barrels full of tallow, giant spools of wool, and crates of oranges. In addition I glimpsed bolts of cotton fabric in several patterns, casks of wine, an elegant mahogany rocking chair, rounds of cheese, and other barrels labeled SUGAR and SALT, all of these presumably just obtained in trade from Captain Craig.

So they were not only pillaging Craig's ship; they were also raiding our stores.

Fury washed through my veins. I thought of how hard the people of the rancho worked for all of those products…how they depended on the rest arriving on a timely basis to supply the villa and feed her people. And they had killed some of the kind guards who had protected Mateo—*please, God, let their lives have at least protected Mateo*—and perhaps others.

I gathered up my skirts and hurried over the dune and to the wall of the storehouse. I was standing with my back against it, holding Javier's dagger, when I saw Mateo lifted from one of the first boats to reach the pirate ship. He struggled against his bonds as he was picked up and bodily hauled aboard like nothing more than a wriggling sack of grain. "No," I whispered. "No!"

Did Javier know they had him? Was he already finding his way out there?

I peeked around the corner and saw four men struggling to lift a massive, heavy crate, one of the last things in the storehouse. Judging by the girth and heft of it, it was another safe. I saw two more dead guards on the ground, with more blood spilled than I had ever seen in my life. I whipped my head back, swallowing the bile that rose in my throat, and took several breaths, fighting my tunneling vision. Because I'd also seen two other Ventura guards, sitting, bound and gagged, backs against a pillar. If I could free them, could we, together, overtake the four pirates that remained and use that last boat to come to Mateo's aid—or Javier's?

The men were counting together—in Portuguese?—and heaved the crate upward on tres. With grunts and straining sounds, they began to move together, out from under the rooftop and down through the soft sands to the last rowboat. When they were twenty paces away, fully focused on their task and appearing to be gaining momentum, I rounded the corner and went to the two young Indian guards, where I used my knife to cut away their bonds.

The first rose and reached for me, looking anxiously about. "You must be away from here, Miss!" he whispered frantically.

The other rose more slowly, and I saw that he had blood trickling down the other side of his head.

"No," I whispered back. "They have Mateo! We must go after them!"

The first man reached for the nearest dead man, rolled him over, and grabbed the sword from his still-clenched hand. "We will go. You go to the villa!"

"I can help," I said, frowning as they both stared at me with wide eyes. Too late, I realized they weren't looking at me—

"Oh, that you can, miss," said a low voice behind me, in tandem with the cocking of a pistol. I felt the smooth, round circle of the gun at the base of my skull. "You will most certainly be a *great* deal of help in future negotiations with Don Javier, if you are who I think you are. Now drop that dagger!" he barked.

I looked down the beach and wanted to cry. The four men had set down their heavy load and were returning to us, all drawing weapons. I dropped my knife.

"You should have stayed where we had left you," said one of the pirates to the Ventura guard. And then he drew his sword, whirled, and practically cut the man's head from his body.

I gasped as a spray of blood splattered across my face and chest, warm at first, then chilled by the wind. I turned and vomited, and as I vomited, I heard them murder the second Ventura guard. I threw up again, not daring to look.

My stomach empty, I rose and looked at my captor for the first time. He was a stranger, with long, straight black hair and creamy skin the color of *café au lait*, not as dark as the rest of his Portuguese crew. He pointed the gun at my chest, lackadaisically looking me over from head to toe and back again, a slow, leering smile lifting the corners of his mouth. I supposed he was handsome, in a way, nearly as big as Javier and with sculpted cheeks, a long, straight nose, and full lips. There was a dimple in the cleft of his chin.

But I thought I'd never seen anyone uglier in my life. "You… *murderer*," I seethed, hands clenched. I was aware of the others, moving in on me from all sides, just waiting for their boss's order to come after me.

"Believe me, miss, I've been called worse," he said in perfect Spanish, not Portuguese. "And I tried to leave a couple behind alive, to show—"

I used his momentary distraction to shove upward, grabbing hold of the gun with one hand and ramming my fist into his throat with the other, hard enough to make him let go. The gun went off, and the other men hesitated, as if stunned that a girl could do such a thing. But, as the pirate captain staggered backward, clutching his throat and gasping for breath, I swung my body, lifted my skirts and roundhouse-kicked the nearest man, my boot connecting with his jaw and sending him reeling. I cocked the heavy gun again—one bullet left—and fired at the man barreling toward me.

I turned my head before I saw the bullet's results, confident that it had to be a lethal—or at least crippling—blow. Another man grabbed me from behind, pinning my arm against my chest as he pulled me toward him. I managed to wriggle my left arm free, reached behind me, and grabbed his nose, tearing away the soft flesh at his nostrils. He screamed and let me go.

But the next man tackled me, driving the breath from my lungs. I was just thinking about a move in which I might be able to get my leg up and in front of his neck—if it weren't for my cursed skirts—when he lifted a fist and belted me across the cheek.

I felt the blow as if I were outside my body. I recognized the pain, but it was distant. And my last thought as I lost consciousness was this: *I'm sorry, Javier. Mateo. So, so sorry…*

I felt the rise and fall of waves before my other senses finally helped me figure out where I might be. Slowly I lifted my head. It was throbbing so hard, I could hardly bear opening my eyes.

I was at sea. As in, *on-board-a-ship-at-sea.*

"Ahh, there you are, my dear. At last," said the captain, stroking my cheek, making me wince from the pain there, even though his touch was light.

I forced my eyes open. Or one eye, actually. The other refused to open—because it was swollen shut? I struggled to remember what had happened. But, as I blinked, I saw that I faced an enraged and red-faced, gagged Javier, bound in a chair before me. And to my side was Mateo, similarly bound, but unconscious.

Slowly, I took stock of my situation. I was in a chair, bound heavily around the chest, wrists, waist and feet. Totally immobile.

I struggled against the scratchy ropes for a sec, which seemed to amuse the captain. Then I tried to talk and realized I was gagged, a filthy rag in my mouth, held there by a band around my head.

Recognizing the salty taste of sweat, disgusted, I began to choke. The captain watched me a moment, waited until Javier began to rock his chair in agitation and fury, until he casually reached forward and untied my gag. I spit out the wad in my mouth, retching for a moment, dizzy. I gasped, regained my composure, and sat up straight, closing my eyes and forcing myself to breathe slowly. *Get a grip, Zara. Think. Think!*

I felt his finger swipe across my lips. "She has lovely lips, does she not, Don Javier? How much are those lips worth to you, intact?"

I blinked, and stared up and over at him as he moved to Mateo, trying to pull four images into one. "Or how much is your little brother's life worth?" he asked, waving to Mateo's inert form. He was still unconscious. "It must eat at you, thoughts of your elder brother, gone, and now this one, so near to his own death..."

"What did you do to him?" I spat out, my voice raspy and dry, wanting nothing more than to cease his taunting of Javier.

The pirate captain glanced back at me before studying Mateo again, as if appraising artwork in a museum. A curiosity. "The boy thought he might be a hero," he said, glancing back at me over his shoulder as he continued to pace in a circle around us. "Let's just say he's young yet."

My eyes met Javier's.

I'm sorry. So sorry, I said to him silently. If I had done what he'd asked...gone home, rather than stay and try to fight...Well, he and Mateo might have still been captured, but I would likely not have been a part of the stakes.

He frowned, but his whole expression was protective rage. Love. Worry.

Which *encompassed* me, in an odd sort of manner.

"And you—Señorita Ruiz, I take it? You, my dear, have cost me. Two men dead. Injuries to two others." He refused to admit that I'd hurt him too, but I saw him lift a hand to his collar and pull the starched edge away from a purpling bruise.

I wanted to laugh.

"Who are you?" I said, my voice still raspy. "What do you want?"

"I am Captain Santiago Mendoza," he said, waving a small circle in the air as he bowed. "I'd kiss your hand," he added, rising, a wry look in his dark eyes, "but well, you recognize my difficulty in that."

My skin crawled as he looked down my body and up again. I knew it was a scare tactic. Menacing, somehow, to Javier, more than me. When his eyes returned to mine, I was staring straight at Javier. *It will be okay. Somehow, some way, it will be okay,* I willed him to know.

Because something in me, in spite of these crazy odds, told me it was so.

Had God brought me back a couple of centuries to fall in love with a man and his family, only to die at the hands of a pirate?

No way.

The knowledge of it sent a surge of adrenaline through me and lifted my chin.

But Javier stared back at me with nothing but fear and righteous, impotent rage.

Which made me feel the same, of course.

"What do you want, Captain Mendoza?" I rasped out.

Wordlessly, he poured a cup of wine and brought it to me.

I sipped, desperate, feeling the tart wine fill my mouth to the full and slop down the corners of my mouth and down my cheeks, chin, and neck. But oh, the relief of that liquid sliding down my parched throat! I swallowed with relish, leaning my head back against the tall, deeply carved face of the chair.

Captain Mendoza took the opportunity to run his fingers up my throat and jaw—making my eye spring open—and then lifted his red-stained fingertips to his mouth, licking them.

I swallowed hard. Hated him, with every fiber of my being. How could someone be so horrible?

Then he gave Javier a meaningful look and resumed his circuit around the three of us, hands clasped behind his back. "You asked what I want, Señorita," he said, as if still trying to figure out his demands, when it was more than clear that he'd long since determined them. "And as near as I can fathom it, the vast potential of Rancho Ventura is at my fingertips," he said, pausing to lift my chin and look over at Javier for a long moment. Then he moved on to Mateo, grabbed hold of his dark curls, and roughly raised his head.

Mateo stirred, squinted, and squirmed, starting to rise to consciousness.

Javier grunted and struggled against his bonds anew.

"Free Javier's gag," I said to the captain. "This is his deal to make, not mine."

Mendoza stared at me, and, behind him, I saw the swing of the light on a chain, moving in an arc with the waves. All at once, I became aware of the creak of the timbers all around us, the thrum and energy of sails unfurled, carrying down here, to the hold. The washing sound of water moving past, surging with each wave, deep enough to make us all lean one way and then the other.

We were on the move. Far from Rancho Ventura. Farther with each wave.

How long had we been at sea? How far were we from home?

Home, I acknowledged internally. *Rancho Ventura.*

The captain moved to free Javier's gag, and he spit out the rag from his mouth.

He turned away when Mendoza offered him a cup of wine, sneering in his direction. "When I am free—"

"When you are free," the captain easily interjected, resuming his pacing around us, "you and I shall sup on occasion as good friends. Perhaps even accept a friendly wager? I hear of your fondness for a hand of cards. But for now, *Don* Javier, you are *not* free, and these are the terms of my demands…"

We waited, the three of us, the gradually rousing Mateo, Javier, and me. Surrounded by four burly, armed guards in the shadows—my brain finally took them in—and the pacing captain.

"I am going to set you free, come daybreak, in a rowboat, to make your way to shore and back to the rancho to collect the same sum you handed to the presidio scum, my price for your precious little brother," he said, miming an arc across Mateo's throat with Javier's own dagger. "And as for *this* sweet, intriguing creature," he said, lifting my chin with the cool flat of the blade.

I stared only at Javier.

"I take it she has stolen your heart? This girl, whom no one knows?"

"*De veras*," Javier whispered, staring back at me, pledging his love with those two words in a way that I didn't think any other might ever match. *Indeed.*

He hadn't had to say it, admit it. But he had.

"Be careful of such women," Mendoza said. "There is a reason that our mothers wanted to know those we might pledge our hearts to—and their kin."

"I know all that I need to know," Javier ground out, still looking only at me.

"Well then," Mendoza said wryly, "her freedom shall cost you another chest of gold."

Javier's eyes moved to Mendoza, deadly still a moment. "I shall not give you two chests of gold for these two…I shall give you four."

"Javier!" I gasped.

"*Four*," he repeated. "But you shall deliver them to me in

Monterey. Unharmed. *Unmolested*," he emphasized, looking to Mendoza with a deadly intensity that sent a shiver down my back. "And I shall never see you or your crew again. Ever."

The captain cast him a wry grin, brows lifting. "Four chests of gold when I asked for but two? Clearly, you are not the gambler that others said you were," he scoffed.

"You, Captain," Javier said, staring at him with a sneer, "have no idea *who* I am and what *threat* I might be. Harm either of these two, and I shall *hunt* you down. *Destroy* you. No, *kill* you…in slow, *exacting* measure," he grit out.

"Such grand talk!" Captain Mendoza scoffed. "May I remind you that it is I who hold your loved ones' lives in the balance? To say nothing of what might transpire for your widowed mother, sisters, and brother, far behind us? Ahh, yes, Señor Ventura, I am well aware of *all* who hold your heart."

I closed my eyes again, unable to combat the fear of what I might have brought down on those I loved.

Those I loved.

I *loved* them.

Not just Javier. But Estie. Francesca. Jacinto. Mateo. Doña Elena.

I loved them as my own.

My own *family*.

And Javier?

As I stared at him, I couldn't imagine him gone. Away from me. It baffled me that I had ever been ready to leave him for my own time. *What had I been thinking?*

It came to mind, then, my third wish. *Adventure.*

My blood was pulsing at a faster rate than I could ever remember. *Okay, Lord, maybe this is a bit too much adventure…*

Somehow we had to get out of this. Some way.

Because this love that I felt for Javier, for his family, couldn't end here or now.

Or ever.

HISTORICAL NOTES

Most of my research came from these five books: Hayes's *Historical Atlas of California*, Dana's *Two Years Before the Mast,* Beebe and Senkewicz's *Lands of Promise and Depair*, Robinson's *Land in California,* and Cleland's *The Cattle on a Thousand Hills.*

However, I took fictional license on a variety of fronts for the sake of the story. To begin with, my depiction of the Venturas' villa is highly romanticized. There were vast ranchos like this, as well as villas that housed big families and many servants, but I somehow doubt that many in this time would be quite this pristine and sophisticated. Alta California, of course, was still a pretty rough frontier, and a family was more apt to concentrate on survival than impressing visitors. Still, with cities like Monterey within reach, I didn't think it entirely implausible…which is enough for most fiction writers.

Along that vein, I placed the Venturas' rancho *north* of Santa Barbara, somewhere along the Central Coast (intentionally vague!), and gave them Bonita Harbor, when according to *Two Years Before the Mast*, there were no such wonderful, perfect landfalls for ships wishing to trade with the rancheros, between Santa Barbara and Monterey. They *did* anchor and trade here and there along the coast—it just was much more arduous than I depicted in this fictional, idyllic harbor. Even though I named the family "Ventura," it should not be confused with the real Ventura, or the San Buenaventura mission, which is actually *south* of Santa Barbara.

In addition, there were other missions between Santa Barbara and Sonoma (Junipero Serra founded nine himself), but I have chosen not to include or describe them; they'd been "secularized" in 1833—dividing mission lands into land grants that became new ranchos—and I assumed many of them were largely abandoned by 1840; I also wanted to increase the sense of the Venturas' isolation from any other "civilization."

My description of the *charreada* was abbreviated—it was typically nine events, and didn't include steer-wrestling (they did do something called steer-tailing, which was more complex, even more dangerous, and yet harder to visualize as I attempted to describe it). Nor was the divvying-up of one rancho's cattle from another's an official "event"—I just thought it sounded like chaotic fun, and it was something that rancheros periodically did, so I made it part of this gathering.

ACKNOWLEDGMENTS

Many thanks to my editors, Paul Hawley and Rachelle Rea, for their fine work in getting this book into presentable shape. Also big thanks to my River Tribers who volunteered to be beta-readers and proofers and horse/rodeo-checkers and Spanish-correctors: Jaime Heller, Marylin Furumasu, Paige McQueen, Rebecca Peake, Rebekah Howe, Courtney Adams, Ashlee Humphries, Samantha Booth, Danielle Linnea Groat, Sarah Jo Day, Julie Grant, Maria Teets, Baily Latham, Beth Wickward, Shannon Long, Katharine Trojak, Melanie Harris (belated thanks for your help on *Deluge*, too!), Abby Olivera-Ruiz, Lydia Joy Blackstone, Staci Murden, Katie Breeland, Sharon Miles, Crystal Hay, Andrew and Debbie Spadzinski, Julie Schmidt, Becky Molitoriz, Sammi Jo Tuinstra, Elizabeth Long, Paula Oyedele-Caleb, Melody Lee, Carolina Santander, Calli Lynch, Joy Doering, Sabrina Vogt, Rel Mollet, Erin Cullipher, Tatiana Moore, Bree Boettner, Karalyn Foster…Lilian Berner, Marcy Cherry, and Hannah Donor deserve special thanks, too. Clearly, it takes a village, and there is none better than my River Tribe! Gracias!!

River Tribe reader Graziella LiVolsi flew from Arizona to Oregon to be my cover model for *Three Wishes* and *Four Winds*—much of it at her own expense. I just can't get over her excitement about taking part, her generosity in helping fund the process, and last but not least, her incredible beauty. From the start, she *became*

Zara Ruiz, as soon as I saw her sweet face. Photographer Jennifer Ilene—a phenomenally talented woman I met on a mission trip to Uganda—took the awesome cover shots. Bobbi and Audrey from Western Costume in Hollywood helped me find the perfect dresses for the shoot and got them there on time. The amazing florist, Katie (Ponderosa & Thyme, Salem, OR) donated the pretty flowers. (If you're getting married in Oregon or have a special event coming up, trust me, you want her to do your flowers. Super-cool work!) Kerry Nietz helped format this book for e-release. Many thanks to all.

CHECK OUT THE ORIGINAL SERIES!

Loved this time-slip romance? Want to see where it all began?

The original River of Time Series, set in fourteenth-century Italy, is available in paperback, ebook, and audio from your favorite retailers!

Book I: WATERFALL

Book II: CASCADE

Book III: TORRENT

Book IV: BOURNE & TRIBUTARY

Book V: DELUGE

ABOUT THE AUTHOR

Lisa T. Bergren is the best-selling, award-winning author of over forty books in all sorts of genres, with more than three million copies sold. Her most recent fiction works include the historical Grand Tour Series (*Glamorous Illusions, Grave Consequences, Glittering Promises*), the dystopian-fantasy Remnants (*Season of Wonder, Season of Fire, Season of Glory*), and the time-slip romance series, River of Time (*Waterfall* et al). She lives in Colorado with her husband, three children, and a little white dog.

For more information, please see her web site, LisaTBergren.com—where you can find out about upcoming releases, events, and sign up to receive her quarterly e-newsletter. Or join her on:

- Facebook.com/RiverofTimeSeries
- Facebook.com/LisaTawnBergren
- Twitter @LisaTBergren

CPSIA information can be obtained
at www.ICGtesting.com
Printed in the USA
LVOW12s1804040516
486686LV00006B/453/P